Margaret And Edgar

Fen Flack

Flack Publishing

Flack Books, 23 Stourport Road, Bewdley,
Worcestershire DY12 1BB, UK

www.flackbooks.weebly.com

First edition 2018

Cover design by Studio B61 from illustration by Bhavin
Mistry

Printed in the UK by Vernon Print & Design of
Droitwich, Worcestershire WR9 8QZ

ISBN 978-0-9564961-8-8

Characters

Edward, son of King Edmund Ironside and Frida

Agatha, his German-born wife

Margaret, Christina and Edgar – their children

Wulfgar, who had married Edward's widowed mother, Frida

Edie and Wulf, twins – the children of Wulfgar and Frida

Maria, Wulf's Hungarian-born wife

Anna and Elizabeth, Hungarian servants to Edward and Agatha

Wulfstan, Prior of the Monastery at Worcester, who had brought the family from Hungary to England

Earl Harold, son of the late Earl Godwine

King Edward, the son of Aethelred and Emma

Queen Edith, his wife and sister to Harold Godwineson

Harold, known as Harry, son of Ralf, Earl of Hereford and the King's nephew

Malcolm, King of Scotland – see the family tree on p.174

Tostig, Leofwine and Gyrth Godwineson, brothers to Harold and Edith

Aethelwine, Bishop of Durham

Edwin and Morcar, the sons of Earl Aelfgar of Mercia, and their sister, Alditha, whose first husband was Gryffydd of Wales

Stigand, Archbishop of Canterbury

Ealdred, Archbishop of York

Waltheof, made Earl of lands in the East Midlands and later made Earl of Northumbria

Duke William of Normandy – see his family tree on p.129

Merlswein, governor of Yorkshire

Gospatric, a kinsman of King Malcolm and who held land north of the Tyne

Turgot, a Benedictine monk, who would become Prior at Durham

Bishop Odo of Bayeux, half brother of Duke William of Normandy

GLOSSARY

Aetheling – a son of the King, one of those considered worthy to succeed to the throne

Fyrd – a fighting force, raised locally

Shieldwall – a battle formation created by men standing shoulder to shoulder with their shields locked together making an almost impenetrable wall

Thegn (pronounced thane) – a lord, of lower rank than an earl

Witan – the King's council, which included bishops, earls and thegns

English Royal Family Tree

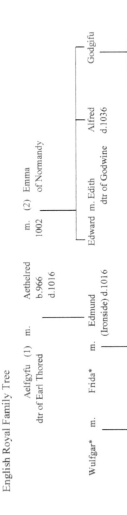

Aelfgyfu (1) m. Aethelred m. (2) Emma
dtr of Earl Thored b.966 1002 of Normandy
d.1016

Wulfgar* m. Frida* m. Edmund Edward m. Edith Alfred Godgifu
(Ironside) d.1016 dtr of Godwine d.1036

Edie* Wulf* Edmund Walter Fulk Ralf
b.1024 Edward m. Agatha b.1017 of Mantes Bishop Earl of
(twins) b.1016 d.1064 of Amiens Hereford
d.21 Dec.1057

Margaret Christina Edgar Harold
b.1045 b.1049 b.1051 (Harry)
(Conjectural dates of birth)

*"Frida" is a fictional name for a real woman; the other characters are entirely fictional.

The Godwine family

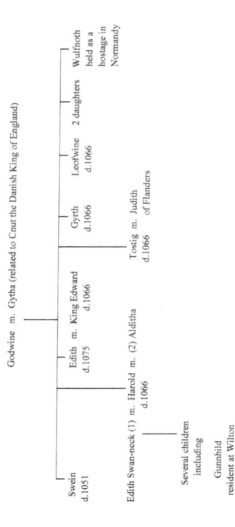

Godwine m. Gytha (related to Cnut the Danish King of England)

Swein
d.1051

Edith m. King Edward
d.1075   d.1066

Gyrth
d.1066

Leofwine
d.1066

2 daughters

Wulfnoth
held as a
hostage in
Normandy

Tostig m. Judith
d.1066   of Flanders

Edith Swan-neck (1) m. Harold m. (2) Alditha
d.1066

Several children
including

Gunnhild
resident at Wilton

Map of Scotland

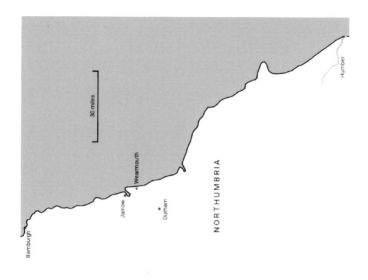

Map of the far north of England

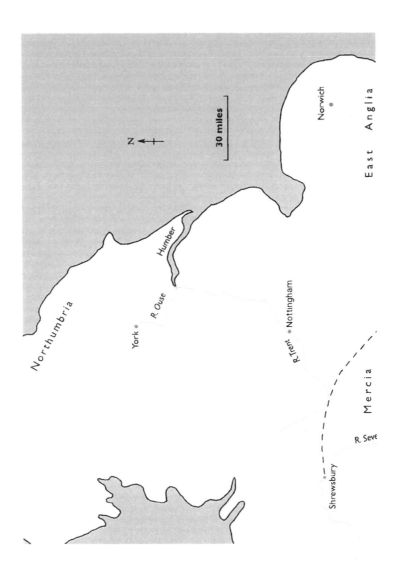

Map of northern England

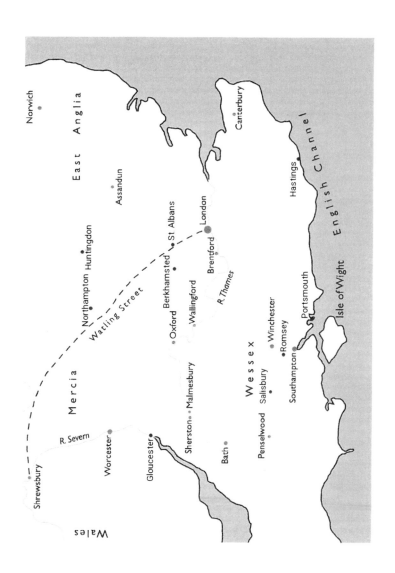

Map of southern England

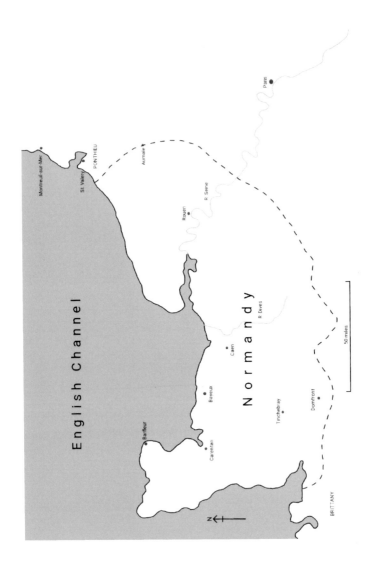

Map of Normandy

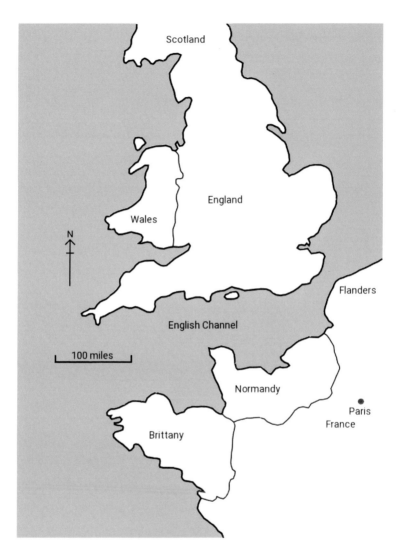

Map showing England, Normandy
and the English Channel

The book could not have been done without the help of:

The ACW group in Leamington Spa, Bewdley Bards, Birmingham Central Library, Janet Bowen, Martin Flegg for the maps, Angela Harvey, Margaret Hawkins, The Hive at Worcester, David Johnson, Liz Munslow for proof reading and support, Beverley Wenman, and the David Wilson Library at the University of Leicester.

There are three narrators and each has a symbol to indicate they are now telling the story.

Edie, the daughter of Wulfgar

Wulf, her twin brother

Andrew, Wulf's son

Each time the narrator changes, there is an indication of the year and the place of the action.

CHAPTER 1

London, late August 1057

"The King is not here."

I knew then that something was wrong.

The man making this statement was tall and handsome and looked to be in his thirties. He had a moustache, but no beard and stood erect and motionless, giving the appearance of supreme confidence.

"Not here?!" exclaimed Prior Wulfstan. "But I sent word of our imminent arrival."

We were in the courtyard of the King's palace in the heart of London on a warm August day, weary after a rough crossing of the Channel.

The tall man's cold eyes hardly blinked.

"Where is he?" the Prior demanded.

"In Winchester."

"Is he sick?"

"No."

I took hold of my father's arm and leaned in close to him.

"Who is that man?" I whispered.

"I think he's Earl Harold Godwineson, the King's right-hand man," he whispered back.

"Then why is he not here to greet this nephew?" Prior Wulfstan continued.

"There was urgent business to be done in Winchester," Earl Harold replied.

"I'm sure he will come soon, now that he knows I have arrived safely."

My half-brother Edward had stepped forward and had placed his hand on the cleric's arm, as it was clear to all of us that the Prior was very annoyed. Indeed, I'm sure he muttered, "It's outrageous!"

"Lord Edward." The Earl inclined his head slightly, but there was no warmth in his voice or his face. "Harold Godwineson at your service."

"Father, I don't trust him," I whispered.

My father turned and smiled.

"Edie, you have only just met him," he chided. "Give him a chance."

"You have a family, I believe," Earl Harold was saying.

"Yes, my wife Agatha," Edward responded, bringing her forward. "And our three children; my son Edgar is six and I have two daughters, Margaret who is eleven and Christina who is eight. Prior Wulfstan brought us the news of the Witan's decision, so I have returned to serve my country."

"You have come from Hungary, I believe," Earl Harold commented.

"That has been our home for the last ten years," Edward replied.

"We have some rooms prepared for you and your retainers."

He glanced in our direction.

"Oh, they are part of the family," Edward laughed. "My mother married Wulfgar and bore him two children."

We stepped forward slightly. My father bowed his head to acknowledge the Earl.

"My son Wulf and his wife Maria, and my daughter Edie," he said proudly. "It is good to meet you, Earl Harold. I knew your father."

"Did you?" He seemed surprised.

"I served King Edmund and went into exile with his sons," my father explained.

"My father died a few years ago."

"I know. We have kept abreast of the news from England."

The Earl raised his eyebrows, but made no comment.

"We are delighted that King Edward and his council have chosen to recall the son of Edmund Ironside," my father added.

"Come inside," the Earl said.

We followed him into the large stone building, which had many rooms.

"Do you remember this?" I asked my father, as we threaded our way through the complex.

"It's changed somewhat. I haven't been here for … it's almost exactly forty years. At that time, your brothers Edward and Edmund were babies, but prisoners at Westminster."

"And Cnut was king, married to Emma," I added. "She was the current King's mother, wasn't she?"

"Yes. Only six months after King Aethelred's death, she married Cnut, and her children by Aelthelred had to go into exile. King Edward's exile was about the same length as our Edward's has been; they have that in common."

"I'm sure they'll get on well – once they meet."

We had been brought into a room where the unshuttered windows let in the sunlight. The stone walls were covered with plain hangings and there were fresh rushes on the floor.

"This room is for you," Earl Harold said. "You have servants?"

"Two from Hungary who serve my wife," Edward replied, indicating young Anna and Elizabeth. "We have no others at present."

"I can provide you with a manservant to meet your immediate needs," the Earl offered. "There are two other rooms here. I did not know about the larger family."

"We can manage," my father responded. "I am happy to sleep in here."

"As the court is not here at this time," the Earl continued, "I will have food brought to you."

"And when are they to meet the King?" Prior Wulfstan demanded.

"I suggest you rest here for a few days before travelling on to Winchester," the Earl answered. "The King has no current plans to come to London. I will go and find a manservant."

He gave a slight bow and left.

"I am so very sorry," the Prior said, sitting down on one of the many chairs. "I cannot understand it at all. I was sure the King would want to meet you at the earliest opportunity."

"It doesn't matter," Edward said. "We have arrived safely. Our long journey is over and now we can relax and get used to our new home. Only Wulfgar remembers England."

He smiled across at my father.

"And much has happened since I left. I think I might even struggle to find my way round London. Forty years ago I went almost daily between this palace and Westminster where you were in the 'care' of the Abbot."

"A prisoner with my brother! But now I am a free man in London and must learn its ways."

"I do not have to return to Worcester just yet and am willing to be of further service to you, my Lord."

"Thank you, Prior Wulfstan. You have already been a great help to us and we value your support."

Little Edgar grabbed Edward's hand.

"Let's explore!" he cried and dragged him from us.

Christina ran off with them, but Margaret went to sit by the Prior.

"The church here in England, it does follow the Pope, doesn't it?" she asked.

"Oh yes," he assured her. "It's like Hungary where you have grown up."

"And *not* like Russia where I was born," she stated. "There they look to Constantinople and the false Patriarch."

"We are one in Christ."

"Exactly! Christ's body cannot be broken," the eleven-year-old declared.

"You will feel at home here because the services are in Latin," the Prior assured her.

I had to smile. I had been present at her birth and loved her dearly, but Margaret had very set ideas about religion, something she had learned from her mother. I thought that one day she would have to learn to compromise. For the time being though, we tended to indulge her.

The chests with our belongings arrived, as did a manservant called Eric, who was very keen to help us.

"I am honoured to serve you, Lord Edward," he said, making a deep bow. "I have served three kings already – King Harold, King Harthacnut and now King Edward, when he is in London."

"You have a Danish name," commented my father.

"I had a Danish father and an English mother," Eric explained. "There has been much intermarriage." He paused. "King Edward has made the court more English, but many of mixed heritage remain."

"Including Earl Harold. I knew his father; he was English with an estate near Chichester."

"Indeed, his mother was Danish. As for the estates, Earl Harold has much land. He is second in wealth only to the King himself."

"I can see you are in good hands," Prior Wulfstan interposed. "I shall leave you to settle in. Eric, I shall be lodging with the Bishop. If Lord Edward needs me, you know where to find me."

Eric nodded and the Prior bade us all farewell. Christina and Edgar were particularly excited about arriving in London, but Margaret made herself useful by helping Anna and Elizabeth to unpack our clothes. Eric brought us a simple meal, apologising that it was not more lavish and promising us something better in the coming days.

"So, Wulfgar, we are home," Edward said, as we sat round the table, enjoying our cold meat, cheese, bread and wine. "You never gave up hope, did you?"

"I think it was Frida who kept England before our eyes," my father commented. "She insisted her sons spoke English as well as learning Norse. She never let you and Edmund forget you were aethelings with a right to be considered for the throne of England."

"My beautiful mother," Edward sighed, "and your beautiful wife. She might still be with us if Edmund hadn't died."

My father looked down at his plate and played with a piece of bread.

7

"We could all see how she gave up wanting to live," I commented. "Edmund was always her favourite, but we didn't mind, did we, Wulf?"

"No, we knew she lived for her royal sons. She would be so proud to see you here, Edward, sitting in the palace in London, acknowledged by the King of England as his true successor."

"It has been a long journey," Edward reflected. "I was taken from here as a small child, forty years ago. I hardly remember our time in Denmark, but I do remember Sweden and Wulfgar's marriage to my mother."

"And then she had twins and I nearly lost her," my father remembered.

"I just about remember our journey to Russia," Wulf said. "I grew up there."

"And there I married my dear Agatha."

Edward touched her hand and they smiled fondly at each other. He had waited many years for a wife, but God had given him a good one – and then three children.

"If Andrew had not found refuge in Russia, we might still be there," Wulf commented.

"That was an awful campaign," Edward groaned. "We wanted to fight at Andrew's side and help regain Hungary, but it was a grim war."

"I shall miss Nadasd," Agatha said. "Andrew gave us a good estate in a beautiful part of Hungary and we were so happy there."

"But this is our true home, Agatha," Edward reminded her. "I am the son of King Edmund, the grandson of King Aethelred, the great-grandson of King Edgar and my true place is in England."

We enjoyed reminiscing about our past, its joys and sorrows, but we all knew we had moved into a new period of our lives. England was where we really belonged. Our lives on the Continent had been simply a preparation for our true destinies. God had brought us here.

We did not know then that our lives would change dramatically and in a way we had not foreseen.

CHAPTER 2

"Edie, Wulf and I are going to find Alfred."

My father's face was bright with excitement. Returning to London meant so much to him. He had been a true servant to Edward and also something of a father to him, as Edward's own father had died when his first son was less than a year old. I really admired my father for his loyalty.

"Alfred?" I asked. "Who's he?"

"My merchant friend, the one who kept us informed about events in London. I've never met him face to face and want to thank him."

"And Wulf wants to find out about trading in England!" I joked.

My brother was near enough to hear what I'd said and he tried to put on a solemn expression.

"Edie, we cannot rely on the King's bounty," he scolded, but I could see his eyes were twinkling. "Father and I must make a living as merchants, as we did abroad."

"Here you might be Alfred's rivals," I suggested.

"Or we could work together."

"I can see you could soon have him working for *you*. You're such a smooth talker."

My brother laughed.

The children wanted to explore the city, so Edward, Agatha, Maria and I took them out of the palace. Anna and Elizabeth came with us, as Edgar and Christina were very likely to run off and we dared not lose them. The two Hungarians were not much older than Margaret, but were very good with all the children and a great help to Agatha in general.

The streets were busy with carts laden with produce for the market. We learned the summer had been a good one and the harvest plentiful, so there was much grain coming in from the country.

The day was warm again and the flies were beginning to buzz around any rubbish that was lying beside the cobbled surface of the streets.

I found myself walking next to Maria.

"You are used to living in a city," I commented. "This is a far cry from our estate at Nadasd."

"Yes, it must be very different," she agreed, "but the children are enjoying all the activity. I know Wulf will want to live here in London, but you will go with Edward, I expect."

"I want to carry on caring for his children as long as I am needed," I agreed.

"You do not mind that you are not married?"

"No, it's never bothered me. Margaret especially is almost like a daughter to me."

"That is good." She paused. "I wish I had a child."

I had never heard her say that before, though I had often wondered, for she had been married to Wulf for several years.

"How old are you now, Maria?"

"31."

As I thought, she was two years younger than Wulf and me.

"There's still time," I said.

She shrugged her shoulders.

"Perhaps I am to be like the Queen of England and never bear a baby who lives."

"She's older than you. Don't give up," I urged, squeezing her hand.

From the busyness of the market area, we made our way to the relative quiet of St. Paul's church. The interior was cool and dimly lit by candles. There were several altars set in alcoves along the side walls, with the central area being uncluttered.

A priest hurried to welcome us.

"We have arrived in London after a long journey and wish to give thanks," Edward explained.

"There is an altar here dedicated to St. Christopher. Perhaps an appropriate place?" the man suggested.

"Thank you."

We spent a few minutes in silent prayer, perhaps each of us praying something different. I was simply glad we had reached London without mishap and could now begin our new life. Maybe Maria prayed for a child. Margaret was very earnest in her devotions, which is more than can be said for her siblings!

Edward gave the priest an offering.

"Please tell us something of the history of this church," he requested.

"There has been a church here since the time of St. Augustine, 450 years or so ago," the priest replied, "but this building is not that old. There was a fire in the year 962 and after that this present church was erected. The dedication has always been to St. Paul."

We began to wander towards the east end with its apse and high altar.

"My grandfather is buried here," Edward told us. "Wulfgar remembers it happening. Edgar, let's find your great-grandfather's tomb."

The priest showed us the place and we each lit a candle to remember a king who had died over forty years before.

"Edgar, King Aethelred was only about your age when he came to the throne," Edward said.

"So I could be King now," the boy answered.

Edward laughed softly.

"King Edward is still alive," he explained. "When he dies, the members of his council – it's called the Witan – meet to decide who will be King. They choose from those who are throneworthy, the aethelings as they are called. I am an aetheling because my father Edmund was a king. If I became King, then, as my son, you would be an aetheling, but you are not one yet."

"Who else is an aetheling?" Margaret asked.

"I know of none except me," Edward replied. "None of Aethelred's other sons had children. The present King's brother was murdered many years ago and my brother Edmund died back in 1051. There are no others of the House of Cerdic, which is why I have been recalled from my exile in Hungary."

"There are no Danes?" I asked.

"None that I know of. Harold and Harthacnut both died childless, but there is a cousin, Swein Estrithson, who reigns in Denmark. I know nothing of him except we heard he had to fight for his crown against our old friend Magnus – oh, and Harold, the King of Norway."

Magnus had been in exile in Russia and was the same age as Wulf and me, so we had become special friends. He was only about ten when he went back to Norway and became its King. I had cried when told of his death several years later.

"I remember Harold," I said. "He was a warrior and no mistake. He'd made a fortune fighting for the Byzantines."

"Enough to win a daughter of the Russian duke and fund his campaign to rule Norway," Edward agreed.

"He has no claim to the English throne, does he?"

"None at all. He should be content with Norway."

Back at the palace, we found my father and brother were full of their visit to Alfred.

"He's sure we can work well together," Wulf declared. "He's really excited about the contacts we have in Sweden, Russia and Hungary, and the exotic goods we can get shipped in."

"He's excited too by our contacts at court," my father added. "He knows we'll get to meet the English aristocracy through Wulf having Edward as a half-brother."

"Everyone benefits," I commented.

"Alfred is going to look out for a suitable place for Maria and me to live," Wulf said. "When the court is in London, we will visit you here, but Winchester is two or three days' journey away, I believe."

"I expect the court will move between several places," my father added. "I remember a meeting of the Witan in Oxford. Edward, your father travelled around much of the country meeting the thegns in their own areas. That was before he was King though. His short reign was spent fighting the Danes. There was hardly time for anything else."

"I certainly want to get to know this land," Edward said. "We'll go to Winchester shortly. Perhaps the King will let me travel and get to know these places that are only names at present."

"I'd be happy to come with you if Wulf can spare me," my father said. "I think, Wulf, you should come to Winchester with us, so that you meet the King and pay him homage. Then we can spend some time in London establishing our business."

"Andrew loaded us with gifts before we left Hungary," Edward said. "We are rich, with jewels and beautiful objects. But I know, little brother, you are itching to use your talent as a trader."

"Hey, not so much of the 'little' these days! I'm as tall as you and have been for years."

Our meal that day was a definite improvement on the first one. Eric had ensured there was fresh bread and roast beef with a rich gravy, as well as some grapes and apples and a good wine.

Later Prior Wulfstan called to see if all was well.

"We went into St. Paul's," Edward told him. "Edgar, what did we find there?"

"A tomb."

"Whose tomb?"

"King Aethelred's."

"Well remembered!"

"He was my age when he became King," he told the Prior, who smiled indulgently.

"I can see you are learning about your heritage," the cleric remarked.

"Wulfgar taught me much while I was abroad," Edward said. "He had served my father and had been with him through many of his trials, so he has been able to tell me about him and even some very personal things. I never knew my father, but I feel I have a real sense of who he was."

"I never met him either, but his nickname of Ironside was well deserved from what I hear."

"He would be proud of what you have become," my father interposed. "Courageous, good and honest. Prior Wulfstan, I have seen Edward grow up to be worthy of the crown of England."

"The King will be very pleased to meet you," the Prior said. "The matter of the succession has been a grave concern for many years. None of us wanted another foreigner to rule us."

The next day, my father took Edward off on a further tour of London. I think they intended to find Westminster where Edward and his brother had been kept as prisoners until the family escaped and fled to Denmark.

"London is a busy place and a rich one," Edward commented on his return, "but I still saw many beggars hoping for alms. They cluster round the churches and ask for money."

"I expect you gave them some," I said.

He shrugged his shoulders. That was his way of saying that he had, but didn't think it worth dwelling on. I had noticed his quiet generosity on other occasions.

The food that day was even more lavish.

"Earl Harold has ridden to Waltham," Eric informed us, "but he brought a special dish for Lord Edward. It is a pigeon stuffed with a secret recipe. And for the rest of you there is more beef, but the cooks have used different herbs today in the gravy."

The children stared with wonder at their father's treat, but there was plenty of other food to keep us all happy.

"The wine is better than I had expected," Wulf commented. "I thought we might need to import some."

"The Italian wine we drank in Hungary was good," my father responded. "There could be a market here for some of that."

We all laughed at him, but he and Wulf were already buzzing with ideas about what they could trade. Agatha, Maria and I were more interested in talking about the ladies' fashions, as we knew we would need to dress in a more English style.

"I will only need to dress like a merchant's wife," Maria said, "except when I come to court, but you will need to wear more jewels than you have been used to wearing."

So we spent a happy evening speculating on how our life in England would be now that we had seen something of its most important city and had a better idea of its society and culture. We knew, too, we still had much to learn.

The morning light was beginning to find its way in through the shutters when Agatha shook me awake.

"Edward – he's ill," she gasped.

CHAPTER 3

"Agatha, what are you saying?" I muttered, as I struggled to focus on her.

"Edward has a fever," she cried. "I've never seen him like this. He is burning and restless."

I got up and hurried back with her to the bed she and Edward were sharing. He was tossing restlessly, but his eyes were closed. I put my hand on his forehead. It was hot and wet with sweat.

"I'll get some water," I said.

Soon everyone was awake and Anna took over my role as a nurse, while Elizabeth quietened the children. Wulf went to find Eric and returned to say Eric had hurried off to tell the Prior.

I found my father sitting at the table, his head buried in his hands.

"Father."

I put my arms around him, sensing his distress.

"He can't die!" he moaned.

"It's a fever, Father. Edward is strong. He will fight it."

He began to shake and I tightened my hold on him.

"His father …"

I knew then what was happening. He had watched King Edmund die, despite all the efforts of the monks at Glastonbury. Nothing had saved the young King and he had gone, leaving Edward a baby and his widow pregnant with another son. My father was reliving that nightmare.

"Edward is not his father," I told him firmly. "He has not spent a summer fighting one battle after another. He is strong and healthy."

He could not be consoled and though I spoke with confidence, I felt a tension inside and a terrible sense of foreboding. Surely God had not brought us safely here, after Edward's exile of forty years, for something awful to happen?

Prior Wulfstan arrived with two monks and was directed to the room where Edward lay. I stayed with my father, trying to comfort him. The Prior soon returned and Wulf joined us too.

"The brothers are skilled in dealing with sickness," the cleric said.

I looked at his furrowed forehead.

He's worried, I thought.

"Have you any idea what has caused this?" he asked.

"He was fine yesterday," Wulf said. "My father and he went off into the city." He laid his hand on our father's arm. "My father is not sick, simply distressed." He lowered his voice. "Edward is his life."

The Prior nodded in understanding. He seemed to appreciate our unusual situation, that we were not royal, but neither were we servants. I truly saw Edward as my brother and suspected my father felt for him as though he was of his own blood.

"You have all eaten the same food, so it cannot be that," the Prior commented.

I suddenly went cold.

"No!" I gasped. "Edward ate something different yesterday. Earl Harold sent him a special dish, a pigeon stuffed with … with a secret recipe."

I caught Wulf staring at me.

"Poison!" I breathed.

"Edie, no! Surely not?"

"Dear lady," the Prior interrupted, "you cannot think the Earl would seek to poison Lord Edward."

I opened my mouth to say something, then closed it. My mind was spinning. The Earl had shown us no warmth. I had a growing feeling he was cold and calculating enough to …

"Where is the Earl?" Prior Wulfstan asked. "He must be told."

"He rode off somewhere yesterday," Wulf answered. "Eric will remember where he's gone. I'll go and find Eric."

Maria came into the room as Wulf went out.

"What news?" I asked.

"The fever is great," she reported. "The monks are trying hard to control it, but there is no response yet."

She was twisting her hands and looked near to tears.

"What is happening to us?" she suddenly cried.

I reached out, took one of her hands and pulled her onto a seat next to me.

"We must pray," the Prior said, and he led us in an anguished cry to God for Edward's healing.

When he had finished, he noticed Wulf had crept in and rejoined us. The Prior raised his eyebrows by way of a question.

"Eric says Earl Harold went to Waltham," Wulf responded.

"That's about a day's ride north," the cleric commented.

"Eric is sending a messenger."

"We cannot expect the Earl before tomorrow at the earliest. In the meantime, the brothers will do their best and we must trust in God to bring deliverance."

We tried to eat and tried to make the children eat, but they were bewildered and unusually quiet.

Margaret snuggled up to me.

"Is my father going to die?" she whispered.

"I don't know," I answered. I couldn't pretend I had confidence in his recovery, for nothing had happened to give me any hope. "We must trust God for the future."

"I do," she said solemnly, "but I don't want my father to die."

"None of us does," I reassured her, but in my heart I wondered if he had an enemy.

Alone with Wulf, I faced my fears.

"From the moment I met him, I didn't like Earl Harold and felt he wasn't a man I could trust."

"But why would he want to harm our brother, Edie? Edward is the answer to the succession crisis."

22

"I don't know. I agree it doesn't make sense. But perhaps Earl Harold thinks Edward will take from him his special position with the King and even perhaps some of his lands. The King having an heir nearly ten years older than the Earl is bound to make a difference at court."

"But I still cannot think the Earl would … poison him."

Later I took some food into Agatha, for she had not left Edward's side. I doubted she would eat it. I also took some for the monks. Edward looked just as hot and restless as he had first thing. I sat by Agatha and took one of her hands in mine. Despite the warm weather, her hand was icy cold.

"Eat something, dear Agatha," I urged. "You are very cold."

"Oh, Edie, I cannot bear this," she whispered, and I could see tears welling up in her eyes. "He is my life and England's hope."

"I know," I said, rubbing her hand gently.

I turned to the monk who was bathing Edward's forehead.

"Is this something he has eaten?" I asked.

"Perhaps, my lady, or maybe he has been with sick people."

"He went out yesterday and certainly he met some beggars, for he gave them money."

"One of them may have been sick. No one else here has a fever, do they?"

"No," I answered. "But my brother did have some special food, different from the rest of us. Perhaps … perhaps it has caused him harm."

"It's possible, my lady. We are struggling to know the cause of the fever, but we are doing our best to deliver him from it." He looked me in the eye and I saw his deep concern. "We pray as we work."

Eric made a bed for Agatha in the room so that she could be close to Edward and we all urged her to try and sleep.

"We will wake you if there is any change," one of the monks said.

By morning there was no change and certainly no improvement. If anything, I thought Edward was worse. I was trying to stay strong and positive for Agatha and for the children, but inside I wanted to weep. Wulf did what he could to comfort our father, but his distress was heart-wrenching. He kept muttering, "Assandun, then Glastonbury, and now this. No, Lord, no!"

Prior Wulfstan came again and stayed with us.

"The word has gone around the city and many are praying for Lord Edward's recovery," he told us. "The brothers are doing what they can here, but … but …"

"He's getting worse," I stated.

He could not meet my gaze. He knew and I knew that Edward didn't have much longer.

In the late afternoon, one of the monks came to us.

"Lord Edward has begun to have fits," he said softly.

Wulf and I went back with him, so that we could be with Agatha. If our brother was going to die, we wanted to be there, but it was a painful sight. Poor Edward was delirious and his body kept arching as though he was in pain, but he did not scream out, only moaned and threw his head from side to side. Agatha was beside herself. I had her enfolded in my arms and could feel her shaking.

How long we sat like that I don't know. The priests anointed him, but were unable to give him the sacrament and I doubt Edward knew what was happening. The light was beginning to fail when Edward gave out a great sigh and his whole body relaxed. He was totally still. I think we stopped breathing too for just a moment.

The monk put a piece of glass near Edward's mouth, but there was no vapour on it. He had gone.

Agatha gave out a great scream and began to weep. She clung to me and together we cried for the loss of our wonderful Edward, a faithful and loving husband and brother. Our world had gone dark.

At that moment Earl Harold walked into the room.

CHAPTER 4

"I can see I am too late," Earl Harold said.

I could not see his expression through my tears. I was vaguely aware of Prior Wulfstan also appearing and of Wulf speaking to them, but what was said I didn't hear. My grief had overwhelmed me.

I can't remember leaving Edward's room, but somehow Agatha and I were pulled away from that awful place of death. In the main room, almost everyone was crying. Maria, Anna and Elizabeth were trying to comfort the children; Edgar in particular was crying like a baby. I sensed my dear brother Wulf was taking charge.

In fact, Wulf proved to be a rock during the next few days. My father was completely broken up and Wulf took on the role of head of the family. He liaised with Earl Harold and Prior Wulfstan with regard to Edward's funeral.

"Agatha," Wulf said sitting in front of her and trying to get her to focus on his face. "Agatha, Edward will be buried at St. Paul's next to his grandfather. He will have a funeral as befits an aetheling."

Her eyes were dulled from crying and she looked at him as though she did not understand. Wulf glanced across at me, as I was sitting next to her. I put my arm round her.

"Agatha, dear, Wulf is talking about the funeral," I said gently.

Tears began again to run down her cheeks. I pulled her into my arms.

"When, Wulf?" I asked.

"Tomorrow. All the arrangements have been made."

I nodded sadly. For the moment my tears had stopped, but I knew they would flow again at the sight of the coffin.

It felt as though all of London came to St. Paul's and all of London mourned. We cried, they cried, and the sense of loss was profound. England's hope lay dead, snuffed out like a candle, gone before his time. He had so much to give. He had learned so much about being a wise ruler through his living in other countries, but all he had learned lay wasted, like his shrunken corpse. We had not simply lost a beloved member of our family – England had lost its hope for a secure future. The problem of the succession had returned.

I looked at Edgar. Today he was not crying, but his face bore no expression. He seemed to be in a dream. Wulf had him firmly by the hand; otherwise I think he would not have noticed when we had to move forward.

Christina clung to her mother and they were both crying. Margaret, however, walked by herself, erect and composed. I think she had determined not to weep in public, but I knew how deeply she felt for I had heard her crying in the night.

The service was fitting for a man of royal blood and when it was over, I thanked Prior Wulfstan for his help. I couldn't bring myself to say anything to Earl Harold.

Back in the palace, my father was still very troubled.

"All Frida wanted was for her sons to return to England and be recognised as aethelings," he sighed.

"And our mother would be proud that Edward did return," I told him. "Father, you did all you could. It's not your fault Edward got sick."

"If God brought us back here, why did he let Edward die?"

I heard the agony in his voice. I shook my head.

"I don't know, but remember this, Edward's family is here. Edgar's very young, but he has royal blood and could one day be King."

He looked at me with such sad eyes.

"We must make a life here," I urged. "This is where God has put us. We must trust him for the future."

"I struggle with my faith. It has been tested much."

"Remember St. Paul. He had a really hard time, rejected, persecuted, but he kept going. God will help us, as he did St. Paul."

"I hope so," he muttered.

"This is a testing time for all of us," I added.

I too could make no sense of what had happened. It had seemed so clear. King Edward needed an heir and my half-brother was his nephew, the son of his half-brother King Edmund. God appeared to have provided an answer and had brought us through many different places and situations to be here, in London, at the right time, but now the heir had died without even meeting the King. I had no answer to the question "Why?", but part of me realised we had to press on with living here. Agatha had, in a moment of grief, talked of returning to Hungary, but that was not the answer; Wulf and I could see that. My father was in no state to make any decisions.

"What will we do?" Agatha agonised, looking at Earl Harold, who was with us.

"I shall send you to Winchester," he stated. "I have business in Essex, so will give you an escort of housecarls. The King will want to take you into his care, I'm sure of that."

There seemed little point in staying much longer in London. We needed to be somewhere that had no painful memories. I, for one, hoped never to be in this palace again. How feasible that would be I had no idea. What would our lives be like now? What would we do? Going to Winchester was simply the next step. Perhaps the King would take control of all of our lives, well, all of us except Wulf and Maria, for I was sure Wulf would return to London as soon as he could, but would not live in the palace.

Until we left London, I had seen nothing of England and as we travelled south-west I was reminded of Hungary with its lush grass. The early September light shone through the yellowing leaves and added gold to the green of the landscape. If my heart had not been so heavy, I might have thought of it as beautiful.

Winchester was a far more splendid city than London, its buildings more graceful, its streets wider and less cluttered. The noise and busyness of London was muted here.

"That's new since I was last here," my father told me, pointing to a great church. "I believe King Cnut is buried there."

"This is a special place?" I asked.

"The heart of Wessex, the home of the great King Alfred. King Edmund made it his base after the kingdom was split."

"But he isn't buried here, is he? I'm sure you told me he was in the west."

"At Glastonbury – that's where he died. We laid him to rest beside his grandfather, another Edgar."

He pulled his horse almost to a standstill and looked around. I paused too.

"This city will have a special place in the heart of every king," he stated. "Young Edgar needs to feel it is his home, the place where he belongs."

I glanced across at my nephew. He was riding with Wulf, seated in front of his uncle, who had control of the reins. He was pale and appeared to be dozing, uninterested in this historic city.

We came to the palace, a stone-built edifice near the church and our party was met by numerous grooms who hurried to take our horses. A man I took to be a steward welcomed us and took us inside.

"You've had a long journey," I heard him say. "We have prepared some rooms for you. Follow me."

We did and found ourselves ushered into our accommodation.

"This room is for your use," he said.

The room was furnished with a table and several chairs. There was a central brazier where a fire burned, taking the chill off the cool interior. Since Edward's death, the weather had turned colder or perhaps we felt more in need of comfort. The heat from the brazier was very welcome.

"There are three other rooms," he continued. "I hope that is enough." He glanced around and I wondered if he had expected such a large party. "I will ask for water to be brought for washing and also some refreshment. I will tell the King you are here and he will see you later."

With that, he was gone and we were left to make ourselves comfortable.

"Will you sleep with us, Edie?" Agatha asked. "I feel so alone."

"Of course," I said, grasping her icy-cold hands and rubbing them gently between mine. "Come, Margaret, let's find our beds."

The children, guided by Anna and Elizabeth, meekly followed my lead, as I took Agatha into the largest room. It was furnished with several beds and had two large cupboards. Was this to be our new home? I knew I had to put my fears and uncertainties on one side, for I had to be a rock to Agatha and the children. They were so utterly lost.

It was some hours before the steward returned.

"The King has ordered me to take you to him," he announced.

At last, we were to meet the person who had recalled his relatives to England.

CHAPTER 5

We followed the steward through several rooms before reaching the main hall. The light was beginning to fade, but the hall was lit with numerous candles, showing it to be richly furnished. The walls were hung with multi-coloured tapestries and there were cushions on many of the chairs. A large fire added to the feeling of warmth and luxury.

The King was seated on a platform with the Queen at his side. My father had told us Edward was in his mid fifties and they had not met for over forty years. The King's hair was greying into white, but his eyes were alert and I cannot therefore say that I thought him old. Close by his side, Queen Edith was much younger. She had a round face, a good complexion and no sign of wrinkles; she also had a sweet smile. Both of them were dressed in beautiful clothes, adorned with jewels which sparkled in the candlelight. We, by comparison, must have looked a sorry sight in our plain clothes. We were entering new territory.

"Come, come!" the King ordered, beckoning us to him. "You are most welcome. But we meet under such sad circumstances. Harold sent word my nephew was laid to rest next to my father. I am truly sorry. His death is a terrible event for England, as well as for you."

He was looking at our group, probably wondering which one of us was Agatha. My father took command of the situation.

"Sire, this is the Lady Agatha, Edward's widow," he said, drawing her forward.

She curtsied.

"I grieve for your loss," the King said, "which is our loss. Our whole country mourns."

I thought she might cry, but she held back any tears.

"Thank you, sire," she whispered.

"And your children?"

"My son Edgar."

Agatha took his hand and drew him forward. He dutifully bowed.

"And my two daughters, Margaret and Christina."

They curtsied.

"And?" The King looked at the rest of us.

"Wulfgar, at your service, sire. My son Wulf and his wife Maria and my daughter Edie."

Maria and I curtsied, while Wulf bowed.

"You are companions?" the King asked.

"Family," my father answered firmly. "Lord Edward was my children's brother."

The King had furrowed his brow, I think in puzzlement.

Earl Harold hasn't told him about us, I thought.

"I married Lord Edward's mother," my father explained and I saw the King nod in understanding.

"Family indeed," he agreed. "You met King Edmund's widow while she was in exile then?"

"No, I served the King, and then her, and went with her and her two sons into exile."

"You served my brother?"

I saw my father smile for the first time in several days.

"Yes, sire, we have met before."

The King gazed at him and shook his head slightly.

"I do not remember," he responded.

"On the King's campaign through Wessex, the battles at Penselwood and Sherston." My father paused. I could tell he was enjoying himself. "I'm sure you remember the battle at Brentford, your ... your courageous attempt to kill Cnut."

Now the King suddenly smiled.

"Wulfgar! Of course! You ... you were at my side."

"Yes, sire, and I remember you believed you would one day be King of England, and God made you that in 1042."

"After my own return from exile."

"My lord, you must have much to share," Queen Edith interposed. "Lady Agatha, I have something the children might enjoy."

She rose and drew us to a table away from the King, leaving him to talk to my father and to Wulf. The children were solemn and large-eyed, but gradually the two girls lost their shyness as the Queen got us involved in a game with coloured counters. Edgar, however, remained withdrawn and could not be coaxed into taking part, despite all her efforts.

Over the next few days, Queen Edith was very kind to us and tried to make us feel at home, though, frankly, it was difficult to relax except in the privacy of our rooms. The royal couple had a definite regal presence. I would describe King Edward as majestic and dignified; I could never imagine him playing raucous games with children. We discovered he had a passion for hunting and there was plenty of forest in Wessex so he would go off frequently with his hounds. He also had several hawks which he had trained to catch prey. I felt he was not a man to be crossed.

Wulf and Maria soon returned to London and my father went with them. There was no point my going too, as Agatha and the children needed me.

"Lady Agatha," the Queen said one day, "your daughters show signs of intelligence and an ability to learn … to learn more than embroidery."

Both Agatha and I looked up from the embroidery we were doing.

"It would be good for them to be educated by nuns," the Queen stated.

Agatha looked across at the table where the girls were playing chess. Edgar was watching them, silent as usual.

"Where would that be?" she asked warily.

"Wilton perhaps, that's where I was educated, or maybe Romsey as that is not far."

"I would want to see them frequently."

"You could go with them," the Queen offered.

"I would not leave Edgar."

"I could go with Margaret and Christina," I said.

"Oh, Edie, you are such a blessing! I would miss you terribly, but … but if you were with them, I would know they would be alright."

I turned to the Queen.

"It's a little soon yet to split the family," I commented.

She nodded.

"Perhaps after Christmas," she agreed.

About this time, we saw evidence of a more vindictive side to the King. News came that a leading thegn had died. There was quite a crowd of courtiers in the hall, including Earl Harold.

"Leofric? You tell me Leofric is dead?"

"Yes, sire," said Harold. "That means the Earldom of Mercia is vacant."

"I know what it means!"

The King had a way of manipulating his bushy eyebrows so that they met in the middle of his brow. I had learned it was a sign he was cross.

"I suppose I'll have to make Aelfgar the Earl, though he doesn't deserve it. He helped the Welsh to rebel and has given his daughter to the King of Gwynedd."

"But he has done homage to you since," Earl Harold reminded him.

The King grunted.

"We'll see," he muttered. "If he steps out of line, I'll banish him again."

I could believe it! But, then, as King, he had to rule firmly, and there was trouble from both the Welsh and the Scots and the King had to ensure the peace of his realm. I wondered how dear Edward would have fared as king of this country. I still grieved that we would never know the answer to that question.

The days were getting shorter and colder. Margaret and Christina seemed to have settled into the routine of the court reasonably well, but Edgar was another matter. We tried to draw him out of himself, but he was sullen and uncooperative. It was as though he had died with his father.

"Edie, I do not know what to do with Edgar," Agatha confided. "He hardly says anything. Today the King offered to show him his hawks; I made Edgar go, but he showed no interest at all."

"He misses his father. They did much together when we were in Hungary."

"I miss him too." There were tears in her eyes. "Will the pain ever ease?"

"Perhaps it will lessen in time," I suggested.

It was difficult for me to know just how she felt, as I had never had a husband. She and Edward had grown very close in their fourteen years of marriage.

None of us were looking forward to Christmas except that my father, Wulf and Maria promised to join us. They came in time to celebrate the mass on

Christmas Eve and to feast well with us in the following days.

"Maria, you are looking a little pale," I said, "and I've noticed you've not eaten much."

She gave me a little smile.

"It's a secret," she whispered. "You must not tell. I think I am expecting a child."

"Oh! That's wonderful!"

"Say nothing, Edie. Just pray it is born alive and healthy."

"I will," I assured her.

In the meantime, our desperate prayers for Edgar seemed to be answered, though not in a way we had expected.

"We have a new member for our family," the Queen told us, as she led a young boy to the table where we were sitting. "His father has just died and he is now my ward."

The boy looked up at us and we smiled a greeting.

"His father was Ralf, the King's nephew, and he is called Harold," Queen Edith explained.

"Do you play chess, Harold?" Margaret asked.

He shook his head without taking his eyes off her.

"Edgar doesn't play either," she added. "We'll try and teach you."

The children gathered at the far end of the table and I was pleased to see that Harold was willing to get involved in their games.

"He is the same age as Edgar," the Queen said quietly. "Perhaps they will be friends."

Over the next few days, we watched with delight as Harold, or Harry, as the children called him, began to talk more and to draw Edgar into the conversations. He had no brothers and sisters, so was very happy to find a new family. I got the impression he hadn't been particularly close to his father, though I'm sure he felt the pain of his death as any child would. Soon, the two boys, so close in age, were inseparable, and Edgar began to be more like the child we had known in Hungary.

As Candlemas approached, Agatha became more agitated.

"I'm not sure I can bear it," she confessed.

"The Queen has decided on Romsey," I said. "It's very close to Winchester. You could even come and visit when the court is here. Margaret and Christina will love the life of prayer and all the learning, and I will be there to make sure they are alright. You will still have Anna and Elizabeth with you."

"The Queen says the court moves around the country, so we could be in Gloucester, Oxford, London. Oh, I shall hate being in London."

"But there you will be able to visit Wulf and Maria and see something of the life they are making. Wulf says trade is very good."

"Your brother could sell anything to the English," Agatha smiled. Then she sighed. "It is such a different life from the one I had imagined."

"Different because Edward is not here, but this is how it would have been had he lived – going with the court around the country, learning what it means to be a king. Now it is Edgar who has to learn and he will – given time."

"How I thank God for little Harry. He has made such a difference."

"We must do what we always have done," I said, "and that is trust God for our future."

CHAPTER 6

London, late April 1058

"Wulf, there is a letter for you."

I took it from Maria's hand and pulled her gently towards me. Her swollen belly touched my torso. I kissed her lips and looked deep into her eyes.

"Is all well?" I asked.

"I think so."

"How much longer?"

"Not much. You and your father are so impatient," she complained.

"Isn't that natural?" I countered. "This baby has given my father some hope, some reason to live, after all that has happened."

"Then we must pray our little one lives and thrives."

The wistful tone in her voice tugged at my heart. I knew how much this meant to her. I had been content to have a lovely wife and no children, but she had felt she had failed me as she had not conceived.

"I think your letter is from Edie."

She was right and I was able to report that my sister was well and that Margaret and Christina were revelling in their new surroundings and all their opportunities to learn.

"Is there any news of Agatha and Edgar?" Maria asked.

"Edie says they are well too. Edgar has a friend at court, a boy about his own age, another relative of the King. They are learning to fight."

"A relative? Could he become King instead of Edgar?"

"I don't think so. The boy's grandmother was King Edward's sister and the female line is never considered for the throne."

"It is good he has a friend. We were all worried about him."

"This boy, Harry, has also lost his father. Edie says they had lands in Herefordshire – I think that's on the border with Wales – but there was trouble with the Welsh and now Earl Harold holds these lands."

"Is he keeping them for Harry for when he is of age?"

"I doubt it," I laughed. "Earl Harold doesn't let go of land once he's got it."

I didn't share my sister's suspicion that Earl Harold had poisoned Edward, but I was wary of him, for I sensed his ambition. He was not a man to trifle with and I was glad our paths didn't cross much. The court had not yet come to London, so I'd had no reason to visit the palace. It would happen soon; Edie's letter told me they would be here for Whitsun. By then, I should be a father. Our child arrived in the middle of May – a boy!

"He looks just like you did, when you were born," my father commented, "in his face that is. You were much smaller, being a twin."

"Can you really remember that?" I questioned. "I'm nearly 34."

He looked up at me and his face seemed to glow.

"I remember it like it was yesterday," he said softly. "My Frida nearly died, but I told her she had to live for me, for you and for Edie. And she did. She was a wonderful woman."

My mother had been dead for five years, but I knew my father still grieved. Edward's death had aged him too and I noticed he was much slower now in everything he did.

"What are you calling him?" he asked.

Maria glanced at me and smiled.

"Andrew," she said, "after the King of Hungary. If it had not been for Andrew and his rescue of our country from chaos, Wulf and I would not have met."

"It's biblical too," I added. "I hope you don't mind we haven't called him after you."

"A Wulfgar and a Wulf is enough in one household," he laughed, and it was good to hear that sound, for my father didn't often laugh these days.

Our baby boy proved to be a great joy to his grandfather and I knew what would happen when Edie saw him.

My sister came to visit as soon as the court arrived.

"Oh, Maria, he's perfect!" she cried and burst into tears.

I simply chuckled.

"You always cry, Edie," I said. "You should be happy."

"I am! I'm thrilled!" she sniffed. "Oh, let me cuddle him."

Our little bundle was held tenderly, but he soon began to cry.

"He is hungry," Maria explained, taking him and putting him to her breast. "I never thought this would happen, but here I am, with a healthy child, who suckles very readily."

"We have many opportunities to pray at the nunnery," Edie remarked. "I will pray for him to grow up strong and healthy."

"What is life like there?"

"We follow the Benedictine rule with its rhythm of work and prayer, but for us work is to learn. Margaret and Christina are both learning Latin and French, as well as studying the Scriptures and growing in their knowledge of music."

"They don't spend all their time embroidering then," I joked.

"Not at all, though they are being taught the intricacies of English embroidery."

"Our mother was skilled in that, do you remember?"

Edie smiled faintly. I think she felt the loss of our mother more than I did.

"Yes, but Agatha does not come from that tradition, so the girls are learning new skills. You must come to court and see how they are blossoming."

"We'll come and bring Andrew, for he's their cousin," I promised, "but I shall be interested to see how Edgar is."

When I had last seen my nephew he was withdrawn and pale, utterly bewildered and lost. I wanted to see if his friendship with Harry had really made a difference.

We went to court the next day and the baby became the centre of an admiring group. I sought out Edgar and found him in the courtyard, practising swordplay with a boy about the same height.

"Edgar!"

He turned and grinned.

"Harry, this is my uncle Wulf. Come and meet him."

"I see you are learning to fight."

"Harry and I are going to be the best knights in England," he boasted.

"I used to fight," I told him, "before you were born. I helped in the war to win Hungary, but thankfully I've had no need to wield a sword since."

"My father fought the Welsh," Harry informed me.

I didn't like to ask if that's how he had died.

"The Welsh and the Scots are always causing trouble, the King says," Edgar stated. "We will help to guard our borders when we're older."

I spent my visit listening to Edgar's chatter and being grateful he was not dwelling on the past. Edie had told me they were in a different part of the palace from the room where Edward had died and that was making things less hard for the family. I was glad Maria and I could return to our own home at the end of the day.

While the court was in London, I took every opportunity I could to be with Edgar. I could never replace his father, but I wanted to be there for him, a grown-up man who was on his side and in whom he could confide if he chose.

Being at court, I learned of a new project.

"The King plans to build a new abbey," Edgar told me, as we sat together in a sunny part of the courtyard.

"Where?"

"At Westminster."

I nearly said, "That's where your father was as a baby," but thought better of it.

"There's already an abbey at Westminster," I commented instead.

"It's not grand enough," Edgar responded. He leaned closer to me. "The King is very pious. They say it's because he's getting old. He wants to build a fine new church ready for his burial there."

"Building it will take several years, so he can't be expecting to die for a while."

"The cost will be enormous, but there are many rich people who want to help." He paused. "When I am King, I will be very rich."

I smiled, not sure whether to encourage such thoughts or not, but I was glad he was looking to the future.

"And I will give Harry his lands back."

"A king is rich enough to be generous," I remarked, and he nodded solemnly.

The following year there was an opportunity to see the court in a very different part of the kingdom. Edie wrote to say there was a plan to visit York and she and Agatha and the three children were all expected to go. Visitors from the Scottish court were also expected to be there.

"I remember going to York," my father said, "way back in 1013, when we had been conquered by Swein, Cnut's father. That was my first time there. It struck me as very Danish – and also very cold and damp. But you could make some good contacts there."

"Trade with Scotland!" I exclaimed. "I can't miss that. Maria?"

"You go," she laughed, "but do come back, for Andrew will miss you."

"I hope you will too," I said, kissing her.

So, with some fellow merchants, I made the long journey to York. Little did I know that it was in that city I would first meet a man who would have a profound influence on our family.

CHAPTER 7

The King was a rare visitor to York, so the court had taken over the Archbishop's palace. It was a fine stone building, but not the equal of the King's residence in Winchester, and York as such struck me as a poor relation of the Wessex capital. The streets were very narrow in places and many bore names reminiscent of the Danish Kingdom that was once here. As my father had warned me, the damp smell of the river pervaded everywhere.

I was greeted by Edgar.

"We've met the King of Scotland!" he cried with great excitement. "He's a real warrior."

"Is that why the court is up here in the far north?"

"I think so. They're doing some kind of peace deal." He winked. "The King is trying to tame the wild man."

I laughed. I had seen plenty of wild behaviour when we helped Andrew reconquer Hungary and I couldn't imagine a King of Scotland could be that wild.

"Are all the family here?" I asked.

"Yes," he said, dragging me off to find them.

"You look well, Edie. Life in a nunnery suits you!"

She rolled her eyes.

"I like the rhythm of life and the peace and quiet and the prayer, but I miss the company of men."

"Really? We might marry you off yet. Any eligible bachelors here?"

"The King of Scotland – I expect Edgar's told you about him – but he's younger than me, not quite thirty, I believe."

"And wild, Edgar says!"

"He's a warrior," she chuckled. "He's always wanting to make his country bigger or rather what he'd say is that he's winning back land the English have taken."

"That's why we're here in York? To encourage him to be content with his current borders?"

"They'll be doing some kind of deal on the quiet. Earl Tostig is involved."

"Ah, this is his Earldom, isn't it? The one place where he can't be bossed around by his big brother?"

"Don't you believe it! We all know what Earl Harold is like." She paused. "I like Earl Tostig. He's a much warmer person and," she lowered her voice, "the Queen's favourite brother from what I've seen."

There were others there whom I had not met before – the Archbishop of York, and a bishop from Durham called Aethelwine, as well as Earl Tostig's wife, Lady Judith. Even Earl Harold's wife, the beautiful Edith Swan-neck, had made the journey to York.

Edgar very happily stayed by my side chatting and telling me all the things he had been doing. He also made sure I met King Malcolm.

There was no mistaking the Scottish warrior. His hair and beard were both much longer than the fashion followed by the English and his clothes were good without being fussy. There were no jewels or rich embroidery on his cloak and tunic! Edie had said he was not yet thirty, but his face had some lines on it, giving the impression of a man who had weathered a few storms. His dark eyes appeared to miss nothing.

"I spent some years in the English court," the Scot told us, "before you arrived, young Edgar."

He grinned at the boy, who grinned back. I had the feeling this was the kind of king Edgar aspired to be, a warrior rather than a pious church-builder.

"Why were you in England?" I asked.

"My father, Duncan, was King of Scotland, but he was murdered and a usurper named Macbeth seized the throne. I sought refuge in England. But about two years ago, with English help, I managed to defeat Macbeth and recover the throne."

"I heard you killed him," Edgar added.

"Not at first. He escaped, but I had him hunted down and another claimant to the throne and … eliminated. There is no one to challenge me now." Turning to me, he added, "I believe you are related to Edgar."

"His father was my half-brother, so he and his sisters are kin, but I have no royal blood like them."

"I would like to meet your sisters, Edgar."

"I'll go and get them," the boy eagerly answered and ran off.

"I am a merchant," I said. "I bring in furs from Russia and Scandinavia, but perhaps Scotland has furs too."

The King's eyes twinkled.

"I can introduce you to the right people," he promised. "I'm sure our furs are just as good."

We did not get very far with our discussion on trade before Edgar returned with Edie, Margaret and Christina and introductions were made. King Malcolm immediately began a conversation with Margaret, who, at thirteen, had all the assurance of a girl on the brink of womanhood.

I was talking to the others and only slowly realised that Margaret was berating the Scottish visitor.

"But it isn't right," Margaret was saying. "All churches should look to Rome and to the Pope. I cannot believe that the Scottish church still holds to ancient Celtic practices."

"If it was good enough for St. Columba, then it's good enough for Scotland," the King responded.

"England rejected the Celtic tradition at the Synod of Whitby," she told him, "and since then has followed the Catholic way. That is very nearly four hundred years ago. Why do you not bring the Scottish church in line with England and the rest of Europe?"

"I haven't really thought about it," he confessed. "I'm far more interested in … expanding my area of influence."

I took that to mean "grabbing territory".

"Margaret has been learning about the history of the church," Edie explained. "Also we were in Hungary at the time of the great schism between the East and the West, so she has long been interested in church unity. Please don't take offence."

"I am not offended," King Malcolm laughed. "I am amused … and impressed. I see you have a fine intellect, Lady Margaret, as well as beauty."

Margaret unexpectedly blushed. Perhaps it was the first time she'd been paid such a compliment.

"You will make a fine consort for a ruler," he added.

"Oh, I wish never to marry, but to be a nun."

The King simply smiled at this declaration.

The next day Edgar wanted me to go with him round York.

"A leader needs to know the territory," he explained, "where the weak points are in the defences of a city."

"Is York likely to be attacked?" I asked.

"Not at the moment. The King of Scotland is unlikely to come this far south, though he may have his eye on a border near the River Tyne."

I was surprised that he was thinking this way at the age of eight, but then I wasn't there all the time.

"You're learning history and geography as well as how to fight?" I queried.

"Oh, yes. My father taught me a lot – he'd got it from Wulfgar. So I know York has defensive walls, like these." He pointed out the thick stone walls. "They are broad enough to be manned," he explained. "Also the river acts as a barrier, so an enemy wishing to capture the city would need boats as well as troops on the land."

"You're learning about strategy as well then," I commented.

"When I'm twelve, my military training begins in earnest. We go out hunting stags and wild boar."

"What has that to do with fighting battles?" I asked.

"We learn to move together as though we're on a campaign. We need to know where everyone is and what they are doing. Also we learn to use the bow and the spear to strike at our quarry and how to use our shields so that we don't get struck."

"You're already quite useful with a sword. Any other weapons?"

"I'll get to use a battle-axe when I'm a bit older and stronger."

For a moment I was back in Hungary and fighting alongside Andrew's troops in that desperate and wretched war to win back the crown for his family. I had been very happy to lay my sword to one side when peace came, but at Edgar's age I had been looking forward to my first battle. Part of me hoped he would never have to fight, but another part of me was much more realistic about the troubled future even an apparently peaceful country like England might have.

Back in the court, Edie pulled me to one side.

"King Malcolm has asked for Margaret's hand in marriage," she whispered.

CHAPTER 8

Our whole family was stunned by the Scottish King's request and powerless to control its outcome. Margaret was certainly old enough to be betrothed, though perhaps not yet old enough to marry, but I don't think any of us had seriously considered someone would ask for her hand yet. As a royal ward, her future would be determined by King Edward.

In the meantime, we ate and drank and chatted to other people at court as though nothing had happened. I had no opportunity to ask Margaret how she viewed the offer, but I knew she wanted to be a nun. Again, it was Edie who told me the news.

"The King has refused," she said, as we walked in a quiet place, away from the crowds.

"You do surprise me. Does he think she is too good a match for the King of Scotland?" I asked.

"No, I get the impression it would have been a very useful alliance and would have kept the Scottish King from attacking England."

"What's the reason then?"

"King Edward is very pious and has grown more so in recent years. He respects Margaret's desire to live as a nun, though he will not let her take any vows until she is older."

"Perhaps he thinks she might change her mind," I suggested.

"Possibly."

"Is King Malcolm affronted?"

"I'm not sure. They all seem still to be talking amicably. Perhaps he has been given some English land instead of an English bride."

The following year, when I heard the Scots had ventured into Northumbria and even attacked Lindisfarne while Earl Tostig was on a pilgrimage to Rome, I did wonder if an alliance with Margaret would have stopped such an action. Whatever deal had been done at York in 1059, the Scottish King felt free to break it in 1060.

In London, I noticed progress was being made with the building of the new abbey at Westminster. Sometimes the King came to see it and then Edgar came too. I also saw my nephew when I visited Winchester, though Margaret and Christina were not always there. I could see Edgar was eager to learn all he could about kingship.

"They are working out a plan to crush the Welsh," Edgar told me with great excitement, when I arrived to celebrate Christmas in 1062. "The King says the Welsh are lovers of theft and plunder, and are always keen to shed blood."

"Isn't Wales a number of provinces with different areas ruled by different people?"

"Someone called Gruffydd has had control of most of it for several years, but the King thinks that if he's removed, the other leaders will squabble and no one will be strong enough to attack us."

"Doesn't the King have a peace treaty with this Gruffydd?"

"He did, but the Welshman led a raid into England in the late autumn, so now the King feels he can have him killed."

Over the Christmas season, some serious planning must have taken place, but Edgar was kept in the dark as to the detail.

"I think Earl Tostig is going to be involved," he speculated. "I keep seeing him and Earl Harold in deep conversation."

I returned to London, but news filtered back of an attack in mid-winter when the Welsh were not expecting it. Earl Harold had captured Rhuddlan, the chief residence of Gruffydd, destroyed it and many ships moored there, but the Welsh leader had escaped. In the late spring the Earl took ships from Bristol round the coast of Wales, while Earl Tostig brought in troops from Chester. This two-pronged approach overwhelmed the Welsh and many of them hid in the high mountains in the north.

This was the position when I joined the court in August.

"The Welsh are very difficult to fight," Edgar told me. "They rarely meet an enemy in a face-to-face battle. I think they don't have the strength, so if their first headlong assault doesn't work, they often run away. They are very agile and only lightly armed, so can move fast. They also have great endurance."

"Presumably they know the land well and where they can hide," I commented. "I hear the mountains are very difficult territory for our men."

"Yes. I think Earl Harold is hammering away at them, hoping they will break."

I hadn't been at court very long when we saw, quite literally, the result of Earl Harold's labours.

We were gathered in the main hall. I was sitting with Edgar and Harry, listening to their latest exploits or, rather, how much better Edgar was at fighting than Harry, when word came that Earl Harold had arrived in the courtyard. King Edward leaned forward in his chair, eager to hear news.

Earl Harold strode in, went up to the King and bowed.

"I bring you gifts, sire," he proclaimed.

Several of his men now entered, carrying the prow of a ship. Others carried golden torques and arm bracelets.

"The Welsh are beaten!" Earl Harold declared. "This is part of Gruffydd's ship and I bring you, sire, some of his treasure."

"What news is there of Gruffydd himself?" the King wanted to know.

"He lost the loyalty of his men. They had had enough of war, of hiding in wretched bogs and dark caves." He paused to take in the utter silence of the hall. "His own men killed him."

A mighty cheer went up, but the King was not smiling. He waved his hands for quiet.

"How do we know he's dead?" he asked. "The Welsh lie. They could be hiding him, ready for another rebellion."

Earl Harold clapped his hands and a housecarl came into the hall carrying a large platter on which something lay covered with a cloak. The man stood in front of the King, and Earl Harold stepped forward to pull the cloak away. Everyone gasped. On the plate was the mangled head of a man, hacked from his body, the hair long and matted with blood, the eyes staring but sightless.

"The head of Gruffydd, sire," Earl Harold proclaimed, and another cheer rose to echo in the rafters.

"How wonderful!" I heard Edgar exclaim. "That is what should happen to all enemies."

Harry had gone pale, but Edgar's eyes were bright with excitement and the sweat glistened on his forehead. It was a moment he was unlikely to forget.

I sought out Edie in her nunnery and told her about Gruffydd.

"He was married to the daughter of Earl Aelfgar of Mercia," she said. "I wouldn't be surprised if she is now brought to court."

"As a prisoner?"

"I believe she has borne Gruffydd two sons. King Edward won't want them becoming rebels when they grow up, so perhaps they will be kept in England."

"Talking of two sons, I have some news. Maria is pregnant again."

"Oh, Wulf, that's wonderful!"

"We thought Andrew was something of a miracle, but I hope in a few months he will have a healthy brother or sister." I paused. "I'm not sure our father will live long enough to see it. He is very slow these days and he sometimes struggles to breathe."

"I'll come back with you to London. Margaret and Christina will be alright here in Romsey and I may be of use to Maria and to our father."

I was glad of her decision for it was a bittersweet time for us – the joy of a new life soon, the sadness of an old life coming to its end. Our father lived to hold his second grandson in his arms, but the following night slipped away in his sleep. We decided to call our new baby Wulfgar.

With all that was happening in 1064, I didn't manage another journey to Winchester, so was pleased when, in the late autumn, the court came to London.

"You've come at a good time," Edgar greeted me.

"How so?" I asked.

"You know Earl Harold went abroad and there was no word from him for weeks."

"He was safe in Normandy, wasn't he?"

"Safe is hardly the word, I believe," Edgar snorted. "Anyway, he's back, much to the King's relief, so we are eating well."

"Have you seen him?"

"No, he's still on the road, but expected very soon."

I smiled. The food at the palace was always good and that evening was no exception. There was plenty of venison and game in rich sauces, white bread and an abundance of fruit.

We were already seated when the Earl came in. He had barely had time to wash the travel grime from his face and I thought he looked troubled.

"Harold, at last!" the King cried.

Earl Harold bowed and kissed the royal hand, before taking his place at King Edward's right-hand side. The feasting could begin.

"So what happened?" the King asked.

We were all busy eating, but everyone was quiet, desperate to know the answer.

"I never made it to Flanders," Earl Harold reported. "An easterly blew up and drove us to Ponthieu."

"Ponthieu! Count Guy is not our friend," the King grunted.

"Indeed, he is not. He impounded my boat and goods and put me in jail, until he realised who I was."

"So, he released you?"

"No, not exactly. He did a deal with Duke William. I have no doubt money changed hands and I was taken into the care of the Norman."

"That was the rumour we heard," the King responded. "I feared for your life and have been worried sick. I couldn't help thinking of Walter."

"Who is Walter, sire?" Edgar asked.

"Walter of Mantes, my sister's son, Harry's uncle. Duke William took him and his wife into custody and …" He shook his head and paused in his eating. "Treacherous man," he muttered.

We had all stopped eating and were looking at the King. He lifted his eyes to meet Edgar's gaze.

"They both died while in his so-called care. He probably had them poisoned; he's like that."

"We don't know for sure, sire," Earl Harold interposed.

The King turned his gaze from Edgar to the Earl.

"So, did you find him kind and generous?"

Earl Harold played with his food.

"No," he admitted, "but he has allowed me to return to England."

"At what cost?" the King demanded.

The Earl resumed his eating, as did the King, but I sensed a confession of some kind was imminent.

"We heard you fought for the Duke," the King resumed.

"He was having trouble with Brittany, so he invited me to join his forces."

"Invited? Did you have the option of refusing?"

The Earl grunted.

"They fight on horseback, so it was a good opportunity to see how they wage war. I thought I might learn something. The Duke was pleased with my contribution. I hoped I had done enough to be allowed to leave."

"You were in debt to him because of Ponthieu?"

"In a way," the Earl admitted. "I felt I had to earn my release. And I thought I had."

"The Duke wanted more though," the King stated. "He's like that. Nasty little bastard, always wanting more, got to prove he's better than anyone else."

There was a pause in the conversation as the serious business of feasting was pursued, but I knew by the look on the Earl's face that even more serious business had been done in Normandy.

Eventually, Earl Harold said, "The Duke made me agree to marry his daughter."

CHAPTER 9

Everyone stopped eating. A marriage alliance between Earl Harold and Duke William's daughter was the last thing we expected.

"What's his game?" the King demanded, and I noticed his eyebrows had met in an angry frown.

"He must see it as an advantageous match," Earl Harold responded.

"Is he trying to get a toehold over here? I won't have him interfering in my country, whether directly or through his daughter. He's a bastard, born out of wedlock, so has no right to be a duke anyway."

"He's a fearsome soldier," Earl Harold commented.

"If you don't marry his daughter, what can he do?" the King retorted. "Bring his army over here and force you? Hardly. Little upstart. I remember him as a cocky lad when I lived in Normandy and now he's grown up to be insufferable."

"Did he make you swear to this agreement?" someone asked.

Earl Harold didn't answer straightaway.

"Yes," he muttered, "but …" Looking round at us, he added, "The oath was made under duress."

"You already have a wife," another voice added.

"They were not married by the church," the King stated, and I sensed a tone of disapproval.

"I don't wish to put my wife aside," Earl Harold replied. "I regard the oath as invalid and will not be pursuing the alliance."

"Duke William could be a dangerous man to have as an enemy," someone commented.

"Harold is more than a match for him," another chimed in, and there was some laughter.

I knew nothing of Duke William, but I knew enough of Earl Harold to believe he would not be browbeaten by a Norman who was the other side of the English Channel.

That he might be browbeaten by rebels within England never crossed my mind, but the following year, he certainly faced a severe challenge.

In late September 1065, I went to see Edgar in Winchester.

"You must come with us into Wiltshire," he urged. "We are going hunting soon."

"The King enjoys his hunting, doesn't he? Are you getting a taste for it too?"

"I love the excitement of the chase, working together – men, horses and dogs – to track down the quarry." His eyes shone with enthusiasm. "Then we sit down to feast on the prey. What could be better?"

I laughed. At fourteen, he was now very much an aetheling, learning about the responsibilities of kingship, but also the benefits of power. Hunting in the King's forests was restricted to the favoured few. I didn't need much persuading to join the party.

"So, Wulf, you are coming hunting with us," Earl Tostig cried, slapping me on the shoulder. "Can you leave your business in London?"

"It's in good hands, as I don't work alone, but can you leave your Earldom? Are you not needed back in York?"

"I have men who can handle the day-to-day business, so I can afford to take some recreation down south."

We made our base at Britford, near Salisbury in Wiltshire, where the King had a hunting lodge. Earl Harold was also there, as well as several thegns from Wessex. I enjoyed the evenings of telling stories and riddles as well as the daytime hunting – all men together, sharing an earthy sense of humour and bedding down on the floor of the main hall around the fire.

"We were meant to have gone hunting in Wales where Earl Harold was building a lodge for the King," Edgar told me, "but near the end of August the Welsh destroyed it. Both Earl Harold and the King were furious."

"That's hardly surprising. I suppose they thought the Welsh had now been tamed, but, of course, they've had a couple of years in which to build up fresh resistance."

"There always seems to be trouble from one direction or another," he agreed. "It isn't easy to be a king. The court will move to Oxford very soon, as there is to be a meeting there of the Witan. Will you come?"

"Maybe. I haven't been to Oxford, so it might be a good idea. You and Harry are learning about so many different aspects of royal life."

It was good spending time with these two youngsters, both made fatherless at an early age, but finding encouragement in each other's company, though of the two Edgar seemed the more aggressive and outgoing. Perhaps he had inherited his grandfather's courage, which had earned him the nickname Ironside.

We were about to enjoy our last day's hunting when a messenger galloped into the yard. A groom took the reins and the man slipped from the saddle, clearly weary from a long ride.

"Terrible news!" he gasped and we almost carried him to where the King was talking to Earl Harold and Earl Tostig. "York," he spluttered.

"What?" cried Earl Tostig. "Fire? An enemy attack?"

"They have killed many of your people, my lord and … and robbed your treasury."

"Who? The Scots? I thought Malcolm was my sworn brother."

"Not the Scots." The messenger struggled for breath. "Men of Yorkshire and men of Northumbria."

"No!" the Earl cried.

"Is this true?" the King demanded. "Englishmen have done this?"

"Yes, it's true," the messenger asserted.

"A rebellion," declared the King and his eyebrows furrowed together. "Harold, go and quash this."

"What about me?" Earl Tostig interposed.

"You'll stay at court until we know what's wrong," the King ordered. "If your people have been killed, you have no men to fight with you and this sounds personal, so it's best to leave Harold to sort it out."

Earl Tostig's face was a mixture of anger and surprise. His Earldom was in uproar, but he had been ordered to stay away.

"We will move the court to Oxford immediately and see what further news we can glean," the King commanded.

Earl Harold and his men went on ahead and the rest of us travelled more slowly north into the heart of Mercia. I rode beside Edgar.

"Earl Tostig has held York for about ten years, hasn't he?" I asked. "Why is there trouble now?"

"I don't know," Edgar answered, "but there have been a number of killings over the last year. I don't really understand it all and I only get to hear odd bits of news. I think there may be a power struggle and Earl Tostig has been eliminating rivals." He leaned closer. "I did hear that two of the men killed had been given safe conduct to his house, but they still died."

"He didn't keep his word?"

"No," he whispered.

"It seems trust is in short supply," I commented, and was sad that Edgar's world was riven with suspicion and treachery. I recalled my father telling me how my mother's first husband and his brother had been betrayed in a similar way while in Oxford. Oxford! That was our current destination.

By the time we reached that city there was further news.

"The rebels have complete control of the north and are marching south. They have rejected Earl Tostig and are demanding a new Earl. They have named Morcar, the brother of Earl Edwin," was the report.

"Where is Earl Edwin?" the King demanded. "He should be here in Oxford. This is his Earldom. Where is he?"

His voice was getting louder and his face was red with rage. The Queen had come from Winchester and she now tried to calm him.

"Harold will bring the rebels to heel and then we shall have peace," she urged.

By the sound of it, Earl Harold needed men from Mercia as well as Wessex. I sensed a real danger of civil war.

When it was discovered that Earl Edwin had already taken the men of Mercia off to meet the rebels, the King calmed down. After a few quiet days, a messenger came from Earl Harold.

"The rebels are at Northampton and Earl Harold has spoken to their leaders. They will not accept Earl Tostig and renew their demand for Morcar to be their Earl."

"Where is Earl Edwin?" the King demanded. "If his brother Morcar is with the rebels, has he not reined him in?"

"Earl Edwin has given his support to his brother and the men from the north."

"What?! How dare he!"

The King rose from his seat and stamped his feet. He also banged his fists on a nearby table.

"I am their King. How dare they disobey me?!"

His face grew redder and redder and I wondered if he might have a fit.

"Tell Harold to come back here!" he screamed.

For the next few days, we tiptoed round the building, trying to avoid the King and his foul temper. Edgar had pleaded with me to stay; I think his world had suddenly become uncertain and I was the one person he felt safe with. I think Harry was feeling the same. They both said they had seen the King get angry in the past, but this time it was much worse. I didn't voice my fears for the King's health.

We were to discover we had every reason to be afraid.

CHAPTER 10

When Earl Harold arrived in Oxford, a meeting of the Witan was called, but it was so chaotic that Edgar, Harry and I were able to be in the hall and hear all that was said. Queen Edith was also there and she wouldn't normally be at such a meeting.

"Tostig, they have totally rejected you," Earl Harold reported. "They will not have you back as their Earl under any conditions. You taxed them too hard."

For a moment Earl Tostig was too stunned to speak; then he found his voice.

"This is all your fault, Harold!" he shouted. "You told me to raise the level of taxes, so that the north paid the same as the south. I was only following your instructions."

"Come now, Tostig, you run your Earldom your way, as I run mine my way. I may have *advised* you to raise taxes. I would not have *ordered* you."

"That's not true!" he cried, going up to Earl Harold and grabbing the front of his tunic.

Now the Queen screamed. She leapt from her chair and rushed to pull her brothers apart.

"Stop this! Stop!"

Both men stepped back.

"Is it just the issue of tax?" a thegn asked, perhaps in an effort to diffuse the quarrel.

Earl Harold glanced at the questioner.

"No, the men of York resent the deaths of some of their leading men."

"I heard it said Earl Tostig had men punished simply out of a desire to confiscate their property," another thegn stated.

"That's not true!" the Earl responded. "I have only punished those who deserved it. I've done much to restore law and order."

"These rebels must be crushed," the King suddenly intervened. "I shall call out the fyrd."

"That, with respect, sire, is not wise," Earl Harold countered. "Winter is near and the men will not want to fight. Besides, we would need a large force to defeat both those of the north and Earl Edwin's men." He paused. "Also, Earl Edwin has Welshmen on his side."

"What? He shall pay for his treachery! Why do men disobey me?"

The King picked up a cup of wine from a nearby table and flung it across the hall. A couple of thegns ducked to avoid being hit as the contents left a red stain on the floor, horribly reminiscent of blood.

"I curse you all, in the name of God Almighty! I am your sovereign, your anointed king. Why am I deprived of your obedience?"

"We are your loyal subjects, sire," Earl Harold firmly stated, in an effort to placate the King.

"Call out the fyrd!" the King demanded.

An elderly thegn now spoke up.

"Sire, fighting our own countrymen is not the answer. We would weaken our land and give a signal to our enemies that we are weak. This is what happened in the time of your father, King Aethelred, and we became subject to the Danes. We must stand together."

Many heads nodded in agreement.

"But we can't give in to them!" Earl Tostig cried. "This is my Earldom."

"Brother, you have lost it through bad judgement," Earl Harold responded.

"It's you, not me!" Earl Tostig answered. "You have stirred up this rebellion to get rid of me!"

Earl Harold stepped back and opened his hands in an expression of innocence.

"Why should I do that?" He sounded genuinely shocked.

"You see me as a rival. You want me outlawed. You can't deny it."

"I do deny it and swear by the name of God Almighty that I've had no part in this rebellion. You have lost their trust, Tostig." He turned to the King, who had slumped in his chair and appeared to be weeping. "Sire, I believe we should accept Morcar as the new Earl, then the men will return home and there will be an end of killing and destruction."

I noticed the Queen was weeping too, unable to bear the pain of seeing her brothers so deeply divided.

"Go," ordered the King, addressing Earl Harold, "and end this assault upon our sovereignty." He had shrunk into his chair and now covered his face with his hands, but we still heard his agonised words, "Why won't they obey me?"

We slipped out of the hall, as did many others, deeply concerned for the King and for our country. The price of peace was Earl Tostig's disgrace and we wondered what he might do next.

The day peace was made with the rebels was the 27th day of October, the eve of the Feast of St. Simon and St. Jude. As mass was said and we remembered these saints, I couldn't help thinking about their turbulent lives, two of Christ's twelve original apostles and almost certainly killed for their faith. It felt like England was on the edge of a turbulent and violent abyss, or had we pulled back? Would there now be peace in our land?

"What do you make of all this, Edgar?" I asked.

"I have been listening to the thegns and it's generally agreed Earl Tostig's rule has been harsh, but the final thing was the raising of the level of taxation."

"The leading men were hit hard?"

"Yes. Earl Tostig blamed Earl Harold for the rise and, well, we know Earl Harold can be forceful, so some people think Earl Tostig was right to blame him."

"But Earl Harold wouldn't want the north to rebel?"

"No." He looked around to ensure only he and I could hear him. "But Earl Harold is a bit of a bully."

"He always manages to get his own way," I agreed, and was suddenly reminded of Edie's suspicion of him. A cold hand seemed to grip my heart.

Harry joined us.

"Are you going back to London now?" he asked.

"Yes, I've been away for over three weeks. I think I should return."

"The court will come to London for Christmas," Edgar said. "The new Abbey is to be consecrated. Everyone will be there."

"Then I shall see you both very soon."

They both grinned.

"The consecration will be a splendid occasion," Harry commented.

Back in London, the city was full of news of the northern rebellion. We heard they had accepted peace and returned home, but not without leaving a swathe of destruction in their wake. The shires of Nottingham and Northampton were said to have been devastated. That was not all. Rumours began circulating about Earl Tostig. Some said the Queen was urging he be given other land, having lost his Earldom, but that his brother was opposing this. Eventually, news came that he had left England with his family and surviving retainers and had taken up residence in Flanders, the ruler there being his brother-in-law. Whether he had been outlawed or gone of his own volition, no one was sure, but there was a general agreement that he was bound to come back. Earl Tostig was not a man who could be humiliated without retaliating. He was a dangerous person to have lurking angrily abroad, planning revenge.

When the court arrived in December, it was obvious to everyone that the King's health had declined. Word went through the city like a fire. He had been King for 23 years and had brought peace and stability after the end of the Danish line of kings. The sense of insecurity was palpable.

"I can't believe how changed the King is," Edie said to me. "I haven't seen him since August. He was strong and well then, but now he is so frail and … mithered."

"It's this business of the northern rebellion and Earl Tostig leaving England that has aged him," I explained. "I did wonder. He went into terrible rages over it and wept like a child."

"I fear he may not be well enough to attend the consecration of the Abbey."

"I see Prior Wulfstan is here in London. We haven't seen him for a while."

"He is Bishop of Worcester now," Edie said, "so he often attends court. You'll see he's deep in conversation with Margaret; she asks him questions about theology whenever she has the opportunity."

Edie was right about the King. He attended mass on Christmas Day, but by the time of the consecration service three days later, he was reported to be confined to his bed. Some of the time he was asleep, but there were rumours of feverish dreams and even a prophetic vision of the destruction of his kingdom. The city seemed to be holding its breath, praying for his survival, but expecting his death.

When I rose on the morning of the 6th day of January, I could hear cries in the street. I rushed to the door.

"What's happened?" I asked.

"King Edward has died," a man hurrying by stopped briefly to tell me. "Earl Harold has been proclaimed the new King."

CHAPTER 11

I hurried to the palace, desperate to find Edgar. He was with a group of thegns.

"Wulf, have you heard what's happened?" he cried.

"I've heard King Edward has died, God bless his soul, and ... and that Earl Harold is to be the new King. But ... but how can that be?"

"How indeed," Edgar snorted. "He isn't an aetheling. He doesn't have any royal blood in his veins."

"He had Danish royal ancestry, as a descendant of Harold Bluetooth," a thegn responded.

"But no *English* royal blood," Edgar countered.

"He says King Edward commended the kingdom to him," another thegn reported.

"Yes, of course my uncle could ask him to protect the realm, but he cannot have meant him to be King. I should be King. I am the true heir, born of the House of Cerdic."

"You are young and we need a strong military leader," someone argued.

"My great-grandfather Aethelred was made King when he was six and older people helped him rule until he was of age. I am not too young."

"You may well be right that the crown should be yours, but Earl Harold has powerful backing."

"He has the military might to bully people into submission," Edgar grumbled.

"Has the Witan already chosen him?" I asked. "The day has hardly begun."

"The Witan has already met," one of the men reported. "We could see the King was very near the end."

"Who was with him when he died?" I wanted to know.

"The Queen and Earl Harold, Stigand Archbishop of Canterbury, and Robert Fitz Wymarc, the palace steward," a thegn said, "and a few of his faithful servants."

"So, who is to vouch for the Earl's claim that the King named him as his successor, for I think that is what you are saying?" I asked.

"Earl Harold told the Witan that King Edward had named him as the next king," the thegn said.

"It's a lie!" Edgar shouted. "He's twisted the words to suit his purpose. My uncle cannot have meant him to be king."

"Surely the Archbishop can testify?"

"Archbishop Stigand was saying the King was delirious, but since the decision of the Witan, he has … he has claimed the King had a lucid moment," was the answer.

"You see how it is, Lord Edgar," one of the thegns joined in. "Earl Harold has the backing of the Witan. No one can oppose him. It grieves me to say this, but you are not to be the next king. The crown is already firmly in Earl Harold's hands and later today it will be placed on his head."

"Come, Edgar," I said. "Let's find Edie and the others."

In the privacy of their room, the young man broke down and wept. He even allowed Agatha to try and comfort him.

"I thought something like this might happen," Edie said quietly, as she and I sat apart from the others. "I have never trusted that man. From the first time we met him, I felt he was our enemy."

"We have no evidence, Edie," I argued.

"No evidence he poisoned Edward," she admitted, "but see what's happened now. He has taken the crown that should have been Edgar's. You surely don't believe this was King Edward's intention?"

"I cannot believe the King would choose a man who was not of the royal house, as he had such a strong sense of his family history and of tradition. Only a true aetheling could be King and even though Edgar's father was never King, everyone has regarded Edgar as an aetheling from our earliest days. Indeed, he is the *only* aetheling."

"You see what I mean? Earl Harold has been plotting this for a long time. Behind people's backs he has probably been gaining support for this idea. The Witan, or at least some members of it, must have been privy to his plans and the rest have fallen easily into line because Earl Harold is not a man who can be opposed."

She glanced across at Edgar.

"It's terrible," she whispered. "Poor Edgar. He will have to pay homage to this usurper. I think we are his only friends."

"Any thegns who are unhappy about Earl Harold being King will keep quiet. No one will speak for justice – and it's too late now, as the Witan has already met and made its decision."

"With the King hardly cold in his bed. How despicable!"

Edgar had quietened down by the time Harry arrived.

"Edgar, this is awful," his friend said.

"I know. I should be King."

"Of course you should, but Earl Harold has more power. There's no way of fighting him."

"He's managed to get all the thegns to back him," Edgar complained. "I thought he wasn't that friendly with Earl Edwin of Mercia and his brother Earl Morcar."

"He wasn't, but he's got them onto his side, from what I've just heard, by agreeing to marry their sister. Alditha will be his Queen."

Edgar snorted in disgust. "So, he will put his present wife aside, so that he can be King."

"Earl Harold has the knack of getting his own way," I commented drily.

"We made this journey to England so that my dear Edward could be King," Agatha said. "After his death, I thought at least my son will be King, but now … How I wish we had never come here, but stayed in Hungary where we were happy."

"Dear Agatha, we must do what we have always done," Edie responded. "We must trust in God. Who knows what might happen?"

"Harold might die," Edgar gloated.

"Edgar, don't even think like that," I scolded. "Shortly he will be a crowned King and such talk would be treason. Keep your counsel."

"And pray for grace," Edie added. "You'll need it when you bend your knee to him."

That moment soon came. In the late morning, we joined the rest of the court as King Edward's body was laid to rest in the newly consecrated Abbey. The lofty building burned with numerous candles and the air was thick with incense and the chanting of the monks. His funeral mass was followed immediately by the new King's coronation.

A chair had been placed in front of the altar and Ealdred, Archbishop of York, took his position between the chair and the people. With both his hands he was holding upright a sword, symbol of state power. Earl Harold approached him and the Archbishop stretched out his hands to offer the sword to him. Harold took it. I could not see his face, but I could imagine his feeling of triumph.

The Archbishop then invited him to be seated and thus the new King was enthroned. The Archbishop anointed his forehead and his hands (the sword having been put to one side) and then placed a crown upon his head, an orb in his left hand and a sceptre in his right.

"God bless King Harold!" he cried and we all joined in, some of us without much enthusiasm probably, but there were plenty of voices raised in his support. Only his family – and perhaps Harry – were thinking of Edgar.

All the thegns then had to do homage and pledge their allegiance. I tried to do it without looking at Harold's face, but I couldn't help glancing up at him. All I saw was triumph and cold ambition. At that moment, even I could believe he had killed my brother.

CHAPTER 12

Within two weeks of his coronation, King Harold had married Alditha and had had her crowned as his Queen. The beautiful Edith Swan-neck would not be mentioned again, but no doubt the King had provided well for her and the children she had borne him. He would be hoping Alditha would provide him with an heir. If she didn't, then there was still a possibility of Edgar becoming King.

"Queen Alditha is still young and healthy," Edie told me. "She was married to King Gruffydd of Wales and has two sons, but there is every reason to believe she will give King Harold a son." She sighed. "Sometimes I worry about Margaret and Christina. Alditha is the daughter of an Earl and both her father and her brothers have used her in their alliances. She has been a pawn in the hands of powerful men. Will they be pawns too?"

"Does the King control their future?" I asked.

"Not necessarily. They are still wards of Queen Edith. King Edward respected their desire to be nuns, both of them, and therefore did not arrange marriages for them, but for the time being they are not to return to Romsey, but are to stay with the court. Queen Edith is so bereft and she treats them like her daughters, so they are a great comfort to her."

"And Edgar?"

"King Harold is keeping a close eye on him. He will not be allowed to stir up trouble. The King will soon be travelling to York to receive the submission of all the thegns in the north and Edgar will go with him. Harry does his best to keep Edgar from moaning all the time, but he had no expectation of being King and has a much more pliant character. Edgar is angry and bitter, though he does not always show it."

The court was away in York for just over a month and when Edgar returned, he reported everyone had meekly submitted to King Harold. There had been some fears that Earl Tostig would be reinstated, but the new King had denied that was his intention, and the fact that he had put aside Edith Swan-neck to marry Earl Morcar's sister was taken as evidence of his goodwill. In further appeasement of the northerners, the King had created a new Earldom, carved out of Tostig's lands in Northamptonshire and Huntingdonshire, for Waltheof, the son of Siward, who had been Earl of Northumbria in the past.

Tostig himself was still believed to be in Flanders. Having heard his brother was now King, he might have hoped he would be recalled to England, but, as far as I knew, the King had no intention of giving his brother a place at court and perhaps an Earldom. We feared what he might do, but soon discovered there was a greater threat from a different quarter.

I was at court the day the Norman delegation arrived.

"Who are these people?" I whispered to Edgar.

"They've come from Duke William. Do you remember how King Harold was held a sort of prisoner there about eighteen months ago?" he whispered back.

"Oh yes, he agreed to marry the Duke's daughter."

Edgar raised his eyebrows and nodded.

There was quite a gathering in the hall, several of us being very curious as to why the delegation had come.

"Duke William sends us to express his surprise that you have been crowned King of England and in such haste, the coronation being on the day of King Edward's burial."

"There was no haste," King Harold responded, frowning slightly. "All the court were here in London. The Witan was able to meet and make an immediate decision."

"Duke William says you have no kinship to the late King Edward, whereas he is kin through Queen Emma."

"Duke William is a bastard and has no claim to the English crown," King Harold's voice was clear and loud.

"He claims the late King made him his heir."

"What utter nonsense!"

"He also claims that on oath you became his vassal and agreed to his claim." The Norman speaker looked around him. "Your own men witnessed your taking the oath."

King Harold did not answer immediately. Beads of sweat had formed on his forehead.

"Whatever oath I took," he said slowly, "was not in support of your Duke's claim to England and was made under duress."

"Are we to report that you will not surrender the crown to the rightful heir, Duke William?"

"I most certainly will not," was the emphatic reply.

"We are instructed to warn you that if you do not keep your oath, you will be regarded as a perjurer and usurper, and Duke William will come and take his kingdom by force."

"You tell that damn bastard to keep out of my country!" the King cried. "He has no claim here and if he tries to invade, we will crush him."

News of this encounter swept through London like a spring tide. We merchants were very sceptical.

"Duke William has no boats to speak of, so how could he invade England?" one man said.

"He would need a huge army to conquer us."

"The Danes did it."

"But they had ships and had worn us down over years of raiding. And they got us when we were weak. Now we are a strong and united country."

"This threat is very bad for trade."

No one believed the Norman Duke had the power and resources, but we all felt our business would suffer because of the uncertainty.

The King remained in London, and when Easter came in mid April there were services in the Abbey and feasting in the palace – and no one mentioned

Normandy. In fact, the gossip was centred more on Tostig and what he might be planning, for he was known to have ships and resources at his disposal.

"I tell Agatha to trust God, but I sometimes wonder what the future holds," Edie said one day as she sat in our house watching my sons playing. "Will there be peace for these boys? Will they grow up to be men?"

"King Edward's reign was one of peace," I responded. "There was trouble on the borders, in the west and the far north, but not here in the south."

"King Harold should not have been King, yet no one in England opposes him. Will God bless his reign? I cannot explain it, but I am troubled."

"You've been listening to people talking about the light in the sky," I laughed.

She did not smile.

"I've seen the light. It is very bright and strange. No one can remember ever seeing such a thing before and some do say it's an ill omen. Is God really warning us of some terrible disaster?"

I felt a shudder of cold. My sister had been right about King Harold. Could she be right about this?

"If it's a warning, what can we do?" I asked.

Her troubled eyes met mine.

"Continue to pray," was her quiet answer.

The bright light was the talk of London for a whole week. Then it disappeared as quickly as it had come, leaving everyone mystified.

It was soon after that we heard Tostig had landed on the Isle of Wight. He hadn't stayed long and was next reported to be raiding along the south coast. The King called up the fyrd and set off for Kent to repel him. Tostig had jumped back into his boats. During May, he had tried to land and get support all up the east coast and had even brought ships into the Humber, but Earl Edwin and Earl Morcar had made sure he was pushed out. The last we heard he was in Scotland at the court of King Malcolm with a much depleted force. I doubted we had heard the last of him. The Scottish King would be happy to cause trouble and was said to be Tostig's sworn brother.

Queen Edith had returned to Winchester and taken Margaret and Christina with her. There was a possibility they might go back to Romsey, at least for a while, but the Queen was still in need of comfort, especially with this news of her two brothers at war.

The court remained in London, but we didn't see much of the King himself. After repelling Tostig, he had been expected back there, satisfied that the threat from his brother had been countered. It was the middle of May before I began to get a real sense of what was happening.

"The King hasn't been in London much," I commented to Edgar, when I visited him at court.

"He's with the fleet on the Isle of Wight," was the reply. "Or, at least, that's where he was the last I heard."

"But Tostig has gone north now."

"You remember the men from Duke William? You remember their threats?"

"To invade, yes. But the Duke has no ships."

"He has now. He's got some from Flanders and has also been building. There are spies who keep us informed."

"So, this threat to invade England and claim the crown, this is a real threat?"

"King Harold has called up the fyrd and there are men all along the coast from Southampton to Sandwich and the fleet is on constant alert, ready at any time to sail out from the Isle of Wight to meet the invader."

"I had no idea it was that serious." I was genuinely shocked.

"There is more, Wulf."

I looked intently at his face, the furrowed forehead and the troubled eyes.

"There are rumours Duke William has sought the support of the Pope," he said quietly. "He is making this a holy war, claiming God is on his side."

CHAPTER 13

For the next two months we all seemed to hold our breath. The uncertainty was very bad for trade with Europe, though other doors were still open to us. As merchants, we would pool what information we had gleaned. The consistent report was that Duke William was assembling a considerable force, which was moored at the mouths of the Seine and Dives rivers.

The middle of July came with news from the coast that the fyrd had been refreshed with new men from the countryside. The danger of invasion was still there, but the wind was blowing from the east and preventing Duke William from bringing his fleet to a point where the English Channel was narrower. We began to think the Normans would not come.

By early September, King Harold was faced with a decision. The current fyrd had been on duty for two months and the men were anxious to get back to the land. Supplies were running low and the wind was still from the east. An invasion now looked very unlikely, so the King disbanded the fyrd and ordered the fleet to sail round into the Thames.

Duke William suddenly decided to move his fleet, as I think there was a brief lull in the weather. We heard rumours that there had been a clash at sea between some of our boats and some of his, but that neither side could claim a victory. It was reckoned the weather had again been a factor in causing losses to both fleets. Duke

William was now said to be at St. Valery with his remaining boats. No one could see how he could invade now; he would have to wait until next year. God appeared to be on our side, not his.

I heard the King was back in London, so took the opportunity to go to court and see what news I could pick up. I was always welcome there, as everyone knew I was Edgar's uncle. It was now mid September. Edgar could tell me no more than I already knew – the fyrd had been disbanded, the fleet was now in the Thames and the Duke's fleet had suffered losses.

"So, it looks as though the threat is over," I commented.

We were sitting in the main hall with many people of the court gathered in small groups sharing news. The King was in deep discussion with Earl Leofwine, one of his brothers.

"Can we really relax?" Edgar asked.

"Duke William won't come now," Harry suggested, "and he must be struggling over supplies, having kept his fleet ready all summer."

"A king should never underestimate his enemies," Edgar remarked. "They strike when they think you are least expecting them."

At that moment, a messenger stumbled into the hall and almost fell at the King's feet. Everyone stopped talking.

"Invasion!" gasped the man.

"What?" cried King Harold. "The wind has not changed. He can't have invaded."

"From the north."

"The north?" The King was on his feet. "What do you mean?" He bent down to pull the man up. "Speak up."

"Your brother and the King of Norway, they have ravaged the coast of Northumbria and the city of York is under threat."

"Tostig! The traitor, and in league with that axeman, the so-called Thunderbolt! I must ride north at once."

"Can I come?" Edgar cried.

The King briefly glanced in his direction.

"No, certainly not, this fighting is for men. You are to stay in London." He turned to his brother. "Leofwine, I leave you in charge down here."

Edgar's shoulders slumped and he frowned in annoyance. I put my hand on his shoulder, partly to stop him doing anything stupid and partly to encourage him, to let him know someone was on his side.

No one took any notice of us in the frantic activity that followed. Before the day was out, messengers had gone ahead on fast horses to call up men on the way north and the King himself had left, accompanied by his housecarls. By the time he reached York, he should have been able to gather a sizable force. All we could do, back in London, was wait – and pray for his success.

The city was unusually quiet. We tried to live normal lives, but found it almost impossible. The churches were filled with people praying and I, for one, couldn't sleep. Each day I went to court to see if there was news. I had to wait until the 24th day of September.

"Wulf!" Edgar cried, when he saw me. "A messenger has come to say York fell to the invaders a few days ago."

"The King has fought and lost?" I asked.

"No, he isn't there yet. The Earls Edwin and Morcar tried to stop the enemy, but were overwhelmed. Tostig is back in York with the Norwegian king."

"That will make King Harold's task harder," I commented.

I sought out Edie and found her with Agatha.

"This is terrible news," Edie agreed. "Brother fighting brother and the people of York caught in the middle. I presume they would have had no way of keeping the invaders at bay."

"York is not an easy city to take, but Tostig would know its weaknesses and perhaps they surrendered rather than face the inevitable destruction."

"How I wish we were back in Hungary," Agatha groaned.

"It's good that Margaret and Christina are with Queen Edith," Edie said. "They have written that they are trying to keep her spirits up. Earl Tostig was her favourite brother and this fighting has cut into her heart.

She fears one of the brothers will have to die before there can be peace."

I nodded, for there was no way Tostig would ever be content in exile and I couldn't see the King restoring him to the northern Earldom.

Each day, time seemed to stand still. I was pleased I had my sons, for they were unaware of what was happening and smiled and laughed in their usual way, and that lifted my spirits. Their antics often made me laugh, which was good because there was little reason to laugh at that time, and I noticed how people had stopped telling jokes and sharing riddles which had been common practice when the old King was still alive.

September was almost over when news came again from the north. Many of us had gathered in the palace, thinking there should be word soon, when a messenger came.

"King Harold has triumphed!" he announced, and we broke into cheers and clapped our hands.

"He made very good progress north and many men joined his force. He reached Tadcaster on Sunday the 24th. He was but seven miles from York. There he learned the enemy was eight miles the other side of the city at Stamford Bridge, but that their boats were moored at Riccall, some thirteen miles to the south."

"That was very foolish. Why were they so far from their boats?" a thegn asked.

"They were expecting to receive hostages and had no idea the King could raise an army and reach them so quickly and that meant they were taken completely by surprise."

The messenger paused to get his breath and was given a cup of ale to ease his thirst.

"Our forces came upon them in a river valley," he continued. "Many had no armour and some no weapons, but even so it was a hard-fought battle. The man they call the Thunderbolt was their leader, but he was no match for our King and when he fell, his men deserted and fled for their ships."

"And Tostig?" someone asked.

The messenger paused.

"He too died in the battle. The King offered him a pardon, but he chose to fight and now has paid the full price for his treachery."

No one cheered. For a moment the hall was silent before men started to talk in groups. I slipped off to find Edie.

"I will send Margaret a letter immediately," she said. "The Queen will need her."

I returned to the hall and found Edgar and Harry deep in discussion with some men.

"There were considerable losses at Stamford Bridge," Harry told me. "The King is safe, but he has lost some good men."

"It's good he doesn't have to fight another battle just yet then," I responded.

"But what if Duke William invades?" Edgar asked.

"That's not likely now, is it?"

"Haven't you noticed, Wulf, that the weather has changed?"

I admit I hadn't. I went off to do some business and found, as Edgar had said, that the direction of the wind had changed. As soon as I could, I returned to court and found that everyone was discussing the change in the weather.

Suddenly, the hall was thrown into confusion by the arrival of another messenger.

"A Norman force has landed in Sussex! They've dug in and are raiding the surrounding countryside!"

CHAPTER 14

In one day we had received the best of news and the worst of news. God had given King Harold a great victory at Stamford Bridge, but a foreign invader had arrived who also thought God was on his side.

Earl Leofwine took command of the situation. He dispatched a messenger to take the news to York. He also ordered messengers to go out into the surrounding counties to call up the fyrd, so that by the time the King returned to London, he would have a fresh army at his disposal. There was no way anyone could go into battle with Duke William at this stage.

The news of both events had soon spread through London. In general, most people remained optimistic. King Harold was regarded as a great warrior, who had seen off the Norwegian King and would now see off the Norman Duke. I noticed though that Edgar was disturbed.

"Wulf, I know I've never fought in a battle, but they take a great deal out of a man even if he isn't wounded. And the King made a rapid march north and will now have to make a rapid march back south. He and his surviving housecarls will be exhausted, won't they?"

I looked at his troubled young face.

"Yes," I agreed. "The English fight on foot, not horses. In Hungary, we fought on horses, but a battle was still draining. Some of his men will be wounded and all will be tired. But the fyrd will provide fresh troops."

"But they do not have the skill, experience and discipline of the housecarls," he responded.

What could I say? I was sure he was right.

We waited anxiously for further news, wondering if Duke William would attack a city such as Canterbury or even Winchester, but all the reports coming in said he had built a stronghold at Hastings and was denuding the surrounding area of its resources in order to supply his troops. People who had not fled were likely to be killed.

I think it was about the 8th day of October when King Harold arrived. He brushed aside any praise for his victory near York.

"That bastard Norman is devastating my lands in Sussex," he said. "He must be taught a lesson."

Preparations were well in hand for an army to accompany him south, but as Edgar had said, his housecarls, as well as King Harold himself, needed some refreshment.

A messenger from Duke William was given safe passage to London and was received by the King.

"Duke William has sent me to say that if you resign the crown to him, he will allow you to remain Earl of Wessex."

King Harold snorted.

"Oh, docs he? How magnanimous of him! Does he not know what I have just done to others who invaded my realm? I sent the King of Norway back home in a coffin and I intend to do the same to your Duke."

"Is that the reply I should give him?"

The King paused.

"No," he said slowly. "I will match his generous offer with one of my own. Tell your Duke I will let him return to Normandy unmolested, as long as he makes reparations for the damage he has done to my lands."

It was obvious to all of us that Duke William had no intention of returning home in such a meek way. He had staked his life and reputation on this invasion. He literally could not afford to give up. He would therefore risk that he might return in a coffin, if he failed to wrest the crown from King Harold's head.

The King's final words to the envoy were, "The Lord judge between you and me", which sounded like a quotation from the Old Testament. Both men thought God was on their side.

"The King has dispatched the fleet to cut off the Duke's return to Normandy. He himself intends to march tomorrow," Edgar told me.

"Are his men ready? Does he have an army to lead?"

"He believes they will be ready by the time they reach Sussex, but …" He lowered his voice. "Some are saying he is too hasty."

"Does he think he can take the Normans by surprise, as he did the Norwegians?"

"I don't see how he can," Edgar answered. "The Normans appear to be waiting for an English attack. The situation is totally different." He glanced around, clearly anxious no one heard our conversation. "There is a rumour that Earl Gyrth, his brother, offered to lead the army and this suggestion was backed up by their mother. But the King got angry and said *he* and he alone would lead the army, but I don't know if the story is true."

"It sounds feasible to me. The King wouldn't want a younger brother having a decisive victory over the Normans and getting all the glory."

Was personal ambition clouding King Harold's better judgement? I wondered. The news was bad enough without encouraging thoughts of an English defeat.

The King left London on the 11th day of October with the housecarls who had survived Stamford Bridge and were fit to fight – that was considerably fewer than he had taken north some three weeks earlier.

The next day the Earls Edwin and Morcar arrived in London with their fighting men, accompanied by Archbishop Ealdred, who had been trapped in York by the invaders.

"The King has left already?" Earl Edwin asked, clearly surprised by the news.

"He thinks, brother, he can deal with this Norman upstart without our aid," Earl Morcar answered.

Those of us in the hall who heard this exchange glanced uneasily at each other. The Godwine family and the Mercian lords had not been on the best of terms, but we thought that had been put behind them, now that Earl Morcar had replaced Tostig and their sister was Harold's queen.

"I say, let him get on with it," Earl Morcar added.

"He has taken his housecarls, such as were fit," Edgar told them, "and is expecting a great gathering from the call-up of the fyrd."

Earl Edwin looked at him.

"If you were King, what would you do?" he asked.

I thought I saw Edgar swallow.

"This Norman Duke has a formidable reputation," he commented. "If I were King, I ... I would want the best army I could muster and I would take my time to assemble it."

"You would not rush into battle then?"

"No. We have the advantage. The Duke has limited supplies – that is why we hear he is raiding the countryside around Hastings. We might even be able to starve him into submission."

His voice was clear and I marvelled at his sense of authority.

"The fleet has been dispatched to cut off any retreat," he added.

"So he is like a cornered animal," Earl Edwin remarked. "But you know what that means?"

"He will fight even harder, like the Danes did at Assandun."

Earl Edwin raised his eyebrows.

"My grandfather had cut them off from their boats. They had to fight or die." Edgar paused. "King Edmund lost the battle."

A horrible silence filled the hall and I went cold in the pit of my stomach.

"Then we must go and add our troops to those fighting for the King," Earl Edwin declared. "Come, brother, that is our duty."

He signalled to one of his retainers.

"Prepare to leave London before nightfall," he ordered. He took his brother's arm and said, "Let's see how our sister is before we go."

I went to spend some time with my sister before returning home.

"The Queen will be pleased to see her brothers and to see that they are well," Edie said, "but it is a difficult time for her. All the men in her life are fighting battles and we know many will die on both sides when the King finally faces the Duke." She paused. "And there is something else. I believe she is carrying Harold's child."

"Has she told you?"

"Not in so many words, but I know she has been sick and off her food. I listen to the whisperings of her women. I have said nothing to Agatha and Edgar."

"How is Agatha?"

"When she first married Edward, she was young, but had a strong faith. I expect you remember."

I nodded.

"But his death hit her hard and the seizure of the crown by Harold hit her even harder. She is devastated and struggling to understand why God brought us all back to England."

"She keeps mentioning Hungary, but we aren't going back."

"I know, our life is here now, but God is putting her through a fiery test. She worries too about her daughters in Romsey."

"This invasion from Normandy is a test for us all."

"You think ...?"

"We dare not think of anything, but victory. The alternative is too awful."

Again the churches filled with people praying, praying for a repeat of Stamford Bridge. I could find no peace though and would wake in the night drenched with sweat, glad to find I was not sinking in the mud of a bloody battlefield, but in bed with my wife.

I think it was the fourth day after the Earls' departure that the news came, the news we had dreaded. They had returned together, but without the King.

"We were too late," Earl Edwin gasped. "The battle was over and men were fleeing from the scene. We met them just a few miles from where they had fought." He paused for breath. "The King is dead. Duke William is victorious."

CHAPTER 15

There was utter silence. Had we really heard those words, "The King is dead"?

"It is judgement on the usurper." Edgar's calm statement brought us back to life. "He took the crown which was not his and God has judged him."

All eyes turned on him, but no one spoke. Then Earl Edwin broke into our jumbled thoughts.

"We must call a meeting of the Witan. Aesgar, find the archbishops. Morcar, we need to break the news to Alditha."

Aesgar was the palace steward and he soon had servants running in many directions. Edgar, meanwhile, was still sitting, staring into the fire. I went to his side.

"Wulf." He looked up at me. "I did not wish his death, but it can be none other than the hand of God."

"Does God truly want us ruled by foreigners?" I gasped.

"No, we will fight this Norman."

"But what with?"

At that point, Harry came running in.

"I've heard the King is dead!" he cried.

"The Earls Edwin and Morcar have brought the news," I said quietly. "We don't know much more at this stage."

"The Duke has won?"

"He's only won *that* battle," Edgar joined in. "We aren't giving in."

"But our army? How many survived?"

"More news will come, I'm sure of that," I said, sounding more confident than I felt.

The meeting of the Witan must have been a small gathering. There were the two archbishops and also some other bishops who were in London, but the number of thegns was few. Some had gone south to fight with the King, while others were far from London on their estates. I think Archbishop Ealdred probably took charge, but, of course, neither Edgar nor I were allowed to be there.

I went home to comfort Maria and that was where Edie found me as the light was beginning to fade.

"The Witan has made a decision," she told us. "There is to be no surrender to Duke William and they have elected Edgar as King."

Maria gave a little cry of surprise and I think I gasped.

"He is to be King?" I stuttered.

"There are some who felt Harold seized the crown ... when he should not have done so, but their voices were too few back in January," she explained. "Edgar is closer kin to King Edward than Duke William."

"He is the only aetheling," I agreed. "And they will back him?"

"Earls Edwin and Morcar have pledged themselves and their troops to fight for him."

"He is so young," Maria said.

"Fifteen, certainly old enough to be King, though he could do with wise heads around him," I acknowledged.

"Archbishop Ealdred is a wise head," Edie answered. "Queen Alditha is leaving in the morning. Her brothers are sending her to Chester. If necessary, she can flee from there to Ireland, where her family has friends."

"If she gives birth to a son, he will be an aetheling," I stated, "for his father was a king."

"The threat to Edgar is not from the Queen's unborn child, but from the Norman aggressor. I fear what our future holds."

We had every reason to fear. Over the next few days, survivors of the battle began arriving in London, giving us more details of the fighting. The King had had his troops in a good position and their shieldwall had done well against the Norman cavalry, but there had been some break-up of the wall in the late afternoon. No one was sure how King Harold had died, but all asserted he and his brothers, Gyrth and Leofwine, and many of the housecarls had fought hard and had died where they fought – brave and loyal to the bitter end.

"It is difficult to get news," Edgar told me. "We think Duke William is probably expecting a total surrender, but we aren't going to surrender."

"So, what's happening?" I asked.

"We are strengthening the defences of London and I have sent out to call up the fyrd."

"Are there still men who can fight?"

"Of course." He paused. "But you're thinking we have lost our best warriors?"

I nodded.

"Earls Edwin and Morcar could lead them," he added.

And their only experience of war is the battle they lost near York, I thought, but did not voice my thoughts.

A few days later, we heard the Normans had moved east from Hastings, burning Romney and taking Dover, which surrendered without a fight.

"He can now get reinforcements and supplies from across the Channel," Edgar groaned, and it was the first time I had really seen him despondent. "Wulf, if Duke William conquers England, he could have me killed."

What could I say?

"Your father was here in London as a child and in grave danger of being killed," I began, "but God rescued him."

Edgar's eyes were large with concern as he gazed at me.

"If God has a purpose for your life, surely he will spare you?" I added.

I think my words may have helped, for the next day he was more cheerful. Soon afterwards, however, we heard Canterbury had submitted without a fight.

"Aesgar, what is the news of our defences?" Edgar asked.

"They are strong, sire. If we hold the bridge, the Duke cannot cross the Thames and we are safe."

It seemed inevitable that the Normans would come against London next. By now, we were sure the Duke would have heard the English had a new King and had no intention of surrendering meekly.

"When the Danes came against my grandfather, they tried to put a stranglehold on London," Edgar announced, "but we have free access to the north, so can bring in troops and supplies."

"So, a siege is unlikely?" Earl Morcar commented.

"The Duke would be foolish to try it," Earl Edwin agreed.

"What might he do?" I asked.

Everyone shrugged their shoulders.

"First, we make sure he doesn't take London," the young King declared.

We didn't have to wait long. A Norman force did try to capture London bridge, but Aesgar's preparations paid off and the invader was repulsed. We waited to see if a stronger army would then try, but nothing happened and word eventually reached us that the Duke was heading west.

"Wulf! What news is there?" Edie greeted me. "Agatha and I are sleepless with worry."

"We think the Duke is heading west and has given up on London, at least for the present."

"West! You know what that means?"

"You are thinking of Winchester?"

"Exactly."

"Oh, my girls!" cried Agatha. "What will happen to them?"

"Queen Edith holds Winchester as it was part of her dower," I said. "The Duke won't be interested in her, but in her treasury."

"Of course, the royal treasury is held at Winchester," Edie gasped. "The Duke will want that."

"And my girls?"

"We think Margaret and Christina are in Romsey, which is further west," I answered. "I doubt the Duke will go beyond Winchester and as they are not aethelings, they won't concern him."

I spoke with confidence, but, frankly, I had none. We all knew what happened to vulnerable women when warriors were victorious – they were part of the spoils of war. So far we had heard of killings and the burning of property, but there were bound to have been other atrocities. I found it hard to calm the real fears of Edie and Agatha.

Several days passed before we had any further news. I was at court when a breathless messenger arrived.

"There has been terrible destruction," he gasped. "When the Duke could not take London, he went west and has been laying waste the land."

"Not just foraging for supplies – is that what you mean?" Earl Edwin asked.

"Far more than foraging," the messenger confirmed. "He's been burning townships and killing everyone in his path."

"There is nothing to stop him," Earl Morcar responded.

Every face there was registering the horror of what we were hearing.

"He went through Kent, Sussex and into Hampshire," the messenger continued.

"Winchester?" Edgar asked anxiously.

"He has not damaged Winchester."

"Because he has not got that far?"

"Because Winchester has submitted."

There were groans from several of us.

"The Duke sent troops to demand the surrender of the city. Queen Edith and the leaders there agreed on the basis that they would do homage to him and pay him a rent in future."

"That was very lenient!" Earl Edwin cried.

"It has not been like that anywhere else," our man added. "Towns that resisted have been burned, others have submitted, but on payment of great sums of money."

"And where is the Duke now?" Edgar wanted to know.

"It is thought he is at Wallingford."

"He can cross the Thames there," Earl Morcar mentioned. "Oxford is now vulnerable and also the Duke can come east and cut off London."

"We should surrender." The voice was Harry's.

Edgar looked at his friend, but the look on his face was far from friendly.

"What did they call your father?" he said slowly. "Wasn't it Ralf the Timid? So, will you too be known as Harold the Timid?" He paused, not expecting a reply. "As for me, I will not go down in history as King Edgar the Timid. We fight on."

The only glimmer of light in this terrible darkness, at least for me, was that the Normans had not attacked Winchester, nor gone further west. For the time being, Margaret and Christina were probably safe.

The mood in London was recalcitrant, but we weren't suffering like other parts of England were. Edgar talked of fighting, but how could we? We had forces, but nothing to match the rampaging Normans.

When I went to court the next day, I had an uneasy feeling, and soon after my arrival Archbishop Ealdred hurried in with news for Edgar.

"Sire," he said, kneeling, "Archbishop Stigand, I regret to tell you this ... he has left London."

"So?" Edgar was puzzled.

The Archbishop rose to his feet and was clearly struggling to look Edgar in the eye.

"It is thought he has gone to Wallingford to submit," he reported quietly.

"The Archbishop of Canterbury has gone to join the enemy," snorted Edgar. "The rat! Well, we can manage without him. You aren't going too, are you?"

"No. I will stay with you, sire, for as long as I can."

"Thank you."

Just then, Aesgar ran in.

"Sire, they've gone and taken their men with them!"

"Who have?"

"Earls Edwin and Morcar," Aesgar gasped. "You have no one to fight for you but the traders of London."

CHAPTER 16

Edgar looked stunned.

"Are you telling me," he asked very slowly, "that the Earls have taken all their fighting men and left London. They have abandoned me?"

"They've gone, but no one knows where," Aesgar answered.

"They did not leave with Stigand," Archbishop Ealdred reported. "Might they have gone out to attack Duke William's forces?"

"Very unlikely," a thegn responded. "Earl Edwin was concerned that the Normans were now ravaging his Earldom of Mercia, but there is no way their small force could match the Normans."

"I heard a rumour they thought London could not hold out much longer," another thegn said.

"So, they are rats too, leaving us to be killed." Edgar's voice was bitter. "Aesgar, I think we need a meeting of the Witan. Please gather everyone you can find."

I went and stood near him and he soon beckoned me over.

"Wulf," he whispered, "I can't see a way through this."

"The Normans have the upper hand," I quietly confessed. "They have an army that is free to move wherever it chooses and which faces little opposition. If the Earls have gone to fight the Duke, I doubt they could achieve much."

"They have run back north, I'm pretty sure of that. They see how the land lies, that London could soon be cut off, with the rest of the country having no stomach to fight." He paused. "King Harold was known widely and admired as a military leader, but few people know who I am, and if they do, they know I am young, have no military experience and really no backing."

I put my hand on his shoulder. He covered it with his own and looked up into my face.

"People are dying out there and their homes are being burned," he said. "It is better that I surrender to the Duke, that I die to save my people."

"It may not come to that," I answered, without much confidence.

The Witan met or rather what was left of it. A few other leading men were found to have slipped out of London unseen.

The mood in the city was still very hostile. Wounded survivors of the battle had been sneaking in to take refuge from the Norman ravaging and they were not in a mood to surrender. They all had stories of friends dying beside them and spread rumours of the mutilation of corpses, though I couldn't see how they had still been there to witness that. What was clear was that no one wanted Duke William as their King and they preferred a great-nephew of the beloved Edward, even if he was a callow youth.

When I next had a chance to talk to Edgar, he was very despondent.

"I think we should surrender, but the Witan is not so sure," he told me. "They say Londoners will fight."

"They would," I agreed. "I've spoken to enough to know they hate the idea of Norman rule and have scores to settle for those slain at Hastings."

"But the Normans will not come here yet," Edgar argued. "They will burn and kill all around us. This has happened before. Don't you remember your father telling us stories of when he was a young servant of my grandfather?"

I frowned, trying to remember.

"The Danes came," Edgar said. "They took the north and then marched south. London held firm, so they took Winchester and Oxford and pretty well the whole country. Then King Aethelred fled abroad and they never had to fight for London. The Duke could do the same."

"Have you said this to the Witan?"

"Yes, but they say I lack experience."

"You do, but maybe you do not lack wisdom."

I felt for him. He had the weight of the country on his shoulders, but didn't have the muscle to override older voices that spoke against his suggestion.

The next day brought news that the Normans were now moving east, through Buckinghamshire towards Hertfordshire. Soon London could be encircled. The Witan met again and this time I think they must have listened to Edgar, for when I went up late in the day, I found a fresh decision had been made.

"We are to surrender," he said. "A messenger has already gone to make contact with the Duke and tell him of our decision." He looked up at me. "You will come with me, Wulf, won't you?"

"Of course."

"I think I have a couple of days. I'm not sure what will happen when he hears this news."

None of us knew. Some thought the Duke would try to ride into London, but others said that would be too dangerous for him and he was more likely to want Edgar and his thegns to go to him – wherever he was. Thinking about it, the latter course of action made more sense. The Duke might face an angry mob in London, but secure in his camp, surrounded by his men, he would be safe and we would be the vulnerable ones.

We heard the Duke was dug in at Berkhamsted and that was where he called us to go and surrender to him there. Maria cried in my arms, but I tried to reassure her.

"The Duke has no quarrel with me," I said. "I am not an aetheling, I am not a thegn, I am simply a merchant."

I hoped I was right. There was no way I could leave Edgar to face this on his own, for we had no idea what the Duke would decide to do with the young King.

There was very little talking among the group as we travelled from London to Berkhamsted. The dull, misty, clammy weather of mid November reflected our mood.

The group was led by Archbishop Ealdred and included other bishops and thegns – in effect, the whole of the Witan that had been meeting in London. Some of the thegns had family members with them, in case the Duke demanded hostages.

At Berkhamsted, we found a temporary hall had been erected, in which a fire burned in an effort to keep at bay the chill of late autumn. There was no welcome or offer of hospitality. Our group was kept outside, though Edgar and I were near enough to the entrance to see inside the candlelit shelter. Everywhere there were Normans and one could feel how they gloated and sometimes see it in their faces. I put my hand on Edgar's shoulder and could feel he was shaking.

Archbishop Ealdred had gone in first to meet the Duke. I hoped he would speak up for young Edgar, but I don't know if he did. Then we were called in. We had no weapons and were completely surrounded by the invaders. If they chose to slaughter us, there was nothing we could do to save ourselves.

Duke William was sitting in a chair on a raised dais. He was stocky, broad-chested and had a receding hairline. His clean-shaven face was expressionless. My first impression was of a man who was supremely confident and who was in absolute control.

"The English Witan," he declared, using an interpreter, and I could hear the scorn in his deep voice. "You have taken a long time to come crawling to me."

I tightened my grip on Edgar's shoulder. He had lowered his head slightly, so that he did not have to look in the Duke's face, but I kept my eyes on our host. He was scanning our group and his gaze came to rest on Edgar and then on me, as he saw how close we stood. I returned his gaze; I would do homage, but I had no intention of letting him break me.

"We are here now," Archbishop Ealdred was saying.

"The Archbishop of Canterbury has already done homage to me," the Duke commented, "as have some of your thegns."

None of us was going to accuse Stigand of being a rat.

"Your King Edward made me his heir and Harold Godwineson swore an oath to fulfil this promise. He broke his oath, but God gave him into my hands and he paid for his perjury with his life."

We listened in silence, knowing that he lied, but not daring to challenge him.

"Edgar." The Duke spoke his name and needed no interpreter.

Edgar looked up. Instinctively, we both stepped forward. I squeezed his shoulder and let go. He held his head high and went to kneel before the Duke.

"Were you crowned?" he asked.

"No, my lord."

"Then I do not recognise you as the King of England. Swear you will be loyal to me as your King."

Edgar duly did fealty and the rest of us followed suit. There was then some discussion about hostages. Edgar was not among those chosen and he remained standing close to me.

The oaths and promises were not all on one side, as the Duke himself promised to be a "gracious lord", whatever that meant.

At length, the bargaining (if that's the right word!) was complete and the Duke ordered we receive refreshments. It was made clear we would not be returning to London just yet and I guessed we would be allowed to return when the Duke, whom I should now call the King, chose to make his triumphal entry into that city. I wondered if there was any way I could get word to Agatha that Edgar had not been summarily executed.

This was probably what I was thinking about as we sat in small groups, surrounded by Normans, to eat. I was surprised to feel my shoulder gripped firmly and to hear a voice say, "Come to King."

CHAPTER 17

I stood before King William. I was trying not to be intimidated, but I could feel my heart thumping fast under my tunic.

I suddenly found the boldness to say, "I speak Norse", at which he raised his eyebrows and waved away his interpreter. He then spoke to me in that language.

"Edgar is your liege lord." The King made it sound like a statement rather than question.

"He is my brother's son, sire." Did my voice quiver? For certain my mouth was dry.

He frowned slightly.

"You have royal blood?"

"No, we shared a mother. My father was a free man and not of the House of Cerdic."

"You supported Harold?"

"He had no royal blood."

"Ah." There was a slight smile. "You agree he was a usurper?"

"Yes, my nephew should have been King."

"But he is not." Each word was spoken carefully, deliberately, coldly.

"You have conquered us," I admitted.

"Have I not the right?" There was a mocking tone to his question. I knew he wanted me to endorse what he saw as God's choice.

"You have conquered us," I repeated and met his cool stare.

"Tell me about your nephew. He was not born in England, I believe. I remember coming to the court of the late King Edward and he was not here."

"He was born in Hungary, the son of Edward, the son of Edmund, the son of Aethelred."

"I think I know his pedigree. Why Hungary?"

"His father was exiled as a baby because of Cnut the Dane. He was in Sweden, where I was born and then we had to flee to the land of the Rus."

I saw King William was listening to every word.

"In Kiev, we met Andrew of Hungary and helped him to win his kingdom. He granted the aethelings – there was another at that time, Edmund – he granted them an estate and that's where Edgar was born."

"The other aetheling? Edmund?"

"He died in Hungary."

"But Edward returned to England?"

"In 1057."

For a moment I relived those tragic days of our arrival and saw the contorted face of my brother as he died.

"Edgar was but six when his father died," I added quietly.

"He has known sorrow."

The King surprised me by his comment.

"Yes, but King Edward was good to him and treated him as a son."

"I think you have some wisdom. I expect you to use it. Your nephew has submitted to me. I am his King. He has no claim."

Again the words were spoken slowly, deliberately, with a pause between each sentence. I knew exactly what he was asking of me, but could I do it?

Our time at Berkhamsted was miserable. Clearly, the "accommodation" was poor and we were little more than prisoners. Archbishop Ealdred certainly spent some time deep in discussion with the King, as did a few of the leading thegns in our party, but Edgar and I were left very much out of it.

"What will my life be now, Wulf, do you think?" he asked.

"I've no idea," I replied. "It seems the King is going to let you live, but he doesn't want you causing any trouble."

"That isn't likely," he said, sadly. "I never had much backing before and there will be none now."

"As long as you are no threat, I think your life is safe. He has not made you a hostage."

"Nor is Harry. A hostage usually ensures the good behaviour of the hostage's father and we are both fatherless."

"He knows Harry has no claim. His royal connection is through his grandmother."

"What a desperate time this is," he groaned. "I thought things were bad enough when Harold grabbed the crown, but this is far worse."

What happened in the end was that the King dispatched an advance guard to ensure his safe arrival in London. With these troops went Archbishop Ealdred and a couple of thegns, whose purpose was to declare to the people of London that Edgar was no longer King and everyone had submitted to the Norman, whom they now acknowledged as the King of the whole of England. Of course, he was, in effect, only the King of the southern half of the country, but having London and a coronation there was key to the conquest of the north.

We did hear Londoners didn't meekly accept the arrival of the group of Normans and that there was some fighting, but somehow order was restored and the palace made safe to receive the new King. By now it was December and we should have been looking forward to celebrating Christmas; instead, the coronation was set for Christmas Day.

"He is to be crowned in Westminster Abbey," Edgar told me. "The ceremony is to be just like King Harold's. I think the idea is to say to the world that Harold was a false king and William is replacing him as a true one."

We looked at each other and were probably both thinking that neither was a true king, as neither had English royal blood in their veins, but we were powerless to change the situation.

So, Christmas Day saw us in the Abbey, watching with sad hearts the final triumph of the Norman conqueror. The King swore the traditional oath to govern his subjects well and to defend the Church. He said he would establish and maintain the law, which meant he was totally forbidding the sort of atrocities that had occurred, though we wondered if he had sufficient control of his greedy troops to fulfil that. There had been rumours that the ravaging of the country had continued even after the submission at Berkhamsted.

After the King made his oaths, we were asked to declare our acceptance of his rule. In view of the language difficulty, the question was put twice, first by Archbishop Ealdred in English and then by a Norman bishop. The huge building resonated with our "Yes" and the service then continued. But we had not got as far as the anointing, crowning and enthroning, when there were cries from outside the Abbey.

"Fire! London is on fire!"

I abandoned Edgar and joined many others who ran outside to find some of the wooden buildings near the Abbey were burning. Several of us found what containers we could and formed a human chain bringing water from the nearby Thames to try and douse the flames. It was hard work and at first we had little impact. There were Normans milling around and apparently doing little except shouting at us in a language we didn't know. Eventually a Norman with more authority turned up and got the firefighting better organised. By the time the flames were under control, my face and hands were black and my throat dry from the smoke. I didn't return to the Abbey, but went home to wash. Thankfully, I lived some distance away from where the buildings had burned or I think I would have rushed home to save my wife and children.

Much later in the day, clean, refreshed, but still coughing a bit, I went to the King's palace to find Edgar.

"Wulf, what was happening out there?" he wanted to know.

"Some of the buildings were on fire."

"Was it a protest by the English?" he asked. "That's the rumour at court."

"Hardly! Why should Londoners burn their own homes?" I responded. "There were quite a lot of troops in the area, guarding the King and his magnates I suppose, but they did little at first to stop the fire, so one suspects they started it. But I don't know."

"There was panic in the Abbey. Hardly any of us were left. Many of the King's leading men ran out, as you did. The clergy all stayed – and the King, of course."

"So, the coronation was completed?"

"Yes, but with little dignity. Archbishop Ealdred anointed William, put the crown on his head and seated him on the chair, so he was crowned and enthroned, but somewhat hastily. We kept thinking the Abbey was about to be stormed. We could hear a terrible noise and I thought I got a whiff of smoke, but we really didn't know what was going on."

"It took some time to get the fire under control and, by then, I was filthy."

"I could see the King was trembling from head to foot," Edgar whispered.

"He may have thought he was about to die. If Englishmen with weapons had got into the Abbey, they could easily have hacked him down. He wasn't dressed for a fight."

The general feeling was that the new King had had an inauspicious beginning to his reign. The mood in London was certainly black. The survivors of Hastings and those grieving the slain all hated him and resented the fact he was now their King. Others of us were simply worried, wondering how on earth peace could ever come again to our country.

Was it like this when Cnut the Dane became King? My father was no longer around to tell me, but I thought it was probably very different. Then there had been Danes around for some time and the Danish takeover, after the several battles of 1016, had been peaceful. King Harold's father, Godwine, had been a leading supporter of King Edmund, but when the young King died, Godwine switched sides and gave his support to Cnut. I wondered how many of our English thegns would now switch sides and support King William.

There was also the question of land. The Norman lords who had helped William would expect rewards; they would want estates. Perhaps this was also how the King would subdue the whole of England, by putting his magnates in strategic places with instructions to quell any rebellion and make the local people obedient citizens.

Over the next few months, I think this is what happened. All we experienced as merchants was a heavy tax, no doubt to pay for the troops, some of whom would probably go home before long.

London remained truculent, so much so that the King withdrew to Barking, east of the city. He took Edgar with him, but we still got some news, as Edie and Agatha stayed in London and Edgar sent them short messages every so often. Thus we learned that the Earls Edwin and Morcar had finally submitted to King William, along with many other thegns and the remaining bishops.

As March approached, the news was more disturbing.

"We have heard from Edgar," Edie told me.

I glanced across at Agatha. She was pale and was fidgeting with the rings on her fingers.

"It's not good news?" I asked.

"We're not sure," Edie said. "King William is returning to Normandy – and he is taking Edgar with him."

"A hostage then, if not a prisoner," I commented.

"Will I ever see my boy again!" Agatha cried and burst into tears.

Norman Family Tree

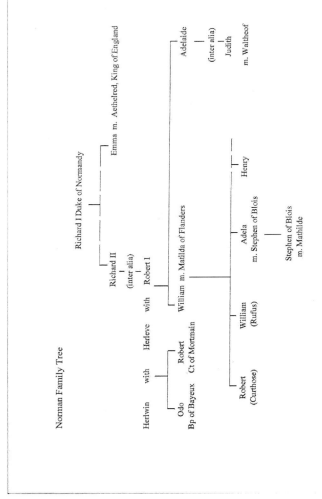

CHAPTER 18

London, Spring 1068

"Edie, there is a letter from Edgar."

I looked up at the sound of Margaret's voice.

"Is he still complaining about being in Normandy?" I asked.

She smiled.

"No, he says he expects to return to England fairly soon."

"Oh, that's good news. Agatha will be so pleased. It's over a year since he left."

"King William's wife is to come to London to be crowned and Edgar will be here for that," Margaret explained.

"The King must think it's safe, that he has truly conquered England now," I commented.

"But has he, Edie?" She was not smiling now. "Wulf says Edgar has been powerless in Normandy, but once he's back, who knows? The Earls Edwin and Morcar will also return."

"Wulf knows more about what is going on in the country than we do."

"If Christina and I were still at Romsey, I think we'd know very little, but, as you say, living here in London so near to Wulf, we know far more. Over this last year, there has been rebellion after rebellion – on the border with Wales, then Kent, then Northumbria, then this latest one in the south west."

"That was probably the most serious," I speculated. "We heard the leaders were the Godwine family, King Harold's mother and his sons by Edith Swan-neck."

"How terrible to be caught up in it, like the ordinary people of Exeter. They have endured a dreadful siege."

"King William is too powerful. I hope Wulf can persuade Edgar to be sensible."

When Edgar returned, Agatha was ecstatic for she had missed him greatly. However, he was living in the palace, which we had long since left to take up residence in an ordinary house near Wulf. Agatha had recalled her daughters from Romsey and we were managing to live through gifts from Queen Edith and from Wulf.

"Edie, Edgar has been granted lands in England," Agatha told me. "That will give us a little income."

"So, he is to become a thegn, managing an estate, is he?" I laughed.

I had tried to be positive for Agatha's sake, but in my heart I doubted a young man of seventeen, who had grown up as an aetheling expecting to be King, would be happy with an estate in the country.

The Queen was duly crowned in Westminster Abbey at Whitsun, but Edgar was more concerned to tell us other news.

"The King had promised Earl Edwin one of his daughters in marriage," he said, "but he hasn't fulfilled that promise and Edwin thinks he will renege. As Earl of Mercia, he had vast lands, but the King has given much of it to others."

"To Normans presumably?" asked Margaret.

"Yes. His right-hand man, William Fitz Osbern, has Herefordshire and Worcestershire and Roger of Montgomery has Shropshire. All of that was once Earl Edwin's, and Earl Morcar is even worse off. He has very little now in the north."

I didn't like the sound of it and had a quiet word with my brother.

"I will try and talk to him, Edie," Wulf promised, "but he is like a dog straining on a leash. I fear that if Edwin and Morcar decide to rebel, Edgar might too."

All was quiet for a couple of weeks and I began to hope Edgar would settle down and accept the situation.

One day, he arrived and was all smiles.

"Prepare to leave London," he said.

"What? All of us?" asked Agatha.

"Yes, you Mother and you Margaret and Christina. And Anna and Elizabeth, of course." He looked my way. "You can come too if you like, Edie."

"Where are you going?" I asked.

132

I hoped he would say to the estate he had been granted.

"York," was his reply.

"York?" we chorused.

"Don't ask anything more at this stage and tell no one," Edgar ordered. "Well, you can tell Wulf, of course, but no one else."

I knew then this was no trip to a country estate. I asked Wulf what I should do – go or stay?

"Edie, if you stay, you are welcome to live with Maria and me, but if Edgar is planning to be part of an uprising of the north, then you may feel you want to be there for Agatha and her daughters."

"Why does he want them with him?"

Wulf thought for a while.

"If he's going to rebel, he doesn't want the King getting his hands on members of his family and using them as hostages." He paused. "At Exeter, the King blinded a hostage in an effort to break the siege."

"Would he do that to a woman?" I was truly horrified.

"If he was desperate enough," Wulf conceded. "Edgar won't want to risk such a thing."

I sighed.

"I believe my place is with Agatha. Her daughters are like my own. Oh, Wulf!"

We clung to each other. We had shared a womb and always found it hard to be far apart.

Our small party slipped out of London and rode north. As I suspected, the two young Earls were the leaders of the rebellion. They had been assured of support in the north and that's where we all headed.

We arrived, weary, in York after several days of travelling. Edgar was excited. I don't think he had really thought through the implications of defying King William. The Earls had, in my view, far less to lose than Edgar. In York, we met another of the rebels – Merlswein – who was governor of Yorkshire. I shook my head at their folly, but no one took any notice of what we women thought. To these men it was a great adventure; they saw themselves as David fighting Goliath and reckoned that, like him, they could defeat the giant.

"Archbishop Ealdred is against our rebelling," Merlswein reported. "He won't give us God's blessing."

"But we have word from Gospatric that the Bishop of Durham will," Earl Edwin answered.

"Gospatric is a good man," Merlswein agreed. "He has control north of the Tyne. Thus the whole of the north is solidly with us."

"Then at least I could recover some of my lands," Earl Morcar said, "though recovering yours, brother, is going to be harder."

"We hold the north first," Earl Edwin declared. "Once England sees that, other men will rise. There is widespread unrest. People only need some encouragement and the King will find he has been left with no safe place in the land."

Earl Edwin's confidence seemed justified when news came that King Bleddyn of Wales, who had caused trouble before, had given his support to the rebellion. That meant the King would be fighting not just in the north, but over in the west as well. Would he split his army? Or adopt some other tactic? I feared these young rebels were much too cocky and I regretted the Earls had such influence over Edgar.

We waited in York. The weather was kind as it was midsummer and no one could have guessed we were at war. Trade continued as usual, much of it with the north or across the sea to Scandinavia.

Then news began to trickle in. King William had left London with a sizable army, so the defences of York were strengthened ready for an attack. But it did not come. Instead we heard the Normans were doing what they had done when they first arrived in the autumn of 1066 – destroying townships and crops.

"Your rebellion is causing ordinary people to suffer terribly," I complained to Edgar.

"There's always a cost," he answered.

"Don't you care?" I challenged.

"This is why we hate the Normans. They burn and destroy, and then take away the land and give it to others. There is poverty, slavery and death. We can't let them get away with it."

A great sadness filled my heart. I knew the conquerors were greedy and rapacious, but I couldn't see how rebelling would resolve that. Surely the King was too strong? I wanted to shout at Edgar, but I knew it wouldn't do any good, as he would shout back at me and dig his heels in even more.

"We need the south and the south-west to rise against the King," Edgar declared.

"There is no news that's happening," I muttered.

"Perhaps they are, but we're too far away to know about it."

A forlorn hope, I thought, but then, what did I know? I said nothing of my fears to Agatha, as she was anxious enough as it was.

The next news we had explained why the King had not yet arrived in York.

"The King is building a castle at Warwick," Earl Edwin announced.

I could tell by the silence with which this statement was received that this wasn't good.

"He is strengthening his grip on Mercia," Earl Edwin continued. "The south has not risen, nor has the west. The Welsh are being kept at bay, probably by Roger of Montgomery."

"We will hold the north," declared Edgar. "That is solidly opposed to him."

I didn't like the way the brother Earls exchanged glances. Edgar, ever the optimist, couldn't see a problem.

York remained busy, but I sensed more tension among the rebel leaders. For two weeks little was said and we continued with our quiet occupations, for there wasn't much we could do except read and embroider.

Then Edgar burst into our room.

"They've gone – the rats!" he shouted.

We looked up puzzled.

"The Earls, Edwin and Morcar, they've gone, gone to make their peace with the King."

CHAPTER 19

Edgar slumped down in one of the chairs.

"Why?" I asked. "Why have they gone?"

"They've given up. They can't see how we can hold out against the might of the King. Edwin probably hopes that by submitting he might get some of his lands back."

"The King has not even reached York," Agatha complained. "They were not tested."

"I know," said Edgar, getting up and pacing around. "And now they've gone, we've lost their men."

"What will you do?" I asked him.

Edgar sighed, stopped his pacing for a moment and then threw up his hands.

"God only knows!"

"Have you asked him?" Margaret retorted.

Edgar looked at her.

"You're the one who spends hours on her knees. *You* ask him!"

"Edgar," Agatha interrupted, "Margaret is right. You need to know the will of the Lord. You have been brought into this rebellion by these Earls, who have now left you. Perhaps you too should submit to the King. Perhaps that is what God would have you do at this time."

"No! We're not giving up yet. And when we win, we'll make sure Morcar gets no share of the north."

This was the second time the Earls had let Edgar down. Wulf had told me that in London they had promised to fight for him, their new King, but had sneaked away in the night. In York they were the mainstay of the rebellion, but again had left their fellow rebels in the lurch. No wonder Edgar felt bitter.

Merlswein and Gospatric, however, continued to back the young man and there was no talk of submission.

Another few weeks passed during which we heard that, having secured Warwick, the King had moved on to Nottingham, where he was building another castle. He was getting ever closer and the feeling of tension in York was rising.

I was not privy to the discussions that went on, but I could tell from Edgar's black moods and outbursts of temper that there was dissension among the rebels. We dared not ask him for news because he snapped at us if we made any comments. However, I was still surprised by what happened.

Edgar burst into our room.

"Pack everything!" he ordered. "We're leaving York."

"Where are we going?" asked Agatha.

"Durham. Today."

It was only once we had arrived there and been given hospitality by the friendly Bishop Aethelwine that we began to get some idea of what was going on. The leading men of York were becoming more and more afraid of what would happen when the King reached the city. Tales had been spread of the Norman destruction of buildings and crops, irrespective of whether these belonged to loyal men or not. Rumours abounded that York would be burned to the ground. Those in power wanted to submit and thus those who wanted to continue the rebellion had to flee.

We felt safe in Durham, but waited tensely to see what the King would do. News reached us that he had occupied York. There had been no destruction, rather there had been the building of another castle.

"This King is too powerful," the Bishop stated. "I advise you to forget this rebellion and make your peace with him."

We women agreed with Bishop Aethelwine, but the men would have none of it. After a few days, it became clear we could no longer stay in Durham.

"I intend to submit to King William," the Bishop told them. "What are you going to do?"

"We have a friend in the King of Scotland," Gospatric declared. "He's my kinsman and will help us."

"We fight on," Edgar agreed.

"Yes," Merlswein added.

With heavy hearts, we packed our belongings yet again and began our journey north. The days were still long and the weather reasonably warm, so we were able to make good progress. We were given hospitality at Jarrow on the River Tyne before continuing our journey by boat, hugging the coast as we sailed to Scotland.

We moored up on the north side of a wide estuary and waited while messengers went to the King. Eventually news came that we were welcome and we headed north to the royal centre, a place called Dunfermline.

I was struck by the number of trees and how green everything was even in the height of summer, but also the rocky nature of the landscape. The court had chosen a naturally defensible position, being surrounded with thick woods and steep crags. We passed many dwellings which were little more than hovels until we came to the centre of the township and the royal enclosure.

"Welcome to Scotland."

King Malcolm rose to greet us. Even on this bright day, his large timber-framed hall was gloomy, with few window openings in its bare walls. A small fire burned, the smoke from which curled upwards to seek a crack in the eaves below the thickly thatched roof. The royal "palace" was hardly impressive.

Edgar led Agatha forward and the rest of us followed. I looked up at the man who stood before us on a raised dais. His face and bare arms were battle-scarred, but his dark eyes were alive with interest and his smile was warm.

"Edgar the aetheling from England, I believe," the Scot continued.

He scanned our group and his eyes rested briefly on Margaret.

"And his family?"

141

"We seek sanctuary," Edgar responded.

The King nodded.

"I heard the north of England had rebelled. I see Gospatric is with you."

"And Merlswein," Edgar added.

"You've had a long journey." He signalled to some servants. "Accommodation for our guests."

We women were given a room, inferior to our home in London, but we could hardly complain, for at least we were safe. We made ourselves as comfortable as we could before being escorted back to the main hall for some refreshment.

We were invited to sit at a table with the King, Edgar and the leading men. Introductions were made.

"I have met your sister, Margaret, before," King Malcolm said. "Nine years ago in York, when King Edward still lived and England was at peace."

"You remember that?" Edgar was surprised. "Margaret was only thirteen then."

"She was on the cusp of womanhood," King Malcolm responded.

Under his gaze, Margaret began to blush and the Scot was kind enough to change the conversation.

"I was gathering some forces to aid your rebellion," he said, "but it was soon abandoned."

"Edwin and Morcar, they left us to fight alone," Edgar snorted. "We stayed for a while with Bishop Aethelwine in Durham, but in the end, he too wanted to submit to William."

"There may be other opportunities," the King acknowledged. "There is no love for the Normans in the north of England."

"My son should have been King," Agatha stated.

"Ah, my lady, I agree, but that Harold Godwineson was too clever and too powerful. King Edward was a good friend to me. I spent some time in the English court before securing the crown of Scotland, but that was before you all came to England, I believe."

"We were happy in Hungary," Agatha added, and I'm sure he could hear the sadness in her voice.

So began our sojourn in Scotland.

"Edgar, this is his palace," Margaret commented, when we were alone as a family. "But there are ordinary men living in better houses than this in England."

"It's a bit rough and ready," he conceded.

"I suppose we can't expect a stone-built palace with carpets, such as the late King had at Winchester, but some wall hangings would help to keep out the draughts."

"You'll be complaining about the way they eat next!"

"Well, you must agree they have no manners. They gobble down their food, talk while they eat and bolt from the table as soon as they have finished. Anyone would think they were in a roadside inn rather than the presence of the King."

It was hardly what we were used to, but at least we were safe, though I wondered how long it would be before Edgar and his friends joined another rebellion. They passed their time honing their fighting skills, while we women were glad of our embroidery. The King would sometimes come and watch us as we worked, often singling out Margaret for his attention.

"This is beautiful work that you do," the King said one day. "We have nothing like it in Scotland."

"It is known as English embroidery," Margaret told him. "There are many women in England making vestments and altar cloths for the churches. I was taught by nuns." She paused. "I want to be a nun."

"Why?"

"It is an ordered and peaceful life of prayer and work."

"More like an escape from the world," the King scoffed.

"No, we pray for the world."

"You could serve God just as well by not being a nun."

"How? I am a woman and therefore I have no power."

"A queen has power."

I looked up and saw the admiration in his face.

He wants to marry her! I thought.

CHAPTER 20

I began to watch King Malcolm to see if my suspicions were right. I knew he had two young sons, Duncan and Donald, and through some careful enquiries, made in a nonchalant way, I learned their mother had died a year or so back.

So he is free to marry, I thought.

I said nothing to Margaret. I knew she would not relish the thought of being courted by a warrior some fifteen years older than her, whose court had little refinement.

There was also the matter of the church. Scotland, we had discovered, was not in communion with the Pope. It followed the Celtic tradition and had refused to accept the Roman ways, even though England had done so four hundred years earlier. It didn't help that the services (which were less frequent than in England) were conducted in Gaelic, not Latin.

Scotland was not a place where we felt at home and as the winter drew nearer it was not a place we enjoyed living, as we found it increasingly difficult to stay warm. The King was generous in providing us with warm cloaks, some of them made of fur, but even though a large fire burned in his hall, it had little impact, as the icy wind found its way in through the many cracks in the walls. Also the days were noticeably shorter and the light so poor, we could no longer embroider. I must confess it was a miserable winter for us.

In mid February, even as the days were getting lighter and our spirits were lifting a little, news came which set the palace buzzing.

"He's been killed," Gospatric reported.

"Who has?" Edgar asked.

"Robert Cumin. The King appointed him to my Earldom, north of the Tyne. He got to Durham, but the people there murdered him."

"And we've news from York too," Merlswein added. "The governor of the castle there has been killed. The north has risen against the Normans."

"We must go!" cried Edgar.

All the men wanted to go and fight.

"What about us?" asked Agatha, in the privacy of our room.

"Do you want to stay here?" Edgar enquired. "I'm sure King Malcolm would be happy for that."

"I want to be with you," stated Agatha firmly.

Edgar glanced at Margaret and Christina.

"I can't wait to leave here," was Margaret's response.

"I want to be with Mother," Christina added.

"Very well, we all leave then. We'll probably make our base in Durham again."

So, Anna and Elizabeth packed our belongings yet again, before we all thanked the King for his hospitality and bade farewell to Scotland. No one was sorry to leave, as we had all found it an alien place. I had lived in Sweden (which I didn't really remember), Russia,

Hungary and England, but none was as bad as Scotland, though I conceded to myself that King Malcolm had tried hard to make us comfortable. We put the wind and the rain, the bogs and the bleakness behind us – or so we thought.

We found Durham had been badly damaged in the recent uprising against the new Earl. He had sought refuge from the rebels in the Bishop's home, but the building had been set alight. The Earl was dead, but we were pleased to find the Bishop had survived.

"I warned Earl Robert not to come," Bishop Aethelwine told us. "I even went to meet him. News of his ravaging of the countryside had gone before him and I knew how it would be, but he wouldn't listen. And now the whole of the north has risen again."

"We will be joining the rebels at York as soon as we can," Edgar said, "but I wish to leave my mother and sisters in your safe hands."

"I will do what I can," the Bishop answered, "but the King will not take kindly to these killings. You can expect reprisals."

Edgar and his men left for York and we were left waiting for news. As the days passed, we grew more anxious. We heard that the castle at York was still in Norman hands, despite its governor having been killed. Clearly the city was not controlled by the rebels as we had thought.

I wasn't really surprised when Edgar reappeared, without Merlswein and Gospatric, and told us the King had taken them by surprise with a huge force and the rebellion had disintegrated. We were to return to Scotland.

We were graciously received back and I suspected King Malcolm was not surprised to see us. None of us wanted to be in Scotland, but at least it was a safe haven and we had arrived there in time to celebrate Easter on the 13th day of April.

"Edie, you will never believe what I've just discovered," Margaret exclaimed. "It is Easter Sunday tomorrow, but the Scots do not celebrate it with a mass. No Holy Communion! No sharing of Christ's body on his day of resurrection!"

"Why not?" I was genuinely shocked and puzzled.

"They say they are too sinful and quote the words of St. Paul in his letter to the Corinthians."

"We are not to take the bread and wine unworthily – is that the passage?"

"Yes, but it means we are to confess our sins first and be in awe of what Christ has done," Margaret said. "None of us is worthy, but Our Lord welcomes repentant sinners at his table."

"This is certainly a strange land with strange customs," I agreed. "Nothing we can say or do will change that. May God give us his grace to live here in peace while we have to."

Spring came later to Scotland than to England, but the scents which came with it touched me more deeply than in England. Perhaps it was because we were so close to woods here. The breeze might be cool, but it smelled fresh and therefore refreshing, lifting my heart a little.

In terms of our situation, there was no reason for feeling more positive. The north was back in the King's hands and even though he'd had more trouble with Harold's sons in the far west, that area too was firmly under his control, from what bits of information we got.

Then something happened which should not have taken me by surprise, but which did.

We were quietly doing our embroidery when Edgar burst in.

"Margaret, King Malcolm has asked for your hand in marriage," he announced.

"I don't want to marry him or anyone else," Margaret declared. "I want to live as a nun."

"Well, you can't," Edgar stated. "I need alliances and your marriage to Malcolm would make a strong bond between him and me. He'll have to fight for my cause."

"That's utterly selfish! Don't you ever think of others?"

"Hark at you! Wanting to be a nun is utterly selfish, tucked away from the world in some cosy place, doing needlework and praying."

"It's not like that! We pray for the world."

"You're being selfish," Edgar challenged. "Christ served others and so should you. And your duty is to marry Malcolm."

Brother and sister glared at each other.

"Margaret dear, I think it is your duty to support your brother in his claim to the English throne," Agatha interposed.

"He submitted to King William at Berkhamsted," Margaret objected.

"I was only sixteen then. I had no option. The army had been destroyed fighting for Harold at Hastings, but I'm eighteen now."

"But you gave him homage, your oath to obey him," Margaret retorted.

"He swore to be a gracious lord, but all he has done is take land from the English and give it to his men," her brother answered. "Foreigners build castles and oppress our people and the King lays burdens of tax on everyone. He broke his oath, so I can break mine."

"Edgar should be King," Agatha stated.

"King William could die," Margaret argued. "Then you could renew your claim."

"The King has sons. I met them when I was in Normandy. Robert, his eldest, is about my age. He expects to be King of England when his father dies."

"Well," said Margaret, "my answer is 'No', at least for the time being. Maybe God will provide you with other allies and you won't need the King of Scotland in your camp."

Edgar stomped off and left us, tense and silent, as no one wanted to talk. Even Agatha said nothing further.

I tried praying about the situation, but wasn't sure how to pray. Rebellion against such a strong king seemed so hopeless and people were dying every time there was an uprising. If Margaret prayed for God to provide her brother with other allies, then her prayer soon got an answer.

CHAPTER 21

Towards the end of July, a letter arrived from Wulf. It had been very difficult to keep in touch and so it was a great joy for me when a merchant arrived at the King's court and had, amongst his wares, this letter for me.

"He writes that he and Maria and the boys are well," I told the others, "and that he is able to trade without too much difficulty. He says London is quiet, by which I presume he means there is little appetite for rebellion there."

"They can make money more easily if there's peace," Edgar scoffed.

"But this will interest you, Edgar," I continued. "Wulf says the King of Denmark is amassing a great fleet of ships and claims to have been invited to come and invade England."

"What? Invited? By whom?"

"Wulf doesn't say. Perhaps it's propaganda. The Danish king knows how volatile the north is and that there are many people living there who have Danish roots. He's reckoning he will be welcomed."

"Not by me, not if he wants to be King of England."

"But perhaps those Danish troops will help to defeat the Normans," Agatha suggested, "and then the English may turn to you as the true English King."

"Does Wulf say when this fleet might sail?" Edgar asked.

"He doesn't know, but thinks it could be in August."

"Where are Merlswein and Gospatric when I need them?" Edgar cried, and left our room, as though he could go looking for them in the palace complex.

These men and their retainers had not, however, fled to Scotland as we had in the previous March and we guessed they might be hiding somewhere in Northumbria.

I looked across at Margaret, but she had returned her eyes to her embroidery and would not meet mine. I couldn't help thinking she was probably smiling inside – God had indeed given Edgar some other allies and she was spared from marrying the King of Scotland.

Maybe Edgar did some praying too, for three days later, Gospatric arrived in Dunfermline, excitedly confirming that the Danes would be setting sail within a month.

"Who's their King?" Edgar asked.

"Swein Estrithson, the nephew of King Cnut," Gospatric told us.

"He's not a young man then," Edgar commented. "He's been King of Denmark for over twenty years."

"He's been putting a story about that King Edward promised him the crown of England," the Earl said.

"Has he indeed? A lie, just like the tale King William told!" Edgar paused. "I heard he'd been invited to invade, invited by Englishmen."

Gospatric looked down at the mug of ale he was drinking and shifted slightly on his stool.

"I've heard that too," he responded. "Perhaps the men of York."

I saw the look on Edgar's face, the way his eyes narrowed and his forehead furrowed.

"Or perhaps you and Merlswein," he accused.

Gospatric shrugged his shoulders.

"Well," said Edgar, "I'll join the Danes and we'll fight together, but Swein isn't having my crown when we win."

Thus, we left Scotland again and sailed down the coast, meeting up with Merlswein in Durham and also Waltheof, who was another Earl throwing in his lot with the rebels. I got a real sense that this time everyone was sure there would be enough power to defeat the Norman King and at least hold the north sufficiently well that he was weakened and would succumb to rebellions elsewhere.

Word came that the Danish fleet was expected at the end of August and the rebel leaders left us in Durham and travelled south, planning to meet up with their allies somewhere to the east of York. We could do nothing except pray and wait for news.

Over the next few weeks, we learned that the Danes were led not by their King but by his brother, Asbjorn. We were relieved to hear that, as it meant any dispute about the crown of England was unlikely at this stage. On a sad note, we heard that Archbishop Ealdred had been devastated by the news of another rebellion, especially one aided by a foreign power. He had been taken ill and had died; that felt like the losing of a friend.

As far as York was concerned, there was no suggestion we should go there. Indeed, the news was that much of it had been destroyed – not by Edgar and the rebels, but by the Normans trying to create a fire break and then letting the fire get out of hand. The rebels had taken it as a sign that God was on their side. This view was reinforced by news of other rebellions – in Shropshire and in the West Country.

The King was being pulled in several directions and we were told he had left the north to be reconquered by his half-brother Robert. That in itself felt like a triumph for the rebels.

I have to admit, though, that I couldn't see how the rebels could win in the long term. The King seemed to have unlimited resources. He was losing hundreds of men (there had been a terrible slaughter in York), yet he recruited more to fight for him and no doubt made them promises of money, if not land. The rebels were at a disadvantage. Many Danes had come to fight, but they were not replenished and from the snippets of information we got, I had the impression they were grabbing booty and then retreating to their ships, which they held in areas inaccessible to a Norman army on foot. What the rebels needed was for King William to be killed in a battle, as Harold had been killed at Hastings, but no battles were taking place, simply some skirmishes. Edgar let us know every so often that he was still alive.

"This is like stalemate in chess," Margaret commented early in November. "I cannot see the King allowing this situation to continue indefinitely."

"What do you think he might do?" I asked.

"He will bring a big force and reoccupy York," she answered. "He will rebuild the castles there if, as we believe, they have been destroyed and he will use York as a base to seek out the rebels."

"They will not meet him in a battle," I remarked.

"Oh, Edie, when can we ever live in peace? I am weary of all this killing and daily wondering if we must seek safety somewhere."

"Edgar will not give up yet," I warned her.

Christmas was fast approaching when Edgar suddenly returned.

"The King has York," he moaned, "and worse than that, he has bribed the Danes to go home."

"What kind of allies are they?" Agatha cried.

"Greedy ones." Edgar sighed deeply. "They were happy to plunder York and the countryside around and fill their boats with booty, but they showed no inclination to help us hold the city against the Normans." He put his head in his hands. "Yet again, the King was too strong for us."

"Where do we go now?" Margaret asked.

Edgar looked up.

"Nowhere for the present," he answered. "I think we are all safe here in Durham. I expect Merlswein to join us too and perhaps Gospatric."

We tried to celebrate Christmas, but none of us could feel any joy. Word reached us King William had appeared in York wearing his crown and all his regalia, apparently having sent to Winchester for them.

"He wants to remind everyone that he is an anointed king," Edgar grumbled.

"Well, he is," Margaret retorted.

I put my hand on her arm and gave her a little frown, as I felt Edgar hardly needed reminding of this painful fact.

The dark days of midwinter were dark indeed, as each day we waited anxiously for news. It was mid January before Merlswein appeared.

"The King is on the move," he reported. "He intends to flush out the rebels and what he is doing to Yorkshire is an abomination."

We all looked at him, puzzled. There was a terrible sadness in the man's eyes.

"He is burning everything as he moves through the countryside," he said. "Crops and buildings are put to the torch. Any people who cross his path are killed."

"This is what he did after Hastings," Edgar commented.

"This is much worse," Merlswein responded. "That destruction was like a trackway through the land; this is the whole area. Before he was showing his power, now he is showing revenge. There will soon be no people left in Yorkshire, for those he has not killed will die of the cold or of starvation."

Margaret began to weep and I could see the news had troubled Edgar, for he was grinding his right fist in the palm of his left hand, an action I had never noticed before.

"Where is Gospatric?" he suddenly asked.

Merlswein shifted on his stool and looked into the fire.

"Is he dead?" Edgar asked.

Merlswein shook his head.

"No, but we shall not see him here." He paused. "I believe he may try to make peace with King William."

Edgar closed his eyes and became very still.

"It's over, isn't it?" he whispered.

He opened his eyes and looked at his mother.

"I see no hope of victory while William lives. I know I should be King, Mother, but too many lives have been lost trying to achieve that."

"King Edward had to wait many years before his time came," Agatha said, "and my dear Edward spent nearly all his life as an exile before his recall to England. Maybe your time will come, my son."

The cause seemed lost, but we were also lost. What were we going to do? Neither Merlswein nor Edgar wanted to submit to William; they preferred exile.

"Flanders is a friendly country, I believe," Merlswein said. "We could make a base there and await events."

"Better that than going back to Scotland," Margaret commented.

"King Malcolm has been all talk, but not provided fighting men," Edgar agreed.

We knew the Normans were working their way through Yorkshire and would then move north towards Durham, so Anna and Elizabeth packed our belongings yet again and we left, believing our next home would be in Flanders. Little did we know when we set out that we would not find refuge in that country.

CHAPTER 22

As we had done before, we moved north to Jarrow to find boats which could take us on our journey. Merlswein had chosen to come with us, so we were a substantial party which took to the sea.

January, however, is not a good time to travel and we had not gone far towards the south when a north-easterly wind got up. We were sailing as close as we dared to the coast, but the wind was pushing us even further. The captain recommended we take shelter at Wearmouth until the wind changed.

"It should be safe enough," Merlswein agreed. "King William is unlikely to have reached the Tees yet. I think he's too busy harrying Yorkshire."

Reluctantly Edgar agreed. He was pacing around the deck and constantly checking the wind direction. When I tried to calm him, he made clear his fear.

"I dare not fall into the King's hands," he declared. "He let me live after Berkhamsted, but I have rejected his forgiveness and been a rebel for the last eighteen months."

"I have been surprised that he is so tolerant of rebels," I replied. "King Cnut had a reputation for summary execution, but I haven't heard that said of King William."

"You're right. He pardoned Edwin and Morcar, so he might pardon me, but I don't want to risk it." He paused. "Of course, there is a difference." The rain was caught on his eyelashes, which made him look as though he had been crying, but I knew he hadn't. "I should be King of England and not William," he stated.

I guessed then that he would not relax until we were safely out of English waters and welcomed in Flanders. In the meantime, our journey to this new refuge was delayed by the weather, as we came into Wearmouth and moored up for the night.

The shouting and the screams woke me. Hurrying on deck, I joined the others as we looked across the water, to see buildings burning in the half-light of dawn, the flickering flames appearing to dance on the dark water.

"It's the Normans!" cried Edgar. "We must sail on!"

"We can't!" the captain answered. "We are trapped here by the wind!"

"Oh, God Almighty, save us!" Agatha pleaded.

"We could disembark and flee on foot," Edgar suggested.

"We wouldn't get far," Merlswein argued, "not with women in our party. We stay on board and send out a scout."

He disappeared to find one of his men. The waiting was terrifying, as we watched more buildings being torched and heard the screams of people trapped inside them. Then Merlswein's man stumbled back on board.

"It's the Scots!" he gasped. "Not the Normans."

161

"The S ... Scots?" Edgar stuttered. "Is ... is their King here?"

"I think so," the breathless scout reported.

"That settles it!" cried Margaret. "Young man, take me to him."

"You can't leave here, Margaret!" Edgar cried. "You'll be killed."

"It's better one person dies than a whole town," she responded. "If I get to King Malcolm, I shall order him to stop."

We were all speechless. She was either being very stupid or very brave.

"I'll come with you." I suddenly found my voice. I could not let her die alone – she was like my child.

"Then I'll come too," Edgar declared.

"No, just Edie and I will go," Margaret said. "We're no threat that way."

What followed was a terrifying ordeal for me – and for her too, I think. Our scout led us towards the mayhem and with every step my heart was beating faster. We held hands tightly, both of us probably convinced we were facing our deaths.

Amazingly, the first Scots we met stopped to stare at us.

"Where is King Malcolm?" Margaret demanded. "You (she pointed to a man near the front of the group), I recognise you from the court at Dunfermline. Tell your King that Margaret, the sister of Edgar the aetheling, is here and wants to speak with him."

There was no trace of a tremor in her voice, but her grip on my hand was so tight, she was crushing the life out of it.

For a moment they hesitated, then the man she had singled out shouted something to the others before retreating through the ranks of warriors. The remaining men continued to stare at us, their bloodied weapons frozen in their hands. Suddenly, they parted and the King marched through. His chain mail was spattered with blood and his sword showed he had been using it to kill. He stopped in front of us.

"Sire," Margaret said, curtseying.

"What, in God's name, are you doing here?" the King managed to say, his face a picture of astonishment.

"And what, *in God's name*, are *you* doing here?" she responded. "This is England. What are you doing burning homes and killing English men, women and children?"

He opened his mouth as though to reply, then shut it.

"Order your men to stop," she continued. "Please."

King Malcolm turned and shouted something in Gaelic. Men began to move off in several different directions. We had no way of knowing what orders he had given them.

"Well?" Margaret demanded.

The King gave a little bow.

"I have ordered them to stop," he replied. "Now will you tell me how you come to be here, in the mouth of the Wear?"

"My brother, mother and sister together with Lord Merlswein are on our way to Flanders, but severe weather has caused us to seek temporary shelter in this harbour."

"Flanders? King William has proved too powerful again?"

"He has control of York and is harrying all of Yorkshire."

"Just like me." The King raised one of his eyebrows and smiled slightly. "I had heard. I thought it a good opportunity to do some harrying myself and perhaps even lay claim to Northumbria."

I felt Margaret's hand tremble a little – whether through fear or anger I didn't know.

"Please bring me to your brother. It will be good to see him again, though I think I had better clean my sword first."

He handed it to one of his retainers, who carefully wiped the blade clean before handing it back. Margaret kept her eyes fixed on the King's face.

"I am ready, Lady Margaret. Lead on."

So, we brought King Malcolm to our ship, where we all took breakfast together, as though we had met by arrangement, rather than in the middle of a pillaging spree. Fires still burned across the water, but we could tell that the King's orders had been obeyed and the killing had stopped.

"Edie, I feel unwell," Margaret whispered, as we finished eating.

She was pale and trembling.

"Excuse us," I said to the rest of the party. I gave Anna a knowing look and we took Margaret below deck to a private sleeping area, where she could lie down.

By now, she was shaking badly and was soon sick. I thought about what we had just eaten, but there was nothing that could have made her ill so quickly. Anna and I tried to keep her warm with extra covers, for she was quivering from head to toe. Then she began to weep quietly.

I lost track of time as I sat by her, desperately praying and wondering how to help her. Then she opened her eyes and looked at me.

"It's the fear, Edie," she croaked.

"The fear?"

"I was so afraid we would be killed, not just me, but you too."

"You appeared to be so bold and brave," I remarked.

"On the outside, yes, but inside I was terrified." She paused to sip a little wine. "My body has taken its toll. It is the fear which has made me sick."

"You are safe now and so am I, and what you did saved many lives, I believe. I'm very proud of you, dear Margaret."

She gave me a faint smile.

"I am so cold," she whispered.

I found another cloak and laid it over her. She closed her eyes again and was soon asleep.

In the mid afternoon, I was aware of our boat moving – we were leaving the harbour. Margaret still slept; the motion didn't disturb her. After about an hour, I left Anna with her and went on board to tell Agatha how she was.

Edgar was at the helm, watching the sea, so I joined him. Looking around, I saw there were more boats than simply ours. There was something else I noticed too.

"Edgar, I can see the coast of England, but it is to our left. If we are heading south to Flanders, surely it should be on our right."

"We are not going to Flanders, Edie," he confessed. "We are being escorted to Scotland."

That explained the extra boats.

"Is this by choice?" I asked. "Or ... or are we prisoners?"

"Not exactly prisoners, but King Malcolm gave me little choice."

I went back to Margaret with a heavy heart. How could I break this news to her?

She stirred as I took my place by her bunk.

"I feel a bit calmer now," she said. "Perhaps I could manage a little food."

I gave her some bread and a small amount of wine and she relaxed back.

"How long is the journey to Flanders?" she asked.

I swallowed and sent up a prayer.

"We aren't going to Flanders, dearest Margaret. We are returning to Scotland."

CHAPTER 23

I had expected Margaret to weep again, but she simply lay there quietly.

"I don't think the King gave Edgar much choice about our destination," I said.

She reached out and took my hand. I felt her squeeze it.

"I am not surprised, Edie. This is my destiny." She turned to look at me. "Our Lord prayed three times for the cup of suffering to be taken from him, but then he said, 'Your will not mine be done'. St. Paul was afflicted by a thorn in the flesh. Three times he prayed for it to be removed, but the Lord did not take it away, but rather told the apostle, 'My strength is made perfect in weakness'."

"What are you saying?" I asked.

"This will be the third time we have taken refuge in Scotland."

I frowned, still puzzled by her words.

"I wanted to be a nun, as I thought I could serve God best in that way," she explained, "but three times I have been taken to Scotland and I know that its King wishes to marry me. I could not see how that could be of service to Our Lord, but today … today I have seen it."

"King Malcolm did what you asked – he stopped the burning and the killing," I responded.

"I doubt he will always listen to me, but I believe God would have me marry him and seek to bring honour to Our Lord in that spiritually dark land. His strength is made perfect in my weakness – that is what I must always remember."

I cradled her hand in mine and found I was crying.

"Don't weep for me," she gently urged.

"It is such a high calling," I managed to say. "Surely the Lord will honour the sacrifice you are making."

"God's will is always the best, even when it proves to be difficult and painful. He will not let me down."

At the beginning of April, Margaret married King Malcolm in the church in Dunfermline, the ceremony being carried out by Fothad, the Bishop of St. Andrews. It was strange to us, for it was done according to the Columban rites, but in the eyes of the Scots they were married and also in the eyes of God. It was plain to me, and possibly to others, that the King adored his bride, even though she did not return his love. She had made it clear she was not marrying to suit Edgar's need of allies, but because she believed it was the will of the Lord. I prayed she would find some happiness in this decision.

"I learned much from Queen Edith while I was in Winchester," she told me one day. "She made sure King Edward *looked* like a king. I believe I should do the same for my husband."

"I grant you he looks more like a warrior than King Edward ever did," I acknowledged. "Are you thinking of dressing him up?" I asked, laughing.

"This is no joke, Edie. When he is not on the battlefield, he should be dressed in far finer clothes than he wears at present and his hall should look like a palace, instead of a … wayside inn. I need to get Wulf to send me the best materials he can find and we also need wall hangings in rich colours to keep the draughts out and to give the court more dignity. *And* I intend to do something about the appalling manners of those who eat with us."

"I noticed you've insisted on praying God's blessing on the food before anyone can start to eat."

"And give thanks at the end before they rush off," she added.

The King indulged these small changes in table manners and I could see that Margaret's reforms were already improving the atmosphere of the court. Getting word to Wulf and receiving his help would take a little longer.

Before we heard from Wulf, we had news from another quarter.

"King Swein has finally arrived from Denmark," Edgar informed us. "He is said to have sailed into the Humber at the end of May, joined up with his brother Asbjorn and been received by the locals with rapture."

We all looked at him, wondering what he would say next.

"Well, I'm not going, if that's what you're thinking," he responded. "Let's see what happens next."

As far as we could tell, no effort was made to capture York. Rather the Danes, or some of them (Swein definitely stayed behind), went south into the Fens and seized Ely. We heard Peterborough was attacked on the 2nd day of June, not by Danes, but by an English gang led by someone called Hereward, and the spoils from the monastery had been taken by the gang to the Danish camp near Ely.

"King William knows how to deal with the Danes," Edgar scoffed. "Greedy devils. He's paid them off, paid them to go back home. That's the end of another rebellion."

"It is as well you did not go," Agatha commented.

At the end of the summer, a familiar face appeared at court.

"Bishop Aethelwine!" exclaimed Margaret. "Welcome to Scotland. My husband is away settling a legal dispute, but you are among friends who can repay the hospitality you gave us in Durham."

"Dear lady, it is good to see you so well, and the rest of your family. I had heard of your marriage."

"Where have you been?" Edgar asked. "We heard the King had declared you an outlaw for helping the rebels last year."

"I took refuge on the island of Lindisfarne for many months," the Bishop explained, "but more recently I returned to Durham. It was clear I could not stay there, for the Norman grip on our country is too fierce, so I resolved to go to Cologne in Germany."

"We passed through Cologne on our way from Hungary to England," Agatha remarked. "The Germans would make you welcome."

"If I got there, they might," the Bishop agreed, "but the wind sent my boat north and so I am in Scotland."

"Make a home here for as long as you need it," Margaret urged. "There are many English here, seeking a safe place away from Norman rule and some will be glad of your ministry." She lowered her voice. "You may know they don't follow the Pope in this country."

"But God is here nevertheless," he quietly responded.

I found myself alone with Bishop Aethelwine the next day and told him of our travels since we had last met.

"The Queen looks very well," he remarked. "She has a glow to her cheeks that I do not remember seeing before. God has certainly led her on an interesting path."

His comment on Margaret's appearance made me look at her with fresh eyes and I could see then what he meant. At the first opportunity I took her to one side.

"Are you expecting a child?" I whispered.

"Yes, but say nothing, for I must tell the King before others know."

I smiled broadly.

"I think he will be very pleased."

"So do I," she giggled.

It was good to see her almost like a girl again, enjoying the thrill of a secret and such a special secret as this one.

Some other news felt, by Edgar at least, to be good was that King William had left England in the early autumn to deal with trouble touching on his Duchy.

"Perhaps he won't come back," he muttered, hopefully.

Other news, however, trickled through that the trouble in the Fens was far from over. The landless and disaffected from various parts of England were apparently forming some sort of group based around Ely.

Bishop Aethelwine stayed for Christmas and even celebrated mass for us English according to the Roman rite, but January brought news that the Earls, Edwin and Morcar, had stolen away from their Norman "hospitality" and were trying to raise a fresh rebellion.

"I cannot stay any longer," the Bishop declared. "I was born in the Fens and served God in Peterborough before going to Durham. I can feel the pull of the marshes and the cry of the oppressed."

We were sorry to see him go. With him went many of the Englishmen who had sought sanctuary in Scotland, but this time Edgar didn't go with them.

"It's all so hopeless," he told us. "I wish them well, but all I can see is more bloodshed and destruction."

He was right. We heard Earl Morcar had joined the rebellion at Ely, but Earl Edwin had died elsewhere. King William had returned and crushed the rebels, imprisoning both Morcar and Bishop Aethelwine. Others fared less well, for some rebels were imprisoned, while others were released after their hands were cut off and their eyes gouged out. We understood the leader called Hereward had managed to escape.

The only light in this dark and terrible time was Margaret's pregnancy. She had been remarkably healthy all the way through, coping with any awkwardness with a holy serenity resulting from her quiet hours of studying the Gospels. King Malcolm indulged her every whim and she used the opportunity to get wall hangings put up in the hall, which had helped reduce the winter cold. Some splendid clothes had arrived from Wulf, which had taken the King by surprise, but which he wore because it pleased his wife.

Agatha was all of a quiver and it took me back to the time when she had given birth to Margaret as her first child. Her labour had been hard, but Margaret's was not so prolonged and she soon held a son in her arms.

"The King says I may call him Edward after my dear father," she said, and we were all delighted.

Scottish Royal Family Tree

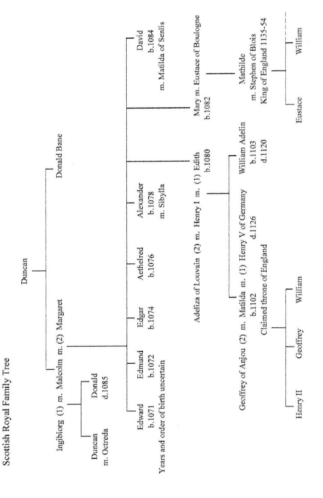

CHAPTER 24

The spring and summer of the year of Our Lord 1071 were happy and peaceful times for us. Agatha and I delighted in Edward. Agatha was convinced she could see her late husband in the baby; I couldn't, but said nothing. She had been a widow for over thirteen years and this little one was a real comfort to her.

Margaret was pleased to let us rear her son. Now that she had her figure back, she concentrated on dressing like a queen. Her linen shift was topped by a long tunic of fine and brightly dyed wool, with the border and sleeves being richly embroidered. Her belt was encrusted with jewels.

She was still seeking to improve the table manners and to do this she sometimes bribed the King's companions with extra wine, so that they would sit quietly until everyone had eaten and thanks were given for the meal. Visitors and newcomers to the court quickly learned to fall in line.

Margaret also persuaded the King that we should eat from platters and drink from vessels made from gold or silver, rather than horn and wood. Some of our dishes were made only of these precious metals, but others were gold or silver plated, though still looked impressive.

The King himself had succumbed to her desire that he look more regal and agreed to the increasing variety of wearing apparel she suggested. She hired a better class of servant to accompany him and insisted they also dress smartly.

King Malcolm allowed his wife to spend money on the church too. The building in Dunfermline (where they had married) was modest, far too plain for a royal chapel. Margaret had it extended, endowed it with beautiful precious vessels and an exquisite crucifix, as well as the vestments created by our English embroidery.

Scotland began to feel less like the barbaric country we had encountered three years earlier. Only Edgar was restless and that was understandable. We women had a role and divided our time between Edward, reading and our embroidery. He was a man without a purpose and I felt for him.

Soon after Christmas, Margaret conceived again, but if we had hoped for another quiet year, we were to be disappointed.

There was no news of any more rebellions. It seemed as though the whole of England had submitted to the Normans. There was little fight left in anyone, even Edgar, who had become morose and lethargic, not even bothering to practise his swordplay.

Then, in April, word came from Wulf that there were rumours the King was gathering a great force, including many ships. No one could see why he needed this unless ... Wulf feared the King might be heading our way.

"Why should he attack Scotland?" Margaret demanded.

"Because I shelter English rebels," King Malcolm answered, "and because I have you as my wife."

"Why should he object to our marriage?"

"Because you are of the royal House of Cerdic and your grandfather was a King of England," he explained. "King William will have taken fright by the audacity, as he would see it, of my alliance with English royalty."

"So you think he could be planning a campaign against you?" she asked.

"I am a thorn in his side," he admitted.

The King gathered his advisers and we waited anxiously to see what might happen.

We were working on a new altar cloth when Edgar came in and slumped in a chair. I glanced at his forlorn face.

"He thinks I should go," he said at last.

"Go where?" Agatha asked.

"He suggests Flanders and I think that's probably the best option."

"Why?" she demanded.

"Mother, King Malcolm doesn't have a great army that can fight the Normans. He has warriors who are very good at border raids, grabbing booty and slaves and retreating back here." He paused. "The King thinks there could be a plan to blockade the eastern sea access. Why else is King William using ships? It's what the great King Athelstan did way back, though I doubt William knows our history. As well as the ships, he's likely to bring men to fight and we all know how fearsome they are. The Scots wouldn't stand a chance."

"Is he suggesting you go now?" she whispered.

"Soon, before I'm likely to get trapped here. And you and Christina will come with me. Edie, you have a choice, of course, for I have no authority over you. You can come if you like or stay with Margaret."

I moved across to take Agatha's hand.

"Dearest Agatha, we have been there for each other from the moment we met. It is so hard to say goodbye, but I feel my place is with Margaret."

Agatha hugged me.

"Dear Edie, I understand and I know you will look after my daughter as best you can."

We both began to cry, for we had become like sisters from our meeting in Russia. She had been sent to marry, a pawn in a diplomatic chess game and couldn't even speak our language. So much had happened since her marriage to my half-brother.

Margaret was equally distressed, as she had never been separated from Christina before. She had known periods of separation from her mother, but this would be a significant change, for none of us could see how we could meet again in the foreseeable future.

So Edgar, Agatha and Christina slipped quietly out of Scotland along with any remaining English rebels. Elizabeth went with them, but Anna stayed with Margaret. We prayed they would all find a safe haven.

It could be many, many weeks before we had word from them.

"The King says we are to travel north, Edie," Margaret told me. "We are sure the news is right that King William is on his way, but he will find the birds have flown."

She was about four months pregnant, so still fairly agile. Even so, the journey through the woods and over the hills was not easy. We passed a lake we were told was Loch Leven before we crossed the River Tay and came at last to Perth, where we hoped to be safe.

"We shall see what happens," King Malcolm explained. "I have scouts in many places and they can bring me news."

Within a month, we had heard of a blockade at sea and praised God that Edgar and the family had left before they were trapped. Then came news King William's foot forces had reached the Firth of Forth and were marching west to find a crossing point. They must have found this somewhere near Stirling, for the next we heard they were heading north-east – in our direction!

"He is bringing boats round into the Firth of Tay," King Malcolm told us. "I need to come between him and his fleet."

We had also heard that on his march King William was destroying small townships and burning what crops he could find. The number of his troops was daunting.

The Scottish King took his hastily assembled force out to meet the invader and left us to pray. I did my best to keep Margaret calm for her sake and for the sake of her unborn child, but it was a terrifying time.

"He doesn't even have forces such as King Harold had at Hastings," Margaret moaned. "It would not be a fight between equals."

"Maybe they will not fight. Let's pray they make peace instead."

Our prayers were answered, for we heard King Malcolm had thought better of pitching his men against the war-hardened Normans. He had sent envoys to King William and they thrashed out a pact.

The treaty was finally agreed at a place just south of the Tay called Abernethy. King Malcolm had to swallow any pride he had and kneel before the conquering Norman, swearing to become his vassal. We weren't there to see this, as we stayed in Perth, and the King said very little about the encounter. However, we gathered the Scot had been granted some manors in England and an annual pension of twelve marks in gold.

"Edie, the treaty has been sealed by the King having to give William hostages," Margaret said.

She fiddled with the edge of her sleeve and I could tell she was distressed. When she looked up at me, there were tears in her eyes.

"He has given him Duncan," she said quietly.

"His eldest son? He's only twelve! Oh, Margaret, is this what happens to royal children?"

"Because my father never became a king, we have been sheltered to some extent from the implications of being royal children, but this is a sad reality. This may be the last time my husband ever sees Duncan, and Duncan's survival will depend on his father honouring the terms of the treaty."

We were a sad group who eventually returned to Dunfermline. Although some of the surrounding countryside had been ravaged, the Normans had not passed through Dunfermline and the palace and church had not suffered. Margaret was able to settle back into familiar surroundings and her usual routine, thankful she had not lost her unborn child.

Not long after our return, an old friend visited.

"Gospatric!" the King exclaimed. "We heard you had submitted to King William and for a high price had purchased back your Earldom."

"That's true," Gospatric conceded. "The King was gracious, but gained a huge financial reward for his 'kind' act."

"So what brings you here? I fear you may be a fugitive again?"

Gospatric looked at his feet and shifted from one to the other.

"The King doubts my loyalty."

"Is that a surprise?" King Malcolm laughed. "How many times have you rebelled?"

"He has dismissed me from my Earldom and given it, damn him, to Waltheof."

"Another rebel who made his peace."

"There is no hope of a successful rebellion now, so I don't see why he doubted me." Gospatric complained. "He has suddenly decided to condemn me for taking part in the massacre of the Norman garrison at York in September 1069 and also for being a party to the attack on Durham earlier that year. Why bring all that up now, long after the events?"

"I heard he has been purging the English church of its English bishops and replacing them with Normans," the Scot commented. "The King tightens his iron grip. Sadly for you, he has tightened it here too. The bastard invaded my kingdom and I had to do a deal with him. He now has Duncan to secure my good behaviour."

"Edgar is no longer here, I take it."

"No, he has gone with his mother and sister to Flanders and that, I suggest, is where you go, for if I let you stay here, I break the terms of my oath."

The two men looked at each other. There was no animosity in the King's words, simply practicality, and Gospatric knew it. He rested with us for a week before continuing his journey.

By October, we had word he had safely joined the others in Flanders and we also had another prince, this one being named Edmund after Margaret's Ironside ancestor.

CHAPTER 25

As part of the English court, Margaret had learned much from King Edward and his Queen and some of this she had soon put into practice in Scotland. She and the King looked like royalty and the court had a far greater air of refinement than it had had when we first came here as refugees.

She had improved the manners at table and had also created a more serious atmosphere. Frivolity was frowned upon, as were dancing and flirting among the younger members of the court. Bawdy songs from itinerant minstrels were censored and no one dared gamble or play with dice where Margaret might see them.

She could do nothing about the weather, but her introduction of thick and colourful wall hangings had made the hall look more sumptuous and inviting, and it certainly felt warmer. The countryside was rich in game, so we ate well – if we chose. Margaret herself often fasted and at other times restricted the amount she ate.

"I grew used to living by the Rule of St. Benedict when I was at Romsey, Edie, and I feel called to pursue that," she said. "The Scots know nothing of this. I shall have to see what I can do to bring some Benedictine monks here to give an example of holy living."

Seeking to reform the church was a priority, but a difficult aim to achieve. There were so many things that were different and which grated on her.

"They work on a Sunday!" she told me. "They say the day of rest is Saturday, but the whole of Christendom observes Sunday as a day of worship and rest. It's ridiculous!"

"They don't like change," I warned. "You will have to tread slowly and carefully."

"At least they have given in over Lent," she crowed.

"Ah, yes, when we first came Lent began on the Monday after Ash Wednesday, exactly forty days before Easter."

"Now it begins on Ash Wednesday as it should, but we do not fast on the Sundays."

It was a small triumph and a change the King had allowed, but he did not indulge her in all the changes she wanted to make. I doubted she could ever achieve her dream of bringing the Scottish church in line with that of Rome.

Even if she could not change others, she did at least lead by example. She gave her time and money to feed the hungry and tend the sick. She endowed churches and entered into debate with priests and others. I know that she wrote to Bishop Wulfstan of Worcester for advice, which I believe he graciously gave. She was fervent in prayer and immersed herself in the Scriptures. She also taught other young women how to do our English embroidery, so that the plainness of the churches could be offset with the beauty and colour of the vestments and altar cloths.

Margaret may have been a very reluctant Queen of the Scots, but she pursued her calling with a zeal I could not fault. She often accompanied the King on his travels around his kingdom, for she was a good horsewoman. Sometimes I went too, but I was also happy to stay with the children. They would join the annual progress when they were older and needed to be seen by their future subjects.

Edward had just passed his third birthday in March 1074, when Margaret began her third confinement. Again she had been fairly well throughout the pregnancy, but the labour this time proved more difficult, and I have to confess to becoming very anxious. King Malcolm paced the hall, unable to sit down for any length of time and snapping at anyone who irritated him, but he was all joy and smiles when told he had yet another son.

"Will you give this one a Scottish name?" I asked Margaret, as she cradled the little one in her arms.

"No, this one is to be Edgar."

"After your brother?"

"No, after our ancestor who was a wise and respected King of England."

"King William wouldn't like to hear you saying that!" I joked.

She smiled.

"I have a feeling this child will be a king one day. He has already made his presence felt more than the others did."

On the 8th day of July, Margaret and I were in prayer remembering St. Grimbald, whose contribution to the Benedictine life in Winchester had been so significant that he had been canonised. The Scots, of course, had never heard of him! He had lived in the reign of King Alfred and had died in the year of Our Lord 901.

Our meditation was interrupted by news that the court had visitors and we went into the hall to find … Edgar, Agatha, Christina and Elizabeth!

"I have missed you so much, dearest Margaret!" Agatha cried, clasping her daughter's hands and kissing them. "When we heard of the birth of a new baby you had called Edgar, I persuaded my Edgar that we must come. Oh, my dear, you look so well."

"And so do all of you," Margaret answered. "You are very welcome."

It was truly wonderful to see the family again, but I wasn't sure what the King would think. His treaty at Abernethy precluded him from harbouring English rebels, but perhaps if the aetheling's stay was short, the Norman King might not know.

Even if King William did not know, another king did. A few weeks after his arrival, Edgar received a letter.

"I'm being offered a position!" he cried. "Philip, King of France, is inviting me to take charge of the castle at Montreuil-sur-Mer."

"Where is that?" Agatha wanted to know.

"It's on the border of Flanders and Normandy, so the northern edge of the Duchy." He grinned. "It pretty well controls the French exit to the sea."

"So?"

"He adds that from that castle he hopes I would daily annoy his enemies. In other words, I have permission to harass the forces of King William."

We did not receive this news with as much excitement as he did. While we were pleased he might have a responsible position, a role into which he could put his energies, we weren't convinced this was the best one, for it would simply drive a bigger wedge between him and King William.

King Malcolm was more sympathetic, because harassing one's enemies on a daily basis was something that appealed to him. Anyway, Edgar had no intention of refusing the offer, even if we had tried to dissuade him, and he sent a letter of acceptance to France.

"May I stay in Scotland?" Agatha asked him. "I've had enough of travelling and getting used to a new place and people."

She was cradling baby Edgar, while Christina had young Edmund on her lap. Edgar looked at both of them. At 23, he was very much a man now and didn't need his mother, but he was nevertheless head of the family and responsible for their care.

"I still have treasures from Hungary," she added. "Christina and I will not be a burden to the Scottish court."

"And you would like to spend time with your grandsons," Edgar remarked. "Yes, Mother, you and Christina may stay."

Margaret and her husband decided to make sure Edgar and his retainers looked the part, and to this end, the men were given fine clothes, even robes of purple and fur-lined cloaks, together with wares of gold and silver.

Agatha cried as Edgar and his companions went on board for their journey to France. The rest of us watched with, I guess, mixed emotions. Surely he could be doing something better with his life, was what I thought.

Edgar's was not the only departure that summer.

Margaret had been writing not just to Bishop Wulfstan but also to the Archbishop of Canterbury. In 1070, King William had replaced Stigand with an Italian-born, but French-educated monk called Lanfranc. He had been persuaded by Margaret to send some Benedictine monks to Scotland, but King Malcolm was wary of too much contact with the English church, as Lanfranc was known to claim that Canterbury was superior to all other churches in mainland Britain.

The source of Scotland's Christianity was not, however, England, for the Scots looked to Ireland and especially to the ministry of the saintly Columba. The roots of this somewhat different spirituality were deep and Scotland's King had no intention of pulling them out. He indulged Margaret in her desire to make the churches less plain and more sumptuous and allowed her to endow shrines and Christian communities. Margaret particularly admired the hermits who devoted themselves to prayer and who acted as spiritual advisers, and she would give to the good causes they advocated.

The King, however, had no intention of allowing Lanfranc or any other cleric representing Roman Catholicism to have great influence in Scotland and in 1074 he expelled two Benedictines called Aldwin and Turgot from the community at Melrose. I'm sure Margaret was bitterly disappointed, but she didn't show it and she didn't allow it to affect her relationship with her husband. There had only been love on one side when they married, but I had observed how her feelings towards the King had grown warmer. She did not share his bed simply out of duty, but because they had an intimate and close relationship.

Edgar had gone, but what happened next took us all totally by surprise.

CHAPTER 26

I came into the hall to find Margaret giving hospitality to a group of beggars. She would wash their feet on Maundy Thursday, but had never actually brought any into the heart of the palace. She was even helping one of them to remove his tattered tunic.

"Oh, Edie, come and help me!" she cried. "Here is Edgar and some of his men, returned in great distress."

Edgar! I hurried to help.

"I have sent some servants to find them clothes, shoes for their feet and some food, for they are famished."

We had sent these men off with fine clothes and rich possessions including gold and silver, yet here were some of them, barely clothed. We asked no questions until they were all warm, clean and refreshed, by which time Agatha and Christina had joined us.

"Can you tell us what happened?" Margaret gently asked.

"The most terrible storm," Edgar groaned. "Our boats stood no chance and we were thrown onto the rocks and cast upon the shore."

"Oh, my darling boy!" wailed Agatha.

"We were able to save some of the treasure." He pointed to some bundles dumped on the rush-strewn floor. "But we were near to the border with England and had a hard time to make our escape. I lost some men to the Normans and the rest of us have struggled to make our way back here. Oh, God, it was awful!"

Agatha took him in her arms and he wept like a child.

"You are safe now," she murmured, "safe with us."

"How glad I am we didn't go with him," Christina remarked. "I think we would have perished."

Alone with my prayers, I could not help but look back at Edgar's life and feel he had been hard done by. First, he had lost his father when he was only six and I knew that had crushed him. Then he had been cheated out of the crown by a devious and ambitious Harold, only to find when the Witan did make him King that a powerful conqueror stood in his way. He had been betrayed by Earls such as Edwin and Morcar and promised support which had never materialised. Now that, at long last, he had a task he might fulfil well, he had been denied it by the forces of nature.

"I don't blame you, Lord," I prayed. "He has suffered at the hands of men more than at the hands of nature, but can you not bless him now and help him to find a better path through life?"

We were all deeply concerned and when the King returned from one of the many trips he took, I think he and Margaret must have talked at some length in the privacy of their bed, for the King had a suggestion to make.

"Edgar, do you still want to go to France?" he asked, when we were alone as a family.

"I can't say I do," he moaned. "Everything has gone wrong and the offer has turned sour, though I presume King Philip would still be willing to give me the care of the castle."

"You have few options," King Malcolm stated. "You could still try to go to France or you could return to Flanders. I cannot allow you to stay here indefinitely because of my oath, for which Duncan is a hostage."

"I know," Edgar nodded.

The sadness in his voice made me want to weep.

"There is another possibility," the King added.

Edgar looked up, as did the rest of us.

"You could ... make your peace with King William," the Scot said.

"He'd kill me!"

"We don't know that, Edgar," Margaret interposed. "We have not heard of anyone he has executed, but we have heard of many he has pardoned."

"And then left them to die in prison!"

"We would not send you to the King without first being assured you will be pardoned and given some measure of freedom," King Malcolm said. "We realise you are an aetheling and that makes you different from, say, Earl Waltheof, but the King now has a firm grip on the whole of England. He knows you could not raise a successful rebellion against him."

Edgar looked down at his hands and I noticed how bruised and cut they were.

"He might give you some land again," Agatha suggested, "and anyway I still have treasure brought from Hungary. We could find a way forward."

"I'll think about it," he promised.

Very soon, I believe, the King sent a letter to King William and a correspondence began, which ended with the assurances we desperately hoped for.

"The Sheriff of York will meet you in Durham, Edgar," King Malcolm said, "and will escort you all the way to Normandy, where King William is at present. Your journey to Durham is to be by land and I will give you an escort that far."

"I'm grateful," Edgar answered. "And when I reach Normandy?"

"The King has promised me he will give you an estate in England and a pension, though I think you may be expected to live in Normandy, not England."

"We do not wish to go to Normandy," Agatha told him. "Christina and I intend to stay here, at least for the time being."

His head was bowed, as though defeated.

"Come, Edgar," Margaret exclaimed, taking his hands. "See this as a new beginning. You are still the grandson of a King of England and will have an honoured place at court."

"There will be hunting and hawking," the King added, "and perhaps the opportunity to do some fighting."

I could see the heaviness of his heart, for it was not how he had wanted life to be, but his true destiny had been denied him.

King Malcolm and Margaret made sure he was dressed like royalty for his long journey south. He had some retainers and all of them had fine horses to ride and changes of clothes. The farewell was again tearful, but in my heart I felt more positive this time and believed he could at last find some measure of peace.

The escort returned safely from Durham, so we knew Edgar had reached that place and was now in the hands of the Sheriff of York. We did not expect to receive any more news for several weeks. However, before the onset of the bitter weather, there was an unexpected visitor.

I was sitting with my embroidery, knowing that soon the daylight would be too poor for me to sew and praying that the children would not get sick during the winter, when Anna hurried in.

"Lady Edie, the Queen asks you to come quickly to the hall."

I hurried there immediately, with visions of another return by a bedraggled Edgar. In the hall was a group of well-dressed men with piles of baggage.

Not Edgar! I thought with relief.

The man talking to Margaret turned and ...

"Wulf!" I cried, and fell into his arms, weeping.

"Edie, dearest sister, I should have known you'd cry!"

We clung to each other. I was wild with excitement.

"Six years," he said, "and you haven't changed a bit."

He was laughing and I was crying, but eventually we were able to sit down and all our visitors could receive our royal hospitality.

"Why are you here?" I wanted to know.

"I bring goods for selling in Scotland," he smiled. "Usually I send Margaret what she's asked for, but I thought it was time I came in person and as (he grinned) there are currently no rebellions, I thought it was a good time."

"Oh, it is so wonderful to see you. Isn't it, Margaret?"

"It is indeed and when you have caught up with Wulf's news, I will ask Anna to bring in my children."

"And talking of children." Wulf turned to a young man seated next to him. "Edie, do you know who this is?"

I looked at the fresh-faced youth and guessed he was in his teens and nearing manhood.

"Andrew!" I cried. "It must be Andrew."

The lad grinned shyly and I could see I was looking at a young version of my twin.

"Edgar visited us while he was in London," Wulf told us, "so we have seen him and heard his tales of woe. He was well and has now travelled on to Normandy." He paused. "It's good that he is making peace with King

William. The Norman grip on England is unlikely ever to slacken."

"It is very hard for him," Margaret conceded, "but the King and I couldn't see any other viable option."

"Is this why you have come?" I asked. "To bring us news of Edgar?"

"Not just that, but for the moment let me hear yours, and, Margaret, I must meet your sons, the future Kings of Scotland."

CHAPTER 27

I did not think my happiness could be clouded. My brother was here and we were as one again, both anxious to hear each other's news. Andrew was thin and lanky like our father and such a delight, as he took great interest in everything that was going on and how we did things in Scotland.

"Andrew and Wulfgar are both learning to be wily merchants," Wulf told me.

"They learn well from you," I laughed. "And Maria?"

"She is well and doesn't mind she has a houseful of men, though sometimes I am away on my travels."

"We still trade with Sweden and Hungary," Andrew added, "and even with Boris in Russia."

"My sons have had to endure my tales of our life in Europe before we came to England and Wulfgar talks of travelling, though Andrew doesn't have the same desire."

"I came with Father because I wanted to see you," Andrew explained. "I remember you so well from your time in London."

"You have grown up while I've been up here in the north," I said proudly.

Wulf had brought other merchants with him and so the group spent a couple of weeks travelling in Scotland, selling their wares and making deals, the King having provided them with guides and a Gaelic interpreter. The afternoon before they were to travel south again, Wulf asked me to take him into the church where Margaret had married.

As we stood in front of the altar, he put his arm around me and I rested my head on his shoulder.

"There was another reason for my visit," he said. "We are no longer young, Edie. We have passed fifty years and I find I get breathless and tired in a way I never did."

Something cold gripped my heart and I froze in his embrace.

"I may not see you again," he whispered. "But I did not want to leave this world without feeling your warmth beside me just once more."

I could not form any words. Tears began to trickle down my cheeks.

We stood there for some time before we prayed to Almighty God, thanking him for our lives, the love we shared, the richness of our family life and how God had blessed us despite all the difficulties we had faced.

As we shared our last evening meal, I looked at him afresh and realised his face now had lines of age I had never seen before and there was less colour in his cheeks. I tried to be brave as we said farewell the next day, but true to form I wept.

News eventually reached us that Edgar was in Normandy, had done homage to King William and been graciously received. As King Malcolm had hoped, Edgar was granted an estate, apparently in Hertfordshire, and this would give him an income; he was also given a pension of one pound of silver per day. There was news too that Christina had been provided for through the gift of estates in Warwickshire and Oxfordshire, from which she would receive an income.

As we had anticipated, Edgar was now a "guest" at the Norman court – not exactly a prisoner, but there was no suggestion he could return to live in England. Agatha was sad about that, as I suspect she had hoped that she and Christina could make their home with him, but that was not to be. On a positive note, Edgar was among nobles and could pursue such pastimes as hawking and hunting. For the present, King William had no battles to fight. Thus we entered into a peaceful period in our lives, punctuated only by the birth in 1076 of another son for Margaret, this one being named Aethelred after her great-grandfather. The day after his birth came the news I had been dreading – my dear brother had died and gone to be with Our Lord, and Andrew, at nineteen, was now head of that family.

A part of me died with Wulf. The family tried hard to comfort me, but I was not interested in life, even the tiny new life that was sometimes given me to cradle. Somehow I missed the summer that year, each day blurred into the next.

Time does heal and when yet another son arrived in 1078, I was keen to cuddle him.

"This one is to be Alexander," Margaret said.

"That's not a Scottish name, or an English one for that matter," I remarked.

"He is named after the Pope," she said, raising her eyebrows in a slightly mischievous way.

"You'll never get the Scottish church to accept the Pope," I said, "but Alexander is a good name nevertheless."

Another year of peace passed, but in the early summer of 1079, I found Margaret weeping before the altar in the church.

"Whatever is the matter?" I asked, kneeling beside her and putting my arm around her.

"Oh, Edie, my husband is taking up arms again."

I sighed.

"He is a natural warrior, Margaret. You may have been able to distract him with good things within the kingdom, but we know he always has an eye for what is beyond his border."

She began to dry her tears.

"Remember Wearmouth," I said.

"I never want to think of that," she answered, shuddering.

"Harrying others is what Scottish kings have always done when they are not fighting each other and, let's face it, he hasn't done any since your marriage and that's nine years ago."

She was calmer now.

"Why now?" I asked. "And where is he going? Presumably into Northumbria."

She nodded.

"He would like Northumbria to be part of his kingdom, but acknowledged it was William's when he made that treaty at Abernethy." She paused. "He has men who long to fight, to grab booty and add to their riches. He can't hold them back forever – at least, that is what he says."

"King William won't like it."

"King William is beset with problems in Normandy. There has been a rift with his son Robert, so the Normans are busy fighting themselves."

"Does the King really think he can get away with it, that no one will notice?"

She shook her head.

"I don't know," she confessed, "but King William is certainly in no position to respond to an invasion in his kingdom at this time."

In August, the King left with his men, their burning thirst for booty being clear to all of us. We women took to praying. Within a month, they were back with goods and cattle and slaves, crowing about their exploits, but we could not match their excitement.

Alone with Margaret, I tried to cheer her.

"The King is safely back," I said, sensing her low spirits.

"This raid, Edie, has made me realise how much I love him. I was so afraid he would be killed and I would have to face life without him."

"Perhaps it will satisfy his men for a while and he won't go to war again."

"They destroyed many buildings," she admitted, "and have brought back much that they have stolen, but the King told me how he would let no one harm the church at Hexham out of respect for the saints who rest there."

"That sounds like your influence, so we must thank God for that at least."

She gave me a wry smile.

"But how long before King William hears about the incursion?" she speculated.

If the King of England heard about it that year, he was far too busy dealing with a family feud in Normandy to bother with the northernmost part of his kingdom.

"The nobility is split," Margaret told us, as she surveyed a letter from Edgar. "Some back King William and some his son Robert."

"And what's Edgar up to?" the King asked.

"Praise God, he has stayed loyal to the King," she reported. "We don't want him rebelling again."

The Scottish raid into England was nothing compared with a blood feud that broke out the following spring, centred on Durham. I couldn't follow all the complications, but there was enough killing for King William (now reconciled to his son) to act and, in the July, he sent his half-brother, Bishop Odo, to sort it out. This war-like prelate led his army to lay the area waste.

Rumours reached us that he had killed, maimed and extorted money from the guilty and innocent alike, before grabbing some of the treasures from the cathedral. We were appalled to hear he had, allegedly, carried off an ornate pastoral staff.

We waited nervously to see if Odo's remit involved Scotland.

CHAPTER 28

"Bishop Odo is a poor example of a man of God!" Margaret exclaimed. "He is a warrior, more concerned with property than with men's souls."

"He has been a faithful agent of King William," King Malcolm countered. "The King has had to spend so much of his time in Normandy defending his Duchy's vulnerable borders, that he has needed a strong man or two in England."

"Bishop Odo should decide whether he is a man of war or a man of peace," Margaret argued. "He can't pretend to be one and act like the other."

"He's certainly not welcome in my kingdom in any capacity," her husband added.

Margaret could have told the King that his raid wouldn't go unpunished, but if she said this to him in the privacy of their bed, she never said it in public and even things she sometimes said to me were never shared with others.

Theirs was an interesting relationship. They complemented each other in many ways, but inevitably there were differences, some of which were irreconcilable and where one party had to give way. The King gave way on matters he regarded as unimportant, like his grand clothes and the manners of the court, but Margaret had to give way on the matter of war and some aspects of church life.

We all heaved a sigh of relief when we heard Bishop Odo had returned south. However, in the autumn, news came suggesting that King William intended King Malcolm should pay for breaking his oath.

"Scouts tell me there is a Norman army advancing north through Northumbria," King Malcolm reported. "It's not headed by the Bishop, but by the King's son, Robert."

We waited in Dunfermline. Margaret was heavily pregnant, her child being expected any day, so there was no way we could travel north, as we had done before. This made the King doubly anxious. He was gathering an army and receiving constant reports on the progress of the Normans.

"They cannot cross the Firth of Forth," he declared. "I believe you are safe here."

"If you fight, then you could die," Margaret complained. "I couldn't bear that."

He tenderly took her hand.

"I will try to be wise," he said. "They will march west towards Stirling, so I must lead my men that way too." He kissed her hand and I heard him whisper, "Pray I return."

We all did that.

He had barely been gone a day when Margaret went into labour. Even when a little girl was safely delivered, we dared not rejoice too much, as we feared she may soon be fatherless.

"Will you wait until the King has returned before you name her?" I asked.

Margaret was resting, weak and exhausted from the birth, while I sat by her, cradling the tiny bundle.

"No." Her voice was very quiet. "She is to be Edith."

"After Edward's queen?"

"She was good to me and I learned so much from her about how to be a queen, though I didn't know then that I would ever be one." Her eyes flickered open and she looked at me and smiled slightly. "She treated me as a daughter, but she is not the only Edith who has mothered me."

I returned her smile and felt a glow of warmth.

Edith was a week old before we had news her father was still alive. King Malcolm had met Lord Robert and the Norman army at Falkirk – and the Scottish leader had realised he was no match for the aggressor. They had sat down together, shared food and wine, and agreed a treaty which basically was a renewal of the one made at Abernethy. Thankfully, no blood was shed and it was agreed no harm would come to Duncan, who was still in the Norman court. Hostages were again given by the Scots, but no child of King Malcolm was included this time.

"What is Lord Robert like?" Margaret asked the King, as we sat eating together after his return.

"Stockier than his father. His nickname is Curthose, 'shorty pants'. He's about Edgar's age, in his late twenties I'd guess, and a man I could do business with."

"Did he have any news of Edgar?" Agatha asked.

"Yes, I think they got on well. He says Edgar is in good health and enjoying life at court." He paused. "I hope Lord Robert is King of England when his father dies."

"Will not Edgar be considered?" Agatha said.

King Malcolm did not look at her, but took a mouthful of venison.

"Mother, King William has too many sons of his own," Margaret interrupted. "We have to face the fact that Edgar's chances ever of becoming King of England are very remote."

The look of sadness on Agatha's face was heartbreaking.

"But Agatha," I said, "you will have a grandson who is King of Scotland."

I said it, but I knew it did not mean as much. Scotland was still seen as a barbaric nation, poor and on the edge of civilisation, while England was rich, refined and respected.

We heard that on Lord Robert's way back south, he had stopped at the River Tyne and built a new castle, which reinforced the Conqueror's claim to Northumbria. On reflection, Scotland had not been badly treated, and with hindsight we were all glad it was Lord Robert who had been sent to punish the Scots and not Bishop Odo.

Two years later, we heard that King William had imprisoned Bishop Odo in Rouen, but we didn't hear what he was accused of. By then, another princess had been born and she was named Mary.

About this time, there was a newcomer to the court – Lord Murray, a widower, who had left his sons to run his estates and had come to be an adviser to the King. He was about sixty years of age and a fine figure of a man, who often entertained us with his tales.

"I have visited the holy island of Iona," he told us. "I have seen there the shrine dedicated to St. Columba. The west coast is a wild part of the Kingdom and many Norse have made their home there."

"I was born in Sweden," I ventured to share, "and grew up in Russia, both countries populated by the Norse."

"I have not travelled east," he confessed. "You must tell me about those lands."

So we would often spend a pleasant afternoon in conversation.

"Your mother was the Queen's grandmother," he said. "Have I got that right?"

"Yes, she was the widow of the King of England, so Margaret has royal blood, but I have none."

"I think she must have been a woman of great beauty, for you both share fine features," he commented.

His words made me blush, for I was not used to such compliments.

"I can see how close you are," he added.

"We have spent much time together, whereas the Queen has been separated from her mother many times and even from her sister."

"Am I right in thinking Lady Christina wishes to be a nun?"

"Both Margaret and Christina were educated at a nunnery, Romsey near Winchester, and the life there was something they admired. If the Queen had not married, I think she would have made a home there. And Christina? Her brother has not forced her to marry and I think her heart may be set on the cloistered life."

"Lord Edgar is still in Normandy?"

"As far as we know. He isn't a great letter writer," I laughed.

Christina was now past thirty and had never shown any inclination to marry. She spent a lot of her time in reading and her day was governed by the hours of prayer. She was really living like a nun already and certainly took little interest in the children. Agatha was beginning to slip into a similar lifestyle.

In the year of Our Lord 1084, Margaret gave birth to another son and this one she called David. I marvelled that King Malcolm had let her name all their children, for David was not a Scottish name either, but the name of the great King of Israel, who had lived two thousand years ago and had united God's chosen people.

"The King and I have been discussing Edith's future," Margaret told me one day.

"Edith?"

"She is nearly five. The older boys are learning to be warriors, except for Aethelred who is with the monks, but Edith must have an education. We are thinking of sending her to Romsey."

"Really?"

"The King will make an appropriate match for her and that is likely to be a man from England, not Scotland, so she must be schooled in womanly arts and given an education appropriate for a princess."

I had spent more time with Edith than Margaret had and I hated the thought of her leaving us, for she was a sweet girl and I had grown fond of her. I was not, however, her parent and so had no say in her future.

"Perhaps next year," Margaret added.

I must cherish my time with Edith while I can, I thought.

The next year had both pain and joy.

CHAPTER 29

The trees were about to burst into life and the melting snow was filling the streams with bitterly cold water, when we had terrible news.

"There's been an accident!"

A servant had rushed into the hall as we all sat at table. The King looked up from his food.

"It's Lord Donald."

King Malcolm was now on his feet.

"My son!" he cried. "What's happened?"

"A riding accident. He was with a group travelling to Stirling and part of the trackway fell into the river. Lord Donald and two others ... they were lost in the torrent."

"Oh, God, no!"

"Their bodies?" asked Lord Murray.

"Have been recovered," the servant reported.

I had never seen the King cry. As a hardened warrior, he was used to death, often causing it himself. His first wife had died, but we weren't here then to witness any grief. Now I saw him weep, with Margaret trying hard to comfort him. At 23, Lord Donald was the eldest of the King's sons still in Scotland.

Lord Donald's body was brought back to Dunfermline for burial. That was such a sad day. Margaret was particularly distressed and, when we were alone, I took her hand and sought to help her.

"I cannot be consoled, Edie. Lord Donald died unshriven."

"But we believe in a God of mercy, don't we? Yes, he had no time to confess his sins and be absolved, but can we not trust in the steadfast love of the Lord?"

"Dying unshriven haunts me," she confessed. "I try so hard to please Our Lord."

"Don't forget his grace. Our entry into heaven is a gift we cannot earn."

I fear my words had little effect. Margaret had spent her formative years believing in discipline, the prayer and fasting she pursued; too often her God was a demanding one. I didn't have the same experience and saw God as more like a dear father who wanted the best for his daughter and was there to pick me up when I fell down, even as my own father had done all those years ago.

Later that summer there came more bad news, at least, most of us saw it as bad. Andrew, bless him, now wrote to us from London and so we heard that the city and much of the south and east coasts were on high alert because the Danes threatened to invade.

"King Swein died about seven years ago," King Malcolm told us, when I read out the letter. "He was succeeded by one of his sons, Harold, who got nicknamed the Soft. He didn't reign for very long. The King now has another son, one called Cnut. Perhaps he wishes to make a name for himself, like the great king who conquered England all those years ago."

"Don't remind us!" Margaret cried. "He defeated my grandfather at Assandun. We don't want his relative in England."

"Even if it meant King William was defeated?" the King asked, raising his eyebrows.

"Would it help Edgar's cause?" Agatha enquired.

"No," replied Margaret, firmly. "If the Danes conquer England, Edgar will lose even the lands he holds and there would be a price on his head as the grandson of Edmund Ironside."

"Andrew writes the rumour is that King Cnut is amassing a huge fleet and that he learned much from the failure of the two previous attempts."

"He may even have been part of them," the King commented. "The Danes know our land, though they haven't tried to invade the southern part for nearly seventy years."

Later we had news King William had brought over a vast army to protect his kingdom; there were many thousands of paid troops, foot soldiers and archers. These men were dispersed across the land, and the thegns and churchmen were expected to maintain and feed them. England was in misery and in Scotland we waited anxiously to see what would happen.

"Edie, what do you think of Lord Murray?" Margaret suddenly asked one day.

"He … he is a good man, I believe," I answered.

"The King appreciates his wisdom and has asked him to look into making Edinburgh more than just a hunting lodge. It was Lord Murray who impressed upon him its strategic position."

We continued with our embroidery.

"I think he admires you," Margaret said.

"Who?"

"Lord Murray, of course. Haven't you noticed how he often contrives to sit by you and single you out for conversation?"

"I enjoy his company."

"I think he wishes you to enjoy it more," she responded, with a somewhat sly smile.

"Whatever do you mean?" I asked.

"Oh, Edie, I think he wants to marry you."

"Marry me? At my age!"

"Why ever not? You've admitted he's a good man, he's trustworthy, you enjoy his company. You are not too old to be loved."

I stared at her and she returned my gaze.

"You're serious," I said.

"Of course I am and I would be happy to see you married, as long as you didn't leave me. You would have to make that a condition."

I felt myself going very hot and I couldn't concentrate on the stitching. I had never seriously considered marrying, as I had been happy to look after Agatha and her children. It was too late to have any of my own, but that there might be a man who loved me was ... was an amazing thought and not an unwelcome one, I discovered.

Next time we sat at table together, I was embarrassed and tongue-tied, too conscious of Margaret's words, but Lord Murray was as charming as ever and after a while I relaxed and tried to be my usual self.

The days were shortening and just before Christmas we heard the Danes weren't coming, at least for the time being, and that King William had sent some of his mercenary troops back to the Continent.

So, we celebrated Christmas with great joy and feasted well.

"You look particularly beautiful today," Lord Murray remarked, in a rare moment when we were alone together. "Your cheeks are glowing."

"It must be the wine," I laughed, and then, suddenly, I became aware of the situation I was in.

"Lady Edie."

Lord Murray took my hand and drew me gently towards him. I felt my heart beating and was sure I was trembling.

"Would you do me the honour ..."

Our faces were now very close and his breath was warm on my forehead.

"...of becoming my wife?"

I tilted my face upwards and was surprised at how soft his beard felt on my cheek. His lips touched mine. I didn't want to pull away; rather I pressed myself against his sturdy frame and felt him engulf me. It was sheer bliss!

When we pulled apart, he looked deep into my eyes and said, "So, will you marry me?"

"I cannot leave Margaret."

"I will make sure you never leave her."

"Then ..." I couldn't stop myself from smiling. "Yes!"

The King and Queen were delighted. I'm sure they had talked of it in the privacy of their bed. Now I was to be blessed with the same intimate relationship they had enjoyed for nearly sixteen years.

We were married at Candlemas, the hall being filled with candles both to celebrate the end of Christmas and to celebrate our union.

The only dark cloud in my bright sky was that Margaret had renewed her idea of sending Edith away to be educated. As this idea was aired among the family, it became clear Christina and Agatha were part of the plan. Both wished to live in the nunnery at Romsey, Christina declaring she would make the vows of a nun. They would take Edith with them and Mary would follow in a couple of years. I suspected King Malcolm was already thinking about their marriages. I had been able to marry for love (Lord Murray and I were really very happy together), but these little princesses would have no choice.

CHAPTER 30

For the time being, no one was going south into England, as the threat of a Danish invasion was still a possibility. As spring progressed, so reports reached us of terrible weather in our neighbouring country; thunder, lightning and storms were the cause of many deaths. Then came the pestilence as cattle, sheep and pigs succumbed to illness and nothing would grow because of the weather. Scotland was spared, but we dared not gloat.

We also heard that King William had ordered a survey to be made of all property in his kingdom. He wanted to know who owned each piece of land, how much it was worth, how many ploughs it needed. Each ox, cow and pig was to be noted down.

"He's about to impose a greater level of taxation," King Malcolm speculated.

"But the English are already weighed down with his demands," I countered. "Andrew writes how many free Englishmen who held smallholdings are reduced to poverty and some are even slaves now. England is in a pitiful state."

"Conquerors always do well, at the expense of the native population," Lord Murray commented.

"The monasteries and nunneries will not be spared," the King warned. "He has raided their coffers in the past."

It was the summer before more encouraging news came. King Cnut had been killed by his own men in July, so there would be no invasion. Also King William had called a great assembly at Salisbury at Lammas and afterwards left for Normandy. The English were facing a heavy burden to tax and talking of "Domesday", but the Danes were no longer a threat and the weather had improved. The journey to Romsey could be made.

"Oh, a letter from Edgar!" I cried, about a week before his mother was to leave.

"Is my boy well?" Agatha asked, always anxious for news of him.

"Oh dear, he has fallen out with the King again," I told them. "He's complaining he stood by King William in all his troubles, but has received no reward for doing so. He complains he isn't treated as a prince should be."

"He is not a Norman," Lord Murray said wryly.

"Anyway, he isn't leading a rebellion; at least that's something," I continued. "Apparently, he's off to Apulia in southern Italy. The territory is under Norman control and he's going to help to keep it that way by being in charge of a company of two hundred knights, so this can't be a serious rift. He has no idea how long he will be there."

Parting with Edith was hard, as we were both fond of each other. Margaret had spent far less time with her and she shed no tears, at any rate in public. I was sad to part from Agatha too, but we had long since ceased to be giggly girls and our lives had taken different paths. I

218

certainly wished her and Christina well and prayed they would find solace for their spirits at Romsey. I had fond memories of the nunnery, but had never felt any calling to pursue the religious life. By this time, Anna and Elizabeth had long since been married to local men, so would not be accompanying Agatha south; I thought there would probably be a lay sister at Romsey who could look after her needs.

"My mother has given me one of the special treasures we brought from Hungary," Margaret told me. "It is an ebony-carved crucifix containing a fragment of the cross of Christ."

She showed it to me; it was kept in a gold casket.

"I shall treasure this to the end of my days," she added.

So began a quiet period in our lives. Edward, at the age of fifteen and as the eldest son, was designated as the King's successor and he, Edmund and Edgar often accompanied their parents on visits to other parts of the kingdom. I always stayed behind, happy to be with my husband and with the younger children. Aethelred was living at the monastery at Dunkeld.

In the autumn of the year of Our Lord 1087, the whole family had returned to Dunfermline and we were all together again. As we sat at table enjoying the food and the company, a messenger arrived, having clearly travelled in haste.

"There is news from Normandy," he said, and total silence fell on the hall. "King William has died."

No one broke the silence. We should not have been surprised, for the King of England was nearly sixty and had spent much of his life fighting battles, though of late he had not been winning them.

"He died at the church of St. Gervase near the city of Rouen," the messenger continued, "and has been buried at Caen."

Still no one spoke.

"There is news of the hostages."

"Of Duncan?" cried King Malcolm.

"It is known that in trying to please God and atone for his sins, the King ordered the release of all hostages, including Lord Duncan."

"Praise God! My son can come home now."

I saw Margaret try to smile and there was a definite ambivalence about our celebration. The King hadn't seen his son since the pact made at Abernethy when Duncan at twelve was handed over to the Normans. Now he was a young man of 27. Would his father even recognise him? And what of Edward who felt himself to be the next King, but was only sixteen? I felt in my bones that the news wasn't entirely joyful.

"I wonder what will happen to Edgar?" I said to my husband in bed that night.

"Did you not say once that he got on well with Lord Robert?"

"Do we know what will happen? Will Lord Robert be King of England and Duke of Normandy? I don't think he and his father were on good terms again at the end, and there are other sons."

"William the one they call Rufus and yet another called Henry," he agreed. "Let's hope they don't take up arms against each other."

Further news reached us slowly. King William had designated Lord Robert as Duke of Normandy despite their differences; apparently he had been so designated many years ago and the nobles wished for no change. The King of England was to be appointed by God, or so King William had decreed, but even before his death, he had sent William Rufus to London with instructions to get himself crowned.

"This sounds like a recipe for disaster," King Malcolm declared. "Neither will be satisfied. Robert will want England and William will want Normandy."

"And where is Edgar?" Margaret asked.

"Still in Italy, I believe," I answered. "He gets on well with Lord Robert, but I don't know about the brother."

"Lord Robert is a good man," the King commented. "I can do business with him, but William the Red is another matter."

Privately, I asked Margaret if there was news of Duncan.

"You know we heard all of King William's hostages were released," she said. "I think they all came back to England with the new King, but some were betrayed. Earl Morcar had been released, but he was put in prison in England. Also King Harold's brother, Wulfnoth, had been a hostage in Normandy for over 25 years, yet on his return to England he too was imprisoned. As far as we know, Duncan is a free man, but ... but he seems to have chosen to stay in England and not return home. The King is grieving."

"I'm sure he is, but it must be such a strange situation, for Duncan has been part of the Norman court for a very long time." I squeezed her hand. "At least we know he is alive and free to travel if he chooses."

In my mind, I thought it just as well, as Edward thought the throne was his.

So, we celebrated Christmas without Duncan and none of us mentioned his name. Our lives continued as they had. I was conscious Mary might soon go to Romsey to join her sister, so I spent as much time as I could with her. Perhaps it was very selfish, but I felt the child needed loving. Her mother was too often taken up with matters of the church.

It was soon after Easter when we heard that there was trouble in England.

"Just as I predicted," the King said. "Lord Robert has allies in England, who have risen up against King William and want Robert as King. And do you know who leads the rebels?"

"Not Edgar?" I exclaimed.

"No, not him, thank God, but the far from saintly bishop who devastated Durham a few years ago."

"Bishop Odo?" Margaret asked.

"Indeed. He was released on the death of King William and has been causing trouble probably ever since. The rebellion is widespread."

Scraps of information came our way, with news of ravaging and burning and devastation. We were grieved and distressed, and I prayed Andrew and the family were safe. Durham, Bristol, Worcester, Norwich – all these were places that suffered. We heard nothing though about London or Winchester and thought perhaps these were held strongly by the King.

"The English have rallied to King William and the rebellion has been crushed," King Malcolm told us.

England was at peace again and it was felt safe enough for little Mary to go to Romsey. My husband tried to comfort me by distraction and suggested I went with him to Edinburgh, where he was organising the development of a palace.

The Red William (named, I was told, for his florid face) had been King for over three years before he made an attempt to oust his brother from Normandy and claim the Duchy for himself. From Andrew's letters, I knew the English people were suffering. The King had laid heavy burdens of tax on them (illegally, they claimed!) and the previous year the harvest had been exceptionally late, with men reaping their corn in November. The fighting, of course, was all on the Continent, but the English were paying.

We prayed for peace, but were surprised at how our prayers were answered.

CHAPTER 31

The fighting in Normandy ended some time in early spring, but we knew nothing of the details until the arrival of an exile from the Duchy.

"Edgar!" cried Margaret, as he and a small group of retainers arrived at the court in Dunfermline. "We weren't expecting you."

"No," he agreed. "I had no intention of returning to Scotland, but I have no choice."

King Malcolm was told of Edgar's arrival and soon we had all gathered around to hear his news.

"We thought you were in Italy," Margaret said.

"I was, but when King William died and Robert became Duke, he invited me back. We're like brothers really. He's a good man."

"That's what I thought when I met him," the King commented.

"He settled some lands on me and life was good, until that damn Rufus started meddling. Last year, he got control, by devious means, of the castles at St. Valéry and Aumale and then some other castles, and started harassing Robert. The King of France came to our aid, but Rufus paid him off."

"We heard about the fighting," Margaret said, "but have they not made peace?"

"Yes," Edgar grunted, "of sorts. Amongst other things, they've agreed to be each other's heir. If Rufus dies without legitimate issue, Robert gets England and if

Robert dies without legitimate issue, Rufus gets Normandy. But one of the other terms was that Robert take back the lands he'd granted me and kick me out!"

"Shame on them!" cried Margaret.

"Does Rufus fear your close relationship with Duke Robert?" King Malcolm asked. "Is that the problem?"

"I suppose it must be, but it's damned unfair! I was just beginning to get settled and now I'm homeless again."

I tended to agree that Edgar had been given a raw deal, but there was nothing that could be done – or so I thought. I soon discovered he and the King were hatching a plan to take revenge on King William by ravaging the northern part of his kingdom.

"But we know what will happen," I complained to Margaret. "King William will send a great force against us and the King will have to do homage."

"He was happy to do homage to Lord Robert," she replied, "but he doesn't want to bend his knee to King William." She paused. "I tend to agree with you, Edie, that he won't be able to avoid it and we shall see Normans in Scotland before the year is out. When it comes to war, the King doesn't listen to me."

Edgar went with the King and his warriors on their raid into Northumbria. I say "raid" because I don't think there was ever any serious possibility of claiming Northumbria for Scotland and keeping it, even if King Malcolm would have wanted that.

They got as far as Chester-le-Street, where there was the usual stand-off with a local force, before the Scots returned laden with booty. The next move would be King William's and that happened in September.

"My scouts tell me the large fleet of ships the Normans have sent north has been wrecked off the Northumbrian coast," King Malcolm told us, "but there is also a massive land army heading our way."

"Should we retreat to Perth?" Margaret asked.

The King shook his head.

"You are safe enough here in Dunfermline for the moment," he answered, "especially as they have failed in their efforts to blockade the coast. I'm gathering a force to fight him."

When you cannot be sure of winning, it is wiser to submit, and when King Malcolm saw the army King William had brought, he decided not to fight, and negotiations were opened. Edgar acted for King Malcolm, while we were pleased to discover the Normans were represented, somewhat surprisingly, by Duke Robert.

Margaret and I could have told the King what would happen – and, of course, it did. He had to do homage to King William and give hostages, but was confirmed in his possession of twelve settlements which he had held under the previous King. He was also given an annual pension of twelve marks in gold. We don't know what else they talked about, but one good outcome was that

Edgar was allowed by King William to have back the estates in Normandy of which he had been deprived.

So, we said another goodbye to Edgar, as he was to return with Duke Robert to Normandy and take up his life there.

"I have a letter from Christina," Margaret said a few months after Edgar's departure. "Edith and Mary have left Romsey and gone to Wilton."

I raised my eyebrows by way of query.

"There is an excellent nunnery at Wilton," she said. "Queen Edith was educated there and Christina and I might have gone to it if the Queen had not decided we should be nearer to Winchester."

"Where is Wilton?"

"Wiltshire, about 25 miles or so from Winchester and very close to Salisbury, I believe."

"And why the move?"

"Christina says it was felt they would get a better education there." She paused. "Actually, I think she was finding them ... a bit rebellious, from the occasional remark she has made. It may even be that they will be happier away from their aunt."

I could imagine Christina being very bossy with the two girls, but I said nothing and simply prayed the move would be a good one.

As it happened, we had a letter from Edith telling us they were now in Wilton and giving the impression they were much happier there. She made no comment about her aunt, but I didn't expect her to.

"She says there is another royal there," Margaret said. "One of King Harold's daughters – Gunnhild – her mother, of course, being Edith Swan-neck. She's in her thirties."

"Is she a nun?"

"I don't think so from what Edith says and as she is well past the age of education, I should say she is more like a prisoner."

"Poor woman! Surely she is no threat to the Normans now?"

"It is strange, is it not? A woman is incarcerated and yet an aetheling like my brother has the freedom to live on his estate. I presume she has no powerful friends, unlike Edgar. But the King may fear someone might marry her and perhaps claim the throne."

For once, it seemed there was someone worse off than our Edgar, a royal who had no voice and who had been completely deprived of her standing in society.

"Oh, this is interesting," Margaret added. "Edith says Bishop Wulfstan went to Wilton to see how she was settling in, and while he was there he met Gunnhild, who was suffering from an eye condition, which meant her eyelids were so swollen that she couldn't open them. The Bishop was very moved by her suffering, so he made the sign of the cross before her eyes and immediately she was able to raise her eyelids and see the light. Such a saintly man! Praise God his prayers were heard and poor Gunnhild was healed."

Suddenly, Margaret cried out and doubled up in pain. I helped her to sit.

"Whatever is the matter?" I asked, anxiously.

She was gasping for breath and clutching her stomach.

"Sometimes ... oh ... I am in pain!"

"You are not pregnant?"

"No. I ... I think those days are past."

I sat with her until the spasm passed.

"Margaret, I don't think you eat enough," I chided. "Even when you are not fasting, you eat so little. And you push yourself very hard – you never stop, from morning till night."

"I must serve the Lord."

"He would not have you make yourself ill in the process."

God seemed to her far more demanding than he did to me and I doubted she would take much notice of my opinion.

In the coming days, we distracted ourselves by moving to Edinburgh and making that a habitable home. Margaret had a small chapel on the rocky fortress and enjoyed the challenge of making the court bright with colour. If we were threatened from the south, we could cross the Forth, if it was thought necessary, and retreat to Dunfermline or further north. Margaret made sure there was a ferry service across the firth, one which could be used by everyone, not just the royal family.

There were still times when I guessed she was in pain, but I did my best to encourage her to eat more. She had long pursued a demanding lifestyle, supported by inadequate nourishment. I feared she may be paying the price for that now, or it may be that some serious illness afflicted her.

One day, we went to a church near East Fortune in East Lothian, which was dedicated to St. Laurence.

"He was Archbishop of Canterbury after St. Augustine," she told me, "so of the true church. He was a very courageous man and I wish to honour him."

When we arrived, however, the monks who looked after the church said we couldn't go beyond the nave.

"Dear lady, you are welcome, but our saint was very specific. He said no woman could enter his sanctuary."

"But I have gifts to lay on the altar," she argued. "He would not want me to be barred."

She made to enter the sanctuary, but was suddenly seized with pain.

"Quick! Help me! I'm dying!"

I was at her side immediately. I took the gifts she held and gave them to the monks, and gently led her away. She clung to me until the spasm passed. I was worried about her, but didn't know how to help her.

"Those monks will say St. Laurence stopped me going in," she whispered.

"Does it matter what they say?"

She managed a faint smile and shook her head.

"Are you dying, Margaret?" I asked.

"Sometimes it feels like that, but when the pain passes, I am alright and feel I have many years ahead. The pain in the church was particularly bad."

"You should outlive me," I claimed.

She squeezed my hand.

"I should, but then, what would I do without you? You have always been at my side, Edie, and I pray you always will be."

At more than twenty years her senior that seemed unlikely, but we all knew the fragile nature of life.

The year of Our Lord 1092 began quietly enough. Margaret was still occasionally beset by pain, but was trying to follow my advice and eat more, though after so many years of inadequate nourishment, she was still frail.

Events in the spring, however, caused an uproar.

CHAPTER 32

"I come seeking sanctuary."

A youngish man faced us in the hall. He had left his group of retainers outside with their horses and baggage. King Malcolm beckoned him forward and the man knelt.

"We have not met for some years, but you will know me by name. I am Dolfin."

"Dolfin? The son of Gospatric, my kinsman?" The King rose, pulled Dolfin to his feet and embraced him. "But you rule Cumbria. Why are you here at my court?"

"King William brought an army against me, too large for me to resist."

"He's done what?!" the King exclaimed, banging his fist on a nearby table. "He shall pay for this!"

Margaret reached across and touched his arm.

"You gave him homage and hostages," she urged.

"And what has he done?" he cried. "Broken any pledge to me!"

"I am truly sorry, sire," Dolfin said. "I do not want to cause trouble, but I had nowhere else to go."

"You did right in coming here," the King replied, sitting down and calming down a little. "And I am being a poor host. We must look after you and your men."

So Dolfin and his men were made at home, but I could see the King was brooding, for he often sat silent, with an angry frown on his face.

"Can you explain to me about Cumbria?" I asked my husband, as we lay together.

"King Malcolm is Prince of Cumbria by hereditary right," he explained. "It isn't part of England, but part of Scotland and King William's ousting of Dolfin, who has ruled there on behalf of King Malcolm, is an invasion of another's kingdom, and a downright provocation."

"This is an ungodly act of aggression," was my comment.

"Indeed, but King Malcolm would be foolish to take an army against the Norman, because he couldn't win. Incidentally, Dolfin tells me his sister, Octreda, married Lord Duncan two years ago."

"King Malcolm has never mentioned it."

"The fact that his son has not returned to Scotland pains him and so he doesn't talk of him, but the fact that Lord Duncan has married within the family suggests he hasn't rejected his Scottish heritage in favour of the Normans."

The King was persuaded to send letters to King William objecting to his takeover of Cumbria. It was also said that the English King's promise of money, made when they met the previous year, had not been fulfilled. King Malcolm had many reasons to be aggrieved, but, for the moment at least, was showing a commendable level of restraint. We wondered, though, how long it would be before he would decide to respond with violence.

Remarkably, King Malcolm did not raise an army, but continued to send letters of complaint to King William for the rest of the year, even though we heard that there was now a Norman castle in Carlisle and people from England had been moved to Cumbria to live there and till the land.

Spring in the year of Our Lord 1093 brought news that King William was seriously ill; indeed, there was a real fear for his life. His death would mean Duke Robert would be King of England and I suspect that's what many were hoping for, as he was Edgar's friend and Scotland's friend. All we had received from William Rufus were broken promises.

"There is more news about the King," Lord Murray told me. "He is desperately ill and has been seeking to make amends for his sins because he fears facing Almighty God. He had been holding onto the Archbishopric of Canterbury, but he has now given that to a man called Anselm. He's been granting land to churches and promising to reverse unjust laws. I believe the promises include restoring Cumbria to Scottish rule, which means that even if he doesn't die, King Malcolm should be appeased and Dolfin can be reinstated."

"I hardly know whether to pray he lives or dies," I confessed. "May God's will be done."

King William was confined to his chamber for the whole of Lent, but in late April began to recover his strength and was declared to be out of danger. We daily expected to hear how he would fulfil the promises he made when he thought he was dying.

"I fear he will renege," my husband said. "He is not a man of honour, he doesn't keep his word, and now he isn't going to die, he will go back on all those extravagant promises."

King Malcolm renewed his call for justice, but the King of England wouldn't listen, though his leading men were apparently urging him to make peace with our King.

One day in May, I found Margaret had taken to her bed.

"You're not well enough to go out riding today with the King?" I asked.

"Edie, it's too painful to ride," she confessed. "I'm more comfortable here, but I will rise later and eat with the court."

"You find such pleasure in riding out with him. Can your physician not help you?"

"Nothing he has prescribed has helped."

She looked at me. Her face was pale and lines of pain were beginning to show. At 47, her beauty was slipping away and I feared her life was too, but there were still days when she was as active as ever and appeared to be pain-free.

"I believe King William has invited our King to go to Gloucester to meet with him," Lord Murray confided.

"Will he go?"

"It is his best option, better than fighting, but he will need assurances as to his safe conduct."

The assurances came in the form of ...

"Edgar! How wonderful to see you!" I cried, as he came into the hall in late July.

"Edie, you look as lovely as ever. Marriage must suit you."

"It does. I recommend it," I laughed.

The court was quickly gathered and I soon discovered King Malcolm had agreed to go to Gloucester to meet the English King and talk about their differences. Edgar had been sent to give him a safe passage and had brought with him hostages from King William as a guarantee of the Scottish King's safe return.

The English escort did not stay long and in early August, the King, with all the trappings of royalty and Margaret's pleas to restrain his temper, left for the long journey south. We knew he planned to stop in Durham for the laying of the foundation stones of a new cathedral.

"I have received a letter from Prior Turgot," Margaret told me about the middle of August. "He witnessed the laying of the stones, together with the Bishop and the King. He also says that the King agreed, while he was there in Durham, that the monks would undertake to say masses for the benefit of us and our children, and in return he will restore the lands in Lothian which he has taken. I had talked to him about that, but wasn't sure he would do it. May God bless him for this act."

The days were shortening and the leaves were gathering on the ground, only to be blown into drifts by a chill wind, before we knew the outcome of the meeting. Margaret's health was even worse, as she was now in pain more often than she was not, and I struggled to make her eat anything.

In my anxiety, I tried to pray, to place everything in God's hands. I often meditated on the words of Psalm 55: "Cast your burden on the Lord and he will sustain you, he will never permit the righteous to be moved." I tried to give the Almighty these situations that troubled me, I tried to trust he would resolve them, but I could not rid myself of my fear of the future and my premonition that disaster was lurking.

In early October, the King and his retainers rode into Edinburgh. The moment he stalked into the hall I could tell by the way he was walking that he was angry. Also, he had with him Edith and Mary!

CHAPTER 33

"That damned Rufus thinks he can treat me like scum!" King Malcolm exclaimed, as he threw off his cloak and slumped into a chair.

A servant hurriedly picked up the cloak and, at a signal from me, ran off to tell Margaret he was home. Others quickly brought in some refreshment.

"Edith!" I cried, "and Mary!", hugging them both in turn. "This is a surprise."

They both looked tired from their long journey and Mary seemed a bit bewildered. There was much hustle and bustle until all the baggage had been dealt with. Margaret was helped in by one of her women and took her seat beside the King. We waited for him to speak, but he downed some ale and took some bread and cheese before he told us what had happened.

"I reached Gloucester on the 24th day of August," he eventually said. "We were well cared for on the journey and given reasonable lodgings in Gloucester. Several of the thegns came to speak with me, all expressing their concern over relations between England and Scotland. I thought it was quite straightforward – King William would give me back Cumbria as he had promised, we would renew our treaty, and that would be it."

He paused and no one spoke. We could all see that things had gone badly wrong. Even Margaret was silent.

"Several days passed and still there was no word of when I would meet the King. I wondered if he was ill again. No explanation was forthcoming. Even Edgar could tell me nothing, as he, like me, had expected the King to receive me without much hesitation."

He was venting his anger on the bread, which he tore in pieces and crushed between his strong fingers.

"Then ..."

He slammed down his cup of ale and some of the contents slopped out.

"Then he *demanded* – he did not *ask* – demanded I appear before an English court for my grievances to be considered. Who does that man think I am? Am I not a king? Almost his equal in status? Should I appear before his court like a commoner?"

Still no one spoke. I think we were too shocked. Such behaviour on the part of the English King would have tried a saint and King Malcolm wasn't one of those.

"When I protested, I was told – for I never came face to face with Rufus – I was told I had to accept these terms or go home empty-handed. Well, I could not tolerate such an insult."

Margaret put her hand on his arm in a gesture of comfort. He gently touched it with his.

"Edgar was as devastated and angry as I was," he told her, "but he was powerless to make any difference."

"And Edith and Mary?" Margaret asked.

"I'll tell you later why I've brought them back here."

I thought I would probably be left in the dark as far as the girls were concerned, but there I was wrong, for, before the day was out, Edith had found me in a quiet place and clearly wanted to talk.

"I have missed you so much," she began, squeezing my hand. "You are a true friend in this troubled world."

"It is wonderful to see you again, but I fear it is under very bad circumstances. I dread to think what the King might do next."

"He'll probably go to war, but I'm happy to be here."

"Didn't you like the nunnery?"

"It was alright. I enjoyed learning and my French and Latin are excellent now, but Christina was horrid to me, and then to Mary."

"In what way?"

"She was very strict and unkind. She wanted us to become nuns like her, but I don't want to be a nun and I know my father doesn't want that. Did you know ...", she lowered her voice, "...that he agreed I should marry King William?"

"No!"

"It must have been one of the terms of the treaty they made when they met up here."

"When Lord Robert and Edgar negotiated the terms?"

"Yes. Soon after that King William came to visit Romsey, to *inspect* me." She rolled her eyes. "But he didn't get the chance. As soon as Christina heard there were Normans about to come into the nunnery, she made Mary and me put veils on, so that we looked like nuns and, according to her, we then wouldn't be molested. But the King went off in a huff when he saw I was a nun, though I wasn't! I took the veil off and stamped on it." She suddenly grinned. "I don't mind about King William not wanting me, as no one speaks well of him."

I was speechless for a moment. The thought of dear little Edith being married to this oath-breaking, cruel and godless King horrified me.

"Christina complained to the abbess about my appalling behaviour," she continued, "but all that happened was that the abbess sent us to Wilton."

"So that's why you moved!"

Certain events now began to make sense, including King William's invasion of Cumbria, which might not have happened if he had been engaged to marry the daughter of the Scottish King. I still didn't know why Edith and Mary had returned to Scotland.

"And you liked Wilton?" I asked.

"It was much better than Romsey because we weren't being bossed about by Christina. Also it's where my namesake, Queen Edith, was educated, so it knows how to educate future queens."

"But King William had rejected you."

"There are other kings," she replied, winking. "Not that I have any choice, of course. My father doesn't tell me his plans."

"Has he another husband in mind?"

"He did have." She looked around to make sure we were still alone. "On his journey to Gloucester, included in the aristocratic escort was a man they call Alan the Red – he's got flaming red hair. He has huge amounts of land in Yorkshire. My father discovered he was a widower and not averse to taking a new wife. The match would be a great advantage to both of them, but would need the King's approval."

"So, did King William refuse?"

"He never got asked. Lord Alan said he wanted to meet me, I was to be *inspected* again, so while my father was being kept waiting in Gloucester, Lord Alan came to Wilton."

"Oh, Edith, don't tell me he didn't like you?"

She laughed.

"I didn't have to wear a veil this time, so he did get a good look, but I'm still learning how to talk to men, as I've seen so few, and I was awkward and tongue-tied, unlike my friend."

"Friend?"

"I've written home about her – Gunnhild, the daughter of the late King Harold."

"But she's *much* older than you!"

"Well, Lord Alan's old, really old, and she could talk to him with ease and she made him laugh. And the next thing I knew she'd left the nunnery with him."

"No!"

"Oh, yes! The abbess told everyone Lord Alan had abducted her against her will, but he hadn't. She saw a way of getting out of her prison and she went off with him very willingly."

"I can't believe this!" I cried.

"It's true, Edie. I was there. I could see how they were with each other. And there was also the matter of land."

I frowned in puzzlement.

"Gunnhild is entitled to land held by her mother, Edith Swan-neck," she explained. "She can now get that land through Lord Alan. While she was imprisoned in Wilton, she couldn't touch it."

"I still don't know why you're here," I said.

"News that Lord Alan had abducted Gunnhild quickly got back to Gloucester and my father was furious, naturally. And then there was all this trouble with King William treating him so insolently, that he decided he'd come to Wilton and bring us both back to Scotland. I have no idea what he plans to do with us next."

"You don't seem very worried," I commented.

"I can't control my future," she sighed.

I felt impelled to give her some advice.

"It is very important that you remain chaste," I said. "You will never secure a good marriage if you have already lain with a man. Some may tempt you, but you must resist temptation."

"Unlike Gunnhild," she grinned. "But if I ever do get to marry a king, I know how to behave, for I was a good pupil at Wilton. In the meantime, I need to learn some womanly tricks, perhaps how to flutter my eyelids."

She had a go at practising this and we both ended up giggling.

When I looked back on our conversation, I was struck by how she had matured while she'd been away. She may not know much about how to relate to men, but she had certainly learned much about the political machinations that went on and how women were often pawns in the hands of powerful men. I prayed she would be given a husband with whom there was a meeting of minds and at least some affection and respect. I hoped the plan to marry her to King William would never be revived.

Thinking of King William made me tremble. I feared what King Malcolm would do next and I had every reason to be afraid.

CHAPTER 34

King Malcolm spent the month of October mobilising a force to take into England. Margaret tried to reason with him, but she had little strength and anyway, when it came to war, her husband rarely listened to her. He seemed unaware of how very sick she was and she certainly tried to put on a brave face in his presence.

"He will go and fight," she sighed. "I can't stop him, Edie. He's been insulted and means to take revenge."

"But he can't get at King William," I argued. "He and his men will do the usual ravaging and stealing in Northumbria, before coming back here. Then King William will send an army to punish him."

"King William is a bully. I will not call him a big bully, for I hear he is half the size of my husband." She sighed. "How often short men have to prove themselves and do so in the wrong way! All those promises he made when he thought he was dying – he has gone back on all of them, not just those made to Scotland. What a godless man! I pray he will be punished."

"One day he will stand before the judgement throne of Almighty God and he will have to answer for his wickedness."

"But that doesn't help my husband. Oh, Edie, what will become of us?"

I had no answer. We both knew our lives were in God's hands.

Early in November King Malcolm left Edinburgh with his men. He also had with him Edward and Edgar for whom this would be their first raid into Northumbria, but both were skilled fighters. Margaret had to make her farewells from her bed and I know she shed tears when they had gone.

Soon afterwards, Prior Turgot arrived at court; I am fairly sure Margaret had written and specifically asked him to come. She made the effort to receive him dressed, but still in her chamber. I and some of her women were there too.

As I half-listened to what she was saying to the cleric, I realised she was looking back over her life and in my heart I knew she was preparing for her death. I heard the words "Hungary" and "my dear father" and "King Edward was good to us". She asked him to remember her and her children in his prayers.

"I fear for what may happen when I am gone," she said. "If the King survives, maybe all will be well for a while, but my sons are young and I dread that they may quarrel, though I have tried to teach them to love and to forgive. I beg you to take care of them. Remind them of their calling to a holy life. They are all at risk from pride, avarice and worldliness, and I beg you to censure them if they stray from God's path."

When it became clear she was confessing her sins, I covered my ears out of respect and did not uncover them until I saw the priest anointing her and making the sign of the cross.

Prior Turgot only stayed with us for two days, before he set off for Durham again – with our prayers that he would reach it safely. We had no news of the whereabouts of the Scottish force.

"I praise God the Prior was able to come, Edie," Margaret said. "I feel more at peace now."

Those of us in constant attendance on her included a priest to whom she had often made her confession. She insisted that he be with us and this made me think she must believe her end was very close. There was still no news of her husband and her sons, but we were not surprised by that. We usually knew what had happened when they rode into court laden with booty and their clothes soiled with blood.

On the 13th day of November, Margaret did not rise from her bed. Indeed, she clung to my hand.

"I have such fear, Edie. I don't know what it is, but I tremble in my inner being. Perhaps something terrible has happened."

"Margaret dear, we do not know. Be calm," I urged, "and we will pray for the King."

Her priest read to her from the Psalms and, after a while, she was less agitated.

Three days later, we were encouraged to hear her say she would get up. With the help of her women, Margaret was able to walk to the chapel where she heard mass. She also received the bread and wine reserved for the dying.

After a while, she asked to return to her bed. As she lay back down, she screamed with pain and tossed her head from side to side in her agony.

"Father, please read the Psalms!" she gasped. "Commend me to Christ!"

The priest began to read from the Psalter and all of us were praying quietly.

"The Black Cross, bring me the Black Cross!" she cried.

I hurried to bring in the box brought from Hungary which contained the ebony crucifix with a small piece of Christ's cross. In my distress, I fumbled with the lid and a servant had to help with opening it. We placed the dark piece of wood in her hand and she held it close. Then she lifted it up and began to recite the words of Psalm 55.

"Offer to God a sacrifice of thanksgiving," I heard her say. "Call upon me in the day of trouble."

I was struggling to hold back the tears. Suddenly, there was a commotion at the door and I looked up to see her son, Edgar, stumbling towards her bed. He was dishevelled and blood-stained, barely able to stand. He crumpled onto his knees at her bedside.

"What news?" she urged. "Edgar, what news do you bring?"

The poor young man simply shook his head and started to weep.

"Tell me!" she ordered.

"We ... we were ambushed ... near Alnwick," he managed to stutter, "three days ago."

"And? You must tell me."

"The King ..." he paused for breath, "... was slain." His cries pierced our hearts.

"And?" Margaret whispered. "What of Edward?"

"Carried wounded from the scene ... but we could not save him."

I sank to the floor and buried my head in my hands. In one fell swoop, she had lost her husband and her firstborn. In a foolish act of wounded pride, the King had paid the final price, but his heir had died too.

I roused myself, but I was in no state to comfort Margaret. She, however, lay unmoving, still clutching the piece of holy rood.

"So, Lord, you count me worthy to suffer such grief," I heard her murmur. "By these great afflictions, cleanse me from my sin. Into your hands I deliver my spirit."

She closed her eyes and I watched as her breathing became shallower and shallower until there was no breath at all. The priest gently prised the cross from her hand and replaced it in its box, before he turned to comfort Edgar.

I found my tears had stopped and I was marvelling at the look of total serenity on her face, a look none of us had seen for many months.

I was suddenly reminded of her birth. After a long labour, Agatha had been delivered of her first child, a little girl, and I had cried with joy. Margaret's life had been rich, for she had used her talents and her position in society to help the poor, to encourage the church and to bring the light of Christ to many. She had not failed in her calling, facing sorrow and joy with an unfailing trust in God. Yes, she had her failings, but I knew that even so she would be remembered as a saintly woman.

Now she rested from her labours.

CHAPTER 35

London, late December 1093

"Andrew, there's a letter for you.   I think it's from Edie."

I looked up and took it from Lucy's hand.

"I'm taking Walter down to the market," she said.

I nodded my agreement and smiled as I watched my son waddle out of the house with his mother, leaving me to read my aunt's letter.

By the time Lucy returned, I had packed my baggage and written several letters.

"I have to go north," I told her.   "The family is in deep trouble."

"What's happened?"

"King Malcolm was killed while raiding Northumbria.   His eldest son, Edward, also died. Another son took the news back.   Edie says Margaret was already at death's door and the news took her life."

"So both parents died within a few days?"

"It's worse than that," I continued.   "King Malcolm's brother, a man called Donald, has seized the throne and the family has fled south. They are currently sheltering in Durham."

"Oh, Andrew, how dreadful!"

"I must go there. I shall probably bring them to London, but here is a letter for cousin Edgar telling him what's happened. I hope he will come over from Normandy to help us in this crisis."

"I'll make sure it's dispatched. I see you've written some others too. Leave them with me."

I took Lucy in my arms.

"May God keep you and Walter safe."

"I'm not alone," she murmured. "Your brother will soon be back from Flanders and your mother is still well enough to help me with Walter."

The winter is not a good time to travel, but I had no option. I was truly glad when at last I reached Durham and sought out Prior Turgot.

"Come with me," he said. "They will be very pleased to see you."

The family had been housed in rooms normally used by pilgrims coming to the shrine of St. Cuthbert, but there were few such travellers in January, so there was plenty of accommodation available.

"Andrew!" Edie cried, grasping my hands.

I saw the tears in her eyes and was glad I could bring some comfort.

We gathered round a table and the monks brought us food. I was surrounded by a sea of faces.

"Edie," I said, "you'll have to introduce me, for you are the only person I recognise. I guess the man who is so attentive to you is your husband, Lord Murray."

"I am indeed," the burly man replied.

His grizzled hair gave away his age, but his eyes were bright with interest and intelligence.

"We're very glad you have come," he added. "And Lord Edgar?"

"I've sent a letter to him in Normandy and hope he can be in London soon. Now, Edie, who is who?"

"This is Edgar," she said, indicating what I took to be the eldest of the children.

"I'm nineteen," he declared. "Nearly twenty."

"And this is Alexander," Edie continued. "He's fifteen."

"Nearly sixteen," the lad added, sitting up straight, as if to compare himself favourably with his older brother.

"And the girls Edith and Mary are thirteen and nearly twelve," Edie said. "David is the youngest; he's nine."

I was counting up in my head and was sure Margaret's children numbered more than this, but I said nothing. We enjoyed the food we had been served.

"So, it's an uncle who has grasped the crown," I eventually commented.

"It isn't entirely surprising," Lord Murray answered. "The kings of Scotland are chosen on merit by a custom known as tanistry. Any adult male whose father,

253

grandfather or great-grandfather has been a king is eligible to be considered. Brothers often have a stronger claim than sons."

"King Malcolm's brother must be a good age," I commented.

"He's about sixty," Lord Murray said. "He is known as Donald Bane, Donald the Fair, but his hair is white now."

"Has he been around? No one's ever mentioned him."

"When Malcolm fled to England, Donald Bane fled to the Western Isles," he explained. "That was in 1040." He paused and gave me a knowing look. "He has been biding his time. King Malcolm's sudden death and the fact that the sons he left are young gave him his opportunity. He has promoted himself as a true Gaelic Scot and not tainted by foreigners."

"I'm beginning to get the picture."

I looked round the table at the pale and serious faces which stared back at me.

"Margaret was regarded as a foreigner, was she?" I asked.

Lord Murray nodded.

"He is driving out all the English and Norman people, not just the Queen's children."

"So, Edie, you're not safe?"

"We have talked about it," Edie said, putting her hand on her husband's arm. "We do not want to be parted, but ..."

"I am a Scot," Lord Murray interrupted. "I would be like a fish out of water if I lived in England."

Edie smiled sadly.

"So, Lord Murray will return to his estates in the far west of Scotland and I ... I shall go with him," she said.

"I have been teaching her some Gaelic over the years," her husband added. "I don't think she will be in any danger, but she will be far from her family."

I looked at Edie and realised her face showed lines of age. Her twin brother, my father, had died nearly eighteen years ago.

She must be seventy, I thought. I hope she dies before Lord Murray.

"But I couldn't go before I was sure Margaret's children were safe with you and Edgar," Edie said.

"I will certainly do all I can to promote their welfare and I think Edgar will too. We won't let you down."

Later, I was alone with Edie and took the opportunity of asking her about the missing children.

"Edward was the eldest," she reminded me, "but he died with his father. The second son is Edmund."

"And he isn't here," I remarked.

"He has thrown in his lot with Donald Bane." She paused. "His brothers feel betrayed."

"I'm not surprised. Does Donald Bane have sons?"

"No, and I think that's in Edmund's mind. He is probably seeking to ingratiate himself with his uncle and be his successor, despite his English mother."

"Was there another son?"

"Yes, Aethelred. At a young age he was sent to the monks at Dunkeld and he has taken vows there. His great-grandfather was abbot there and I expect he will follow in his footsteps. He is no threat to the new King, but Edgar, Alexander and David will be when they are older."

"And the girls?"

"They were in the nunnery at Wilton receiving an excellent education, but their father brought them home." She paused. "There was trouble."

"The girls caused it?"

"No, they are good children and shouldn't give you any trouble, but I believe the King had arranged for King William to marry Edith, but he chose not to. Then he had another husband lined up for her, but he ... he chose another."

"Does Edith feel rejected?"

"Not at all. She understands something of the politics of marriage." She took my arm and gripped it. "You and Edgar, between you, somehow you must secure good marriages for both Edith and Mary. We cannot expect their brothers to take such matters to their hearts as they are having to fight for their own survival. Also, there's little by way of a dowry for either of them."

Here was a burden I hadn't really thought about, though perhaps I should have done. With Edie's decision to stay in Scotland, the girls were left with no mother figure.

Edie cried when we said our farewells a few days later. She knew, I think, that she was unlikely to see any of us again, but I knew she was in safe hands, for the Lord had provided her with a fine husband. If something did happen to him, Edie knew she could come south.

Our party included two of Margaret's women as well as men loyal to Malcolm and his sons. The weather wasn't good, but we were not hampered too much and several days of travelling brought us to London, where we found Edgar had come from Normandy.

Once we had settled everyone in various billets (our house wasn't big enough for the whole party), Edgar and I met to discuss our options.

"I think it best if I take the boys to Normandy with me," Edgar said. "There's a bit of trouble between William Rufus and Robert, but that's nothing new and where I have land is fairly peaceful."

"What about the girls?"

"I suggest they go back to Wilton. They aren't in disgrace, are they?"

"Not to my knowledge. I think it was King Malcolm's decision to remove them."

We agreed to call the family together and put our ideas to them.

"We're not sure of the best place for you all at the moment," Edgar began. "Clearly, your father had crossed swords with King William. If he hadn't been killed, I'm sure the King would have sent an army north to confront him. I can't see a place for you in the

English court, at least not yet, so I'm suggesting I take you to Normandy. Duke Robert is a friend and you'll be welcomed."

"We will follow your advice," young Edgar responded.

"I'm only talking about you, Alexander and David," Edgar continued. "I suggest that Edith and Mary return to the nunnery at Wilton."

"Well, we're not going there," Edith stated firmly.

We turned to look at her. She was sitting bolt upright with her head held high and she was clasping her sister's hand.

Edie had said they shouldn't give us any trouble, but they were – already!

CHAPTER 36

The only sound in the room was that of the logs crackling in the brazier. No one spoke. I think we were all too shocked.

"What do you mean?" Edgar asked. "Why don't you want to return to Wilton?"

"We don't want to be nuns," Edith replied. "While our father lived, he ensured we would not be nuns. He was utterly opposed even to our wearing a veil." Her voice was clear and firm, and she met our gaze with barely a blink. "Also," she added, "we don't want to be forgotten."

"You won't be forgotten!" I cried, truly anxious that they should even think that way.

"No, Edith, you and Mary won't be forgotten," Edgar reassured her. "But I confess I don't know what to do for the best. I'm reluctant to take you to Normandy as well."

"It isn't the matter of education," I commented, "so much as living the life of a nun. Is that the issue?"

"Yes. The education the nuns were giving us was excellent, but we don't want to live with them."

I suddenly had an idea.

"I have a merchant friend in Salisbury," I said. "He has two daughters of about your age and I know he is making sure they receive some education. Perhaps he might be willing for you both to be part of his houschold – for the time being."

Edith and Mary exchanged glances.

"Let's all think about it," I suggested. "There is no immediate hurry, as you are safe here in London with us."

Over the next two weeks or so, letters were sent and received and more family gatherings were held until it was finally agreed that Edith and Mary, with their two women servants, would go to Salisbury to lodge with my friend and his wife, while Edgar would take the men and boys to Normandy. I felt a great sense of relief when I returned to London after delivering the girls to Salisbury. Their letters that followed assured me they had settled in well and had resumed their education. I felt I could now concentrate my energy on my trading.

There was, of course, another son of King Malcolm, of whom no one ever spoke, but who now made his mark on history. I heard the news through the merchants' gossip. Duncan, who hadn't lived in Scotland for many years, got the backing of King William to unseat Donald Bane and claim the throne for himself, as the son of King Malcolm. By May, he had succeeded in this venture and had been installed at Scone.

I wrote to Edgar to tell him what had happened and to ask whether the Scottish princes should also return. He suggested we wait and see, and that was good advice for, sadly, King Duncan didn't have a long reign. Before the year was out, he had been murdered and Donald Bane was back in power.

Another death I heard about during the winter was that of Bishop Wulfstan, who had been such a good friend to the family. He had died peacefully at the age of about 86.

Other information reached me through the merchants' network.

"There's been an outrage," a fellow merchant told me, "by the Earl of Northumbria, a man called Robert of Mowbray."

"What's happened?" I asked.

"He's robbed four large Norwegian trading vessels which had gone into one of his North Sea ports. We've complained to the King."

A few weeks passed before he could report that the King, in response to the merchants' complaints, had ordered the Earl to make restitution. Not surprisingly, no response came from the Earl.

"What's the next step?" I asked.

"The King will summon him to come to the court at Winchester this Easter."

"He's not likely to come, is he?"

"No, so he'll be summoned to another court, and if he ignores that summons, the King will take action."

"An army will go north?"

"Yes, I reckon so."

I reported all this to Edgar and in the spring he arrived in London with the princes.

"We are going to Winchester," he explained. "The King has acknowledged that he is responsible for the welfare of King Malcolm's children, so I believe we will be welcomed. And if he needs men to fight in the north, I think we shall go."

"What's the situation in Scotland?"

"Donald Bane is still in power and thought to be backing Robert of Mowbray. It's believed others have joined the Earl, so the King looks to be facing a serious rebellion in Northumbria. The King backed Duncan's campaign and was disappointed that his reign was so brief. I think he'd back young Edgar in a bid for the crown. If we go and fight with the King against the Earl, that could help Edgar's claim, as he's the next in line."

He grinned and rubbed his hands.

"Some fighting, Andrew," he laughed, "and all in a good cause."

So, the young Scots went to war with their uncle and the King. I had to rely on the gossip again, as they sent back no letters to me in London. I learned the King had taken a force up the great northern road, bypassed the stronghold at Newcastle, which was meant to stop him, and then disabled the castle at Morpeth. Robert wasn't giving up that easily, but wouldn't meet the King in an open battle. He was holed up in Bamburgh, but the King built another castle nearby and waited. By the autumn, Robert had been captured and the rebellion was over. The King returned in triumph to hold his Christmas court at Windsor.

In January, the court was to meet in Salisbury and Edgar invited me to join them. I reckoned this would be a good opportunity to see how Edith and Mary were, as well as learn whether the princes had earned King William's favour.

Everyone was in high spirits, despite the raw weather. I found the arrangements made for Edith and Mary were working well and they were both in excellent health. The princes were full of the campaign in Northumbria.

"Robert of Mowbray was the man who ambushed our father," young Edgar told me. "It was good to exact revenge."

"What's happened to Earl Robert?" I asked.

"He's in prison and likely to stay there for the rest of his life," he answered. "He sought sanctuary in a church, so the King can't have him executed. But there's another rebel here that he can deal with differently; he's Count William of Eu."

"I gather there was no big battle."

"Just some skirmishes, but we all fought well."

"Even David? He's only eleven!"

"He stayed at the back, but he's a plucky lad and will make a good soldier. The King is impressed with all of us." He puffed out his chest. At 21, young Edgar was already a fine figure of a man. "I granted a charter," he boasted.

"You what?" I queried.

"I made a grant of Berwick and some other estates in Lothian to Bishop William of Durham and the monks of St. Cuthbert for the souls of my father and mother and my brothers Duncan and Edward and for my own salvation and the salvation of all my predecessors and successors."

"But in what capacity?"

"As the son of Malcolm King of the Scots by the grant of King William and by inheritance from my father."

I stared at him. He stared back and clearly wasn't joking.

"I can't fulfil it – yet," he added, "and actually the Bishop died just after Christmas."

"Are you claiming the Scottish crown then?"

"Yes," he said firmly. "I'm not sure when, but I think the King will give me men who will fight Donald Bane and make me King in place of him. Uncle Edgar says he will back me and join my army."

I couldn't help but smile. I could easily imagine his uncle rising to this challenge. He seemed destined never to be a king himself, but could perhaps be instrumental in ensuring Margaret's son ruled Scotland.

Speaking later to Edgar, he confirmed what the young prince had said.

"It may not be this year," he said, "but I'm sure the King will give him a force to take north. He would rather have a compliant Edgar as King of Scotland than a rebellious Donald Bane. Mind you," he added, "Malcolm was meant to be a vassal of the English King, but he rarely acted like one."

As we stood chatting, we were approached by a man of about Edgar's age.

"Don't you recognise me?" he said, smiling at Edgar.

"No," Edgar responded, frowning and shaking his head slightly.

"Harold, son of Ralf, Earl of Hereford."

"Good God, Harry! I haven't seen you for years!"

CHAPTER 37

"Andrew, look who's here. Harry and I were at King Edward's court together," Edgar said. "Harry, this is my cousin. He's a merchant based in London."

"Then you have seen many changes in recent years," Harry commented, "with the shift away from Scandinavia in favour of the Continent."

"I still have strong personal trading links with the east," I answered, "but we do much trade in Europe too."

"William Count of Eu is about to do battle," Harry said. "Are you coming to watch?"

"Oh, yes," Edgar answered. "I was in the King's force which captured the rebel in Northumbria. Who's fighting him on behalf of the King?"

"I heard it was to be Geoffrey Baynard," Harry replied. "He's a former High Sheriff of Yorkshire and a skilled swordsman. The King has chosen well, for the Count will struggle to avoid defeat."

I followed as they moved off to the courtyard where the duel was to take place. From what I could gather, if the Count won he would save his life, but if he lost, the King could mete out some physical punishment. He was in fact a double rebel, as he had defied the King some eight years earlier. Robert of Mowbray had too, but he wasn't facing this battle ordeal as he had claimed sanctuary in a church in Tynemouth and was now incarcerated at Windsor and unlikely ever to be released. I wasn't sure which was the better option.

There was a big crowd gathered to see the fight. Both men wore chain mail and helmets and carried a shield and a sword. The duel was long and intense, with neither showing signs of weakness, but then I began to wonder if William was tiring. I think Geoffrey sensed this too and redoubled his efforts. The rebel was beginning to struggle and, of course, the crowd all wanted him to lose, so there were no cries of support. In the end, he crumpled and Geoffrey was the victor; William was now at the mercy of the King.

Edgar and Harry went off to talk to other members of the court, while I sought out some merchant friends.

Much later, I caught up with Edgar on his own. We sat under the stars by a brazier with mugs of ale, listening to the minstrels in the hall and enjoying the beauty of the clear starlit sky.

"Harry's father was called Ralf the Timid," Edgar suddenly said. "Good name for the son too."

"He was once your sworn brother, but not now?" I asked.

Edgar grunted.

"Way back we had both lost our fathers, but since the conquest, we've taken different paths." He took a swig of ale. "He gave in, accepted defeat and got an estate. It's called Sudeley, somewhere in the county of Gloucester."

"But you fought King William," I commented.

"For as long as I could, but he was too strong." He sighed. "Perhaps I should have been like Harry and kept my knee bowed. King William might have given me more than he did, but Harry wasn't an aetheling." He shook his head. "The bastard never gave me the respect I deserved."

"Now you fight for his son, perhaps that will change," I suggested.

"I don't fight for Rufus," he whispered. "I'd rather see Duke Robert King of England. I fight for my nephews and hope they can take their rightful place in Scotland."

We were quiet for a while, both deep in our thoughts.

"As we've seen today," Edgar said, "it isn't worth rebelling against Rufus. You could end up like Count William."

"Do we know what will happen to him?"

"It's already happened. He's had his eyes taken out and been castrated. I doubt he will survive. The King is making an example of him, warning others what he'll do to them if they rebel."

"I was only eight at the time of the conquest," I remarked, "so I don't really remember a time when our country enjoyed peace. We've had thirty years of conflict. Last summer, there was even the threat of yet another invasion. Will it ever end? We are nearly crushed by the burden of taxation and many cry for justice."

"We dare not cry too loudly," was Edgar's quiet response.

I looked up at the stars and silently pleaded with God to heal our pain.

"Duke Robert is thinking of taking the cross."

Edgar's words broke into my reverie.

"He what?"

"You've heard about the Pope's sermon? Last November? He's calling on Christians to retake the holy city of Jerusalem from the infidels."

"Really?"

"Yes, anyone fighting in the crusade will receive forgiveness of their sins. I suspect Robert will go. Indeed, it will be a real adventure."

"Are you tempted to go?"

"Yes, but my first concern must be winning the Scottish throne for young Edgar. Then we'll see."

Duke Robert's desire to fight in the crusade to retake Jerusalem was fulfilled more quickly than Edgar's hopes for his nephew. I heard that Duke Robert was able to leave Normandy and take the pilgrim route towards the east in September. He had raised a loan from King William, who now had control of the Duchy until Duke Robert returned and could redeem the loan. I confess I thought it wouldn't be easy to get his homeland back, for once King William got his hands on Normandy, I couldn't see him letting it go – not without a fight.

Edgar had to wait until September of the following year before King William gave his blessing on the Scottish campaign.

"Come with us, Andrew," Edgar urged.

"I'm no soldier," I objected.

"I know that, but I could do with someone who's good at managing the supplies. You'll be able to find us provisions and make sure we don't starve, and vital matters such as these."

Lucy wasn't keen, but I relished the challenge. Also, here was my opportunity to do something to help the family. So, I went north with the force, which was led by Edgar, as he had more experience than the young princes, but they were there too, determined to play their part.

A man in his twenties came alongside me.

"Lord Edgar has asked me to help," he said. "I'm to do whatever you say." He grinned. "Within reason."

I grinned back.

"And you are?"

"Robert Godwineson. My father holds land of Lord Edgar in Hertfordshire."

"You know then that I'm his cousin."

"Yes, and therefore related to young Lord Edgar for whom we fight."

Robert was a good companion on the journey and efficient in helping me with organising supplies, but I could see he was also adept with the sword and eager for battle.

We had penetrated well into Lothian and reckoned we couldn't be very far from Edinburgh when we heard the Scots were coming against us. As we sat round our campfire, relishing its warmth in the cool of the autumn evening, we discussed our options.

"It's good they've come out to fight," Edgar said. "It wouldn't be good to try and besiege Edinburgh. We know how difficult that would be to conquer."

"Can I fight alongside *you*?" young Edgar asked.

"Yes, indeed, we need to be seen, but, David, you need to be well back. If your brothers are killed, you need to be able to escape alive in order to fight again another day."

David scowled slightly, but he was under orders. I guessed his day would come, but not yet.

"Lord Edgar," Robert said, "I must share with everyone that I had a very vivid dream last night. Actually, I'd call it ... a vision."

We turned to give him our full attention.

"I saw St. Cuthbert," he continued. "You know how we stopped in Durham. I prayed at his shrine for justice and for peace." He paused, but no one spoke. "I know it was Cuthbert I was seeing in my vision because I recognised his banner. He told me we would meet the Scots and they would put forward a group of warriors to fight some of us, a bit like Goliath was the champion of the Philistines."

"You're not going to tell me we should pit our David against this band of soldiers, are you?" Edgar gasped.

Robert half-smiled and shook his head.

"No, St. Cuthbert didn't say to do that, but he did say that three of us should go forward under his banner to fight them. And he would give us the victory."

We sat in stunned silence.

"That's still a bit like David and Goliath," Edgar said at last. "In battle terms, it doesn't make sense."

I could feel my heart pounding and my mouth go dry and knew I had to speak.

"I'm no soldier," I began, "but perhaps the way forward is to see what happens."

I sensed every eye on my face and was glad of the half-light of the campfire.

"When we meet the Scots," I continued, "if they line up to fight using all their men, then surely we need to do the same, but if they do put forward a picked group of warriors, then … then perhaps we should respond according to Robert's vision."

CHAPTER 38

The firelight danced on our faces and cast eerie shadows behind us. The wood crackled and spat a little, but otherwise there were only the usual noises of an army preparing to camp, the shouted orders, together with the snorting and scuffling of horses.

"What do others think?" Edgar asked.

The whites of the men's wide-open eyes contrasted with the darkness of the night.

"I say Andrew's right," one voice spoke.

"I should be one of the three fighters," another said. "Last night I dreamed I fought alongside Robert and Richard."

"Richard, would you fight with us if the Scots put forward some warriors?" Robert asked.

"It's a mad idea," Richard scoffed, "but if it's the battle plan of the Almighty, we'd be foolish to ignore it." He paused. "Yes, if that's what the Scots do, I'll be the third man."

I looked at them – three men in their prime, fit, strong, determined and ... a little reckless. But if St. Cuthbert had truly given his guidance, then the victory could be theirs.

"We'll see what the Scots do," Edgar asserted. "If they put up their champions, then the three of you will fight – and God give you the victory."

"I will go through the camp tonight and seek out a banner of St. Cuthbert, so that we're ready," Robert said.

At dawn, there was no sign of the enemy, so we struck camp and began moving further north. About midday, with a pale sun on our backs, we glimpsed the glint of armour. The Scots sent a man to parley and he was met in the middle of a wide dry valley by our man. We waited. Our man returned.

"King Donald Bane accuses you of invading his kingdom," was the message, "and he will fight for the liberty of his subjects."

That sounded like a full-scale battle.

"You can return home in peace; he will not stop you," our man continued with the enemy's words. "But if you do not, a group of his warriors, hand-picked for their skill, will challenge a similar group of English aggressors."

"It's the vision," I said quietly to myself, and I could hear others murmuring something similar.

Edgar looked round. Robert and his two companions were nearby and nodded their consent.

"We will send a group of warriors to fight," he commanded. "That is the message to take to the Scottish usurper."

Our men prepared themselves, while the rest of us watched. In due course, five Scots and their grooms rode forward to the middle where the parley had taken place. Then our three with their grooms rode to meet them. Robert held high the banner of the saint, its silver cross shimmering on the red silk cloth and its silver bells tinkling in the breeze. There were cries of derision from the enemy. They clearly thought us fools for pitting only three against five.

The soldiers dismounted and their grooms held the horses clear of the fighting area, one of our grooms also holding the saint's banner.

"If they are slain," I asked Edgar, "is that it? We concede defeat?"

"The Scots may think those are the rules," he replied, "but I can assure you, Andrew, if our men do fail, we shall fight. I'm not that chivalrous." He winked. "Norman codes of honour don't apply this far north."

The clash of swords made me tremble and I found myself praying far harder than I usually did. Could our three overwhelm their five? Yet as I watched, I realised the groups seemed evenly matched, but I couldn't understand why.

Into my mind flashed a memory of a Bible story. The prophet Elisha was under siege; he asked the Lord to open the eyes of his servant, who then saw a great host which would rescue the prophet. I looked at the fighting with fresh eyes. Were there forces invisible to my eyes who were fighting on our side?

Two of the Scots seemed to be holding back and then took their turn rather than all five trying to fight at once. Then two did attack Robert. I couldn't see very well, but I did see that Robert had felled both of them and a cheer went up from our side.

The fighting was brutal and not brief, but our men had youth and fitness on their side – and St. Cuthbert. Another Scot fell. Now the English outnumbered the Scots.

"Get ready to fight!" Edgar ordered.

Men all around me began to bristle with tension, eager to get at the enemy. On the other side of the valley, there were no cheers now, no cries of derision.

"They're beginning to panic," Edgar told me. "Not long now."

Another Scot fell.

"Forward!" cried Edgar.

Men on horses thundered past me and I briefly lost sight of what was happening. Then I could see the enemy was scattering. Their champions had failed. Goliath had been felled by David and they had lost heart. Some Scots stayed to fight, but there was no doubt that the day was ours.

I organised the bringing up of the supply wagons as we moved north, mopping up any opposition. I caught up briefly with Robert, who grinned broadly and had no serious wounds.

"St. Cuthbert gave us the victory!" he exclaimed. "Praise God, we are the victors here today and young prince Edgar can be King."

I hadn't been in the hall at Edinburgh, but those who had, commented on how it had changed.

"Queen Margaret had coloured wall hangings, but they've all gone," was one remark. "The court here must have been dour and cold."

I gathered Donald Bane was a king in the old Gaelic tradition and his reign had involved a rejection of all things "southern". I suspected young Edgar would want to bring back the colour and pomp which he remembered from his youth; he hadn't been here for four years, but he hadn't forgotten.

"Donald Bane has escaped," Edgar told us, "but we have captured my nephew Edmund."

In all the excitement, I had forgotten that one brother had backed the now-deposed King. I feared the price he might pay, but there seemed to be no hurry to mete out justice.

So we feasted first. I say "feasted", but there were many mouths to feed, the bulk of the army being camped in the surrounding area, while royalty and knights made do with what could be found in the palace.

Once our bodies were rested and fed, the business of victory could proceed.

"Bring Edmund in," Edgar ordered.

He sat on a raised dais with young Edgar at his side and flanked by Alexander and David. The rest of us gathered round, leaving a central space for the prisoner.

Edmund was a sorry sight, his clothes torn and blood-spattered from the battle. No one had allowed him to wash, so he looked older than his 24 years. He glanced at each face on the dais and then fixed his eyes on the rush-strewn floor.

"Well, *brother*, what do you have to say for yourself?" young Edgar demanded, the sarcasm in his voice being abundantly clear to all of us.

Edmund said nothing.

"Come on," his brother urged. "It's a long time since we've seen each other. What have you been doing?"

"Living quietly in my homeland," was the soft response.

"And supporting Donald Bane. At least that's what we heard."

"Yes, because he was made King by the people on the death of King Malcolm."

"And when our brother Duncan came north and claimed the throne, did you then bend your knee to him?"

Edmund would not raise his eyes.

"Indeed, we heard it said you were complicit in his murder!"

Young Edgar rose from his seat and strode down to stand in front of his older brother. They were about the same height, but the victor appeared taller than the vanquished.

"Well, do you confess your guilt?" He spat out the words.

"I do," Edmund said quietly. "I was wrong to encourage the death of my brother Duncan. I had hoped to be King after King Donald Bane's death, as he had no sons."

Edgar strode back to his seat, satisfied with the extracted confession.

"You deserve to die!" Alexander cried.

CHAPTER 39

A few cheers from the assembled knights greeted Alexander's call for Edmund's death.

"You were complicit in the killing of an anointed King," Alexander accused.

"But he's our brother!" David suddenly countered.

Edmund looked across at his youngest brother.

"I am," he said calmly, "and I look back on those days when we lived in harmony and we did not quarrel. I regret what I have done with my life and wish to make amends."

"Your execution will make amends," Alexander argued.

"Or I could spend my time in prayer for you and for those members of our family who have died."

"One at your instigation!" Alexander responded.

His uncle had been quiet, but now intervened.

"We need to talk about your fate," Edgar said. "In the meantime, you are to be made comfortable. Give him food, fresh clothes and water for washing."

Edmund bowed and was then ushered out of the hall.

When he had gone, a stillness settled on the company.

"He should die," Alexander asserted.

"But what did our mother teach us?" David responded.

"To love and to forgive," young Edgar replied.

"You have a number of options," Edgar said. "You could have him killed, for he's admitted his guilt. Or you could let him go free."

"No!" Alexander cried.

Edgar waved him to be silent.

"Or ... or you could confine him ... to a prison or ... or to a monastery where he would be under a harsh rule and expected to pray for you all, as he said."

"He will not die, not yet," young Edgar declared. "I must be installed at Scone like my forebears and Edmund must kneel before me and do homage."

There may have been further discussion among the brothers, but I wasn't privy to it. I felt Edgar was exerting a good influence on the new King, as a hasty decision would be regretted, but a measured one might combine justice and mercy.

As the son of the late King Malcolm, Edgar was duly installed and crowned at Scone and the leading men of Scotland did homage, including all his brothers. Even Aethelred came out of his monastery at Dunkeld to honour the new King.

We stayed a few weeks to ensure that young Edgar was secure. There were rumours Donald Bane had been captured and put to work in a laundry; he was no longer regarded as any kind of threat. It really looked as though King Edgar would fare far better than King Duncan and we were confident as we set off to return to England. With us, in chains, travelled Edmund.

"What is to happen to him?" I asked.

"I have instructions to confine him in a monastery," Edgar replied. "He is to take the tonsure and full monastic vows."

"Alexander didn't prevail then?"

"No, he was outvoted. Mercy and forgiveness won the day. That's what my sister would have urged, for it is the way of Christ. There's no profit in taking a man's life when he can spend his time in prayer and seeking reparation for his sins."

I confess I was glad. Edmund was guilty of fratricide, but forgiveness was a better option than revenge.

"Once you have dealt with Edmund, have you any plans?" I asked.

"Yes. I've been thinking about Duke Robert. He left a year ago to fight for the freedom of Jerusalem. I'm going to try and join him in the crusade." He grinned. "It's better than sitting around all day or even going out hawking. There's a purpose to the fighting."

I wished him well. Later, I heard Edmund had been consigned to a monastery at Montacute in Somerset.

Thus the year of Our Lord 1097 came to a quiet end, with Lucy pleased to see me safely returned and with Edgar gone east to find more fighting. Any news we received from Scotland was good, except for one missive.

Lord Murray had taken Edie to be reunited with those of Margaret's sons who were in Edinburgh and she had wept tears of joy at seeing young Edgar now the

King of Scotland. However, on her return to Lord Murray's estate, she had suddenly but peacefully died. It was as though she knew her work on earth was done and she could move to the next world content.

King William was abroad fighting, we heard, in areas called Maine and Vexin, but in his absence there was much building work being done in London. The bridge, our only crossing here of the Thames, had been badly damaged by flooding over the years and was virtually being rebuilt so that this vital crossing could still be used. I noticed too that even though the construction of the King's White Tower (begun by his father) was finished, there was work on a new rampart to complete its enclosure. However, the talk of the city was the King's most ambitious project, the building of a new hall next to Westminster Abbey. We were astounded at its size, the like of which none of us had ever seen, not even in our trips to the Continent. It was built of stone and was some 240 feet long. Work continued on this hall all through the following year, but early in 1099, we could see it was nearly finished and the rumour was that the King planned to hold his Whitsun court there.

Further news reached me from Scotland that King Edgar would be a guest at this court. As King William's vassal, he was expected to do homage every so often along with other earls and knights and this would be one of those occasions. Indeed, King William himself returned from Normandy in April and went to one of his manors near Huntingdon to escort King Edgar to London. Edith and Mary were to come from Salisbury, so it looked as though much of the family would be reunited. The exception, of course, was Edgar, whom we believed still to be fighting in the east.

"A great army gathered at Constantinople," a merchant friend told me, "and then moved farther east. There is some hope that because the Christian west has helped the Byzantines they will be reconciled to Rome and come again under the jurisdiction of the Pope."

I knew of the schism in the Christian Church, when the East had broken away from the West. This had happened more than forty years ago, when Margaret was a small child. She had been deeply distressed by it and, later in life, horrified to discover Scotland also did not accept the Pope, but she had never succeeded in bringing Scotland in line with Rome and I doubted even a crusader army could bring an empire to the point of compliance.

The date set for the great feast in the new hall at Westminster was the 29th day of May and I managed to get invited. I proudly watched the young Edgar as he carried King William's sword in the crown-wearing ceremony held in the Abbey and we heard the singing echoing through that vast building before numerous men paid homage to the Norman.

The feast was held in the Hall and we were all astonished at its size and magnificence. When someone commented to King William on how large it was, the word came back that the King had replied it wasn't big enough by half for him!

I noticed too that the court officers had a new livery for the occasion. They were wearing fine quality cloth I had imported and their gowns were edged with pearl-grey squirrel fur, another of my imports. I felt quite proud to have played a part in adding to the splendour of the occasion.

I could, however, take no credit for the feast, which was equally extravagant. The meat, such as the tender venison, had probably come from some of the King's hunting forests, but there were spices and even vegetables from the Continent, the like of which we rarely saw.

The King sat at a table on a dais, resplendent in magnificent robes, but these did not stop him from eating heartily. He was flanked by King Edgar and his highest-ranked Earls. I could see Edith and Mary were there too and one man was being particularly attentive to Edith. He looked about thirty, was broad-chested and had receding black hair.

"Do you know who that is?" I casually asked my neighbour and indicated the man in question.

"That's Count Henry. He used to be the King's enemy, but they are now united against their brother, Duke Robert."

"I don't think I've seen him at court before."

"He hasn't been here much in the past, but with their improved relationship, he spends more time at King

William's side than he does in his stronghold at Domfront, in Normandy." He winked. "That's when he's not in some woman's bed." He looked across at Edith, probably not realising I knew her. "He looks as though he's preparing yet another mistress. He likes them beautiful and that one's certainly got the qualities he looks for in his women."

I felt myself go cold inside. If Edith were to marry well, she could not afford to become the mistress even of so important a person as King William's brother.

CHAPTER 40

Two days after the feast, I got my opportunity to do something about Edith. We were gathered in part of the palace, King Edgar, Edith, Mary and me.

"What an amazing occasion that was!" declared young Mary.

At just seventeen, she was blossoming into an attractive young woman, but she tended, in company at least, to be a little overshadowed by the more assured and talkative Edith.

"It's the talk of London," I agreed, "and could be for some time, unless the King intends to make it an annual event."

"Could he afford to?" young Edgar asked.

I glanced around.

"He taxes us hard enough," I said quietly, "but I suspect this was put on as a show to celebrate the building of the Hall and his successful campaigns in Normandy."

"His brother is charming," Edith said. "He was very easy to converse with and very knowledgeable. He was talking of making a visit to Salisbury because Bishop Osmund helped with his education. I was telling him how frail the Bishop has become, so he thinks he might visit before the Bishop dies."

King Edgar and I exchanged glances.

"Count Henry has a reputation," I warned.

"For what?" she said, her face a picture of innocence.

"For bedding every woman he meets," I answered. "He has fathered several children and he is only about thirty. Do be careful, Edith."

"You must remain chaste," her brother added. "You dare not become his mistress as that would ruin your chances of making a good marriage. And the same applies to you, Mary. A dowry is a problem for both of you, but your great asset is that you were both born in the purple, born to a reigning King."

Edith frowned slightly.

"I hear what you say," she conceded. "But who is King William's heir? Our father hoped he would wed me, but he hasn't. Indeed, he has wed no one and appears to enjoy more the company of men."

"He's a soldier," I said. "But as King he should marry and do so fairly soon. His heir has always been regarded as Duke Robert, but he's in the east, fighting to free Jerusalem and he may not return."

"Then it would be Count Henry!" Edith responded, with a mischievous grin.

"Perhaps," young Edgar agreed, "but until he is King, you are to keep him at arm's length. Do you hear?"

"Very well."

I sensed a certain reluctance in her voice. At eighteen, she was certainly old enough to marry, but, for the present, there was no one suitable. Edgar as a King might well have his own ideas on alliances he wanted to make and he might use his sisters to achieve his aims. I was glad I had been able to marry for love.

Very soon the members of the court went their separate ways. I don't know if Count Henry visited Salisbury as he had planned, but I hoped Edith was intelligent enough to know her virginity was a prize possession she must keep for marriage.

The spring brought in a new era, the year of Our Lord 1100, and some looked for portents in the sky, but there were none that were remarked upon. In the late spring, tales circulated of a pool in Berkshire which welled up, not with water, but with blood. Men scoffed at such reports, but others said they had been to see it and knew it to be true. As such a report had also come to us only two years before, it was not taken too seriously, but people did wonder if the year would bring a significant death.

Someone very much alive was my cousin Edgar, who returned in July from his adventures in the east.

"A year ago we captured Jerusalem," he told me proudly. "Robert and I fought side by side. We have seen the place where Christ was crucified and also the tomb from which he rose on the third day. We have walked the streets where he walked. Jerusalem is a very special place."

"So once Jerusalem fell, was that it?" I asked. "Crusade completed?"

"Not really. The enemy wasn't going to accept defeat that easily, but we felt we'd done our job. We took part in a battle at Ashkelon in mid August and then started for home."

"You've taken a long time!"

"We stopped off in Sicily, where Robert found a wife! She's called Sybyl and she's beautiful, so I'm not surprised he fell in love with her. She's also rich and that's going to help in getting back the Duchy. He'll have to pay King William a sizable amount, but Sybyl can help with that. I've left him enjoying his wife."

"So, what now?"

"The first thing is to pay court to the King and get a feel for whether Robert is going to face difficulties getting Normandy back."

"I think he's in Hampshire."

"Ah, hunting perhaps. Will you come with me? I can brighten up our journey with tales from my adventures in the east."

So we travelled to Winchester, where we learned that the King had gone to the New Forest. It was the second day of August, a Thursday, when we set out early to ride to his hunting lodge at Brockenhurst, where we were surprised to find him eating a midday meal.

"I thought, sire, you would already be in the Forest," Edgar said, "but I am pleased to see you are here and I can bring news of your brother."

I noticed Count Henry was among the men gathered round the table. I also noticed he glanced in King

William's direction, but the King was intent on stripping a bone of its meat.

"You're too late," the King spoke through his food. "I've heard Robert has married a rich woman."

"The news has travelled before me," Edgar agreed. "He himself should be in Rouen in a few weeks' time."

The King looked up and smirked.

"He thinks he can just walk back into Normandy, does he?" he scoffed. "He'd better think again."

He downed some ale and belched.

"Does Robert know his son is dead?" the King asked.

Edgar frowned.

"His son?"

"His bastard, the one called Richard. He got killed here in the Forest, back in May, arrow through his heart."

"No ... no, I don't think he knows that."

"Nice welcome home present then," King William laughed.

I had to clench my fists out of sight of everyone. I knew there was no love lost between the King and the Duke, but this was a callous and cruel comment.

"Are you coming hunting with us?" the King asked. "We are a merry pack. I'm not sure you know them all. My brother Henry, Robert Fitz Hamon, Walter Tirel, Henry Beaumont, Robert Beaumont, William from Breteuil." He waved a hand in the general direction of a few others. "Edgar, uncle to the King of Scotland," he added by way of introduction.

"And my kinsman Andrew," Edgar said.

No one was in much of a hurry and it was well past noon when we set out.

"I'm no huntsman," I confessed.

"Lammas marks the first day red stags can be hunted," Edgar said, "so the King's lost a day and a half already, but there will be plenty in the Forest as only he has the right to hunt here."

We let the others ride ahead of us.

"They will fan out," Edgar explained, "and try to chase a deer past the King, but they've all got arrows and are entitled to use them. We'll just enjoy the day and the ride – and later the venison," he added, grinning.

So that's what we did. We soon lost sight of the others in the hunting party and enjoyed the cool shade of the thicker parts of the Forest.

After about an hour, we came into an open area, the sort of place where the killing of a stag would take place. There were no stags in sight though.

"Look!" I said. "Over there."

I pointed to a spot across the glade where a group of men were standing.

"Some of our party," commented Edgar, "and off their horses, so they must have shot a stag. Let's go and see how big he is."

We galloped across the space to join the huddle of knights. I couldn't see the King among them, but Count

Henry was there and the Beaumont brothers and a few servants.

"Have you killed a fine stag?" Edgar called, as he jumped off his horse.

The group parted and what we saw was completely unexpected. Face down on the ground was a man with an arrow through him.

CHAPTER 41

Edgar and I both gasped. We were not looking at a red stag, which would be food fit for a king and his companions, but a human being.

"Who is it?" Edgar cried.

"Who do you think?" one of the Beaumonts said.

He knelt to lift the body slightly, just enough for us to see the face – the florid face of King William!

"Is ... is he dead?" Edgar asked.

"Oh, yes, there's no question about that," Beaumont said rising. He took Count Henry's arm. "Leave Lord Edgar to deal with this. You need to get to Winchester and ..." He whispered something in his ear, but I caught the word 'treasury'.

"Yes, of course," Count Henry agreed. "Lord Edgar, we have sent a servant to take the news back to the lodge. Please attend to the King, as we have urgent business."

Edgar was given no option. The men mounted their horses quickly and were gone, leaving us with three servants and the body of King William.

"How did this happen?" Edgar asked, looking around at those left behind.

"We don't know," one answered. "A tragic accident, we think."

"Like Richard, Robert's son," I suggested.

"Where is everyone else?" Edgar asked.

"The King was alone when we found him," a servant said, "though we weren't far away. His companion was Lord Walter, but we don't know what's happened to him. When we found the King, we called out and soon Count Henry and the other men appeared."

Edgar looked at me and shook his head.

"I hope to God it is a tragic accident," he muttered.

Waiting there in the Forest by the body of the dead King was one of the worst times of my life. My thoughts were racing. Who had shot the arrow? Who would be King now? Would we be faced with civil war?

Edgar and I said nothing to each other, as we were probably both conscious of the servants hearing our conversation. I tried to pray, but my thoughts kept wandering.

It must have been nearly an hour before men arrived with a horse-drawn wagon.

"This is awful," Edgar whispered. "We are to put the King on a cart as though he were a stag. This is what these carts are used for."

"He would be too heavy for us to carry all the way back to the lodge," I answered.

Edgar nodded and took charge of proceedings. Because the day was warm, there wasn't even a cloak amongst us which could be used to wrap the royal body and the King did indeed look too much like the carcase of a quarry killed in the hunt.

When we arrived back at the lodge, we discovered none of the King's men were there; everyone had deserted him.

"I suppose we'd better bury him at Winchester," Edgar said. "King Cnut and his son are both buried there."

"Where's his father buried?"

"Caen in Normandy. And King Edward lies in Westminster, but even London is too far to take a body in August."

Messengers were sent to the minster. There was no bishop there, as this was one of the many sees the King had kept vacant and taken their money for himself. There was a bit of a battle over the funeral as the Church regarded the King as an ungodly ruler, but the Prior, a man named Godfrey, consented to give him a Christian burial. It was a very poor affair, not even attended by Count Henry, and was done early the next morning.

Some of the King's leading men were present at the service, as the King was laid to rest under the tower. I realised none of them had been at the hunt and they were interested to hear afterwards our account of what had happened.

"Count Henry was here yesterday evening," one of them told us. "He seized control of the treasury and had us swear allegiance to him as King William's rightful successor. As you can see, he isn't here. We believe he's preparing to leave for London."

"And that's where we should all go without further delay," another added. "The Count, or rather the new King, will make sure there is a speedy coronation."

I took Edgar on one side and told him about Edith.

"Now Henry's King, he might marry – and he might well marry Edith."

"After what you've said about their meeting last year, it sounds possible. We need to prepare for it."

"I will ride to Salisbury and tell Edith what's happened and then join you in London."

We went our separate ways. In Salisbury, I sought out Edith and Mary and was able to talk to Edith in a quiet corner within sight but not sound of the other members of the household. She was genuinely shocked at my news.

"To die in such a way!" she exclaimed. "With no time to confess his sins – and those are many."

"Some are saying it was the hand of God, for he's taken much from his people and also from the church, but it looks far more likely that it was the careless hand of Lord Walter. But you know what this means?"

Her intelligent eyes met my gaze.

"Count Henry is now the King," she said quietly.

I nodded.

"Have you seen him since the great banquet last year?" I asked.

"I have. He came to visit Bishop Osmund and it was good that he did, for the Bishop died in the winter." She smiled slightly. "I heeded your advice. I was friendly, but demure, and gave him no opportunity to act inappropriately. My virginity is intact."

"He may offer you marriage, but we don't know that and we wouldn't want to raise your hopes and you then be disappointed."

"He's no fool and neither am I. We are the children of reigning kings and I represent the ancient House of Cerdic through my mother." She pulled herself up and proudly added, "I am the great-granddaughter of a King of England. I am a worthy bride for its present King."

"So, you would accept him? I thought as much. We need to write to your brother, but we need to be discreet. I suggest we both send letters. I will write from London. I'm meeting Edgar there, for it's thought there will be a speedy coronation. I pray to God there is, because we don't want civil war."

"Would anyone back a rival?" she queried. "Who is there? Only Duke Robert and he's away on crusade."

"He has survived, has married and is daily expected back in Normandy, but I agree it's unlikely anyone in England would welcome him as King, not unless Henry proves to be a tyrant."

"A God-fearing wife could not prevent that." She smiled seductively. "But she would probably try."

I was back in London in time for the coronation, which took place on Sunday the 5th day of August. Edgar told me it was very similar to the coronations of King Harold and King William, both of which occurred when he was in his teens, but which he vividly remembered. He hadn't been in England at the time of William Rufus's coronation. There was a significant difference though. King Henry made the usual promise to prohibit all iniquities, but he elaborated on this by vowing to put right all the injustices of the previous reign. He was marking himself out as correcting what people hated so much about the reign of his brother. Indeed, another innovation was for his coronation promises to be published in the form of a written document; now he couldn't go back on those promises.

The ceremony had been conducted by Bishop Maurice, the most senior bishop available. Thomas, the Archbishop of York, was far away in Ripon, and Anselm, the Archbishop of Canterbury, was in exile in Lyons. But no one doubted the King was truly crowned.

News had reached Archbishop Anselm very quickly and I think he may even have been preparing to return to England when he received a letter (so we heard) from the new King urging him to come back. The quarrel that had led to his exile was with King William and clearly King Henry was seeking to heal many of the wounds caused in the previous reign.

The King held his court in Salisbury at the end of September, by which time it was believed the Archbishop was back in England and had travelled west. I wondered what else the King might be doing while in Salisbury. I didn't have very long to wait, as two weeks later I had a letter from Edith.

"The King has asked me to be his wife and
I have accepted. However, an objection has
been raised."

Surely not, I thought. Her brother would be pleased
by this union. Why would he object?

"My brother is delighted and has given
his consent."

"So, the objection is not from young Edgar," I
muttered.

"It is claimed that I became a nun while I
was at Romsey or Wilton and therefore I
cannot marry. Believe me when I say I *never*
became a nun and I shall fight *hard* for my
right to marry the King and be his Queen!"

CHAPTER 42

My hand trembled as I held Edith's letter. The family had faced many setbacks since their return from exile. There had been Edward's sudden death soon after their arrival (a year before I was born), then Harold's seizing of the English crown when Edgar was the rightful heir, then the conquest by the Normans and its terrible consequences. Exile in Scotland had admittedly brought some stability to Margaret's life after her marriage to Malcolm, but Edgar had drifted, tossed hither and thither by circumstances, a wanderer with little purpose. And now dear Edith's hopes seemed dashed. I felt she had a mountain to climb, but I knew her to be a woman of spirit. A great-granddaughter of Ironside would not accept defeat!

I kept in touch as best I could with developments over the next two weeks. Edith appealed directly to Archbishop Anselm. I suspected she had met him in Salisbury and charmed him with her "innocence". The Archbishop called a gathering in London of bishops, abbots and leading men to consider the objection. Edith herself told me he had sent an envoy to Wilton to obtain evidence and he may have sent one to Romsey as well.

The Archbishop faced a difficult situation. He had just returned from exile and, while I heard rumours of serious issues over which he and the King could not agree, I was sure he wouldn't want to make their relationship even more difficult. King Henry wanted to marry Edith and she was determined to prove he could. I wouldn't want to be the man who said "No".

As it happened, the council found there was no evidence Edith had taken the vows of a nun. There were tales she had, reluctantly and occasionally, worn a veil, but that had been to protect her modesty.

Early in November, the Archbishop declared the marriage could proceed and the date of Sunday the 11th was set. Edith, immediately after her marriage, would be crowned Queen.

"I am so excited," she wrote. "God has answered my prayers and now I can fulfil my royal destiny even as my mother did. I have decided to take a new name – Matilda – even though I am not ashamed of my ancestry."

She assured me I would always be welcome at court.

The marriage and coronation were splendid affairs and there was much rejoicing. A reigning king had not married since King Edward in 1045 and the Queen we bowed to now was English, well, half-Scottish, but with no Norman blood in her at all. Surely this would help to establish a peaceful reign. Edgar had written from Normandy warning me Duke Robert would fight for *his* right to be crowned. The Duke had been able to walk back into his Duchy without repaying anything for it – because of the death of William Rufus – and with a rich wife he could afford a campaign. Also, many of King Henry's barons had done homage to the Duke and it was rumoured they might prefer him as King. I prayed Queen Matilda would be Queen for many years.

The trouble began in the spring. Edgar told me Duke Robert had written to the Pope to complain about Henry's seizure of the throne, but the Duke didn't seem to have a plan on how to proceed further until Bishop Ranulf Flambard arrived. He was the disgraced Bishop of Durham, who had been imprisoned in the Tower of London, the first time it had been used as a prison. He had escaped and had fled to Normandy and was advising the Duke on how to make a successful invasion, using his "inside" knowledge. Edgar was keeping well out of it, as, although the Duke was his sworn brother, Queen Matilda was his niece and he had no desire to see her toppled from her throne.

I think King Henry had other spies, so Edgar wasn't the only source of information. I also think the King was doing deals I knew nothing about.

I did attend his Whitsun court on the 9th day of June at St. Albans. He and Matilda wore their crowns and other regalia, and the King had many of his chief men renew their oaths of loyalty in return for which he renewed his promise to rule justly. At this court, he stripped Ranulf of his bishopric and lands.

Soon afterwards, King Henry sent out letters calling on all his subjects to be loyal; we had to take an oath to this effect. There was also a summons to go and fight for him against the invader. The Queen persuaded me to go and help with the provision of supplies, as I had done on the Scottish campaign.

On Midsummer's Day, the King led his army and camped near Pevensey. This was the site of his father's invasion nearly 35 years earlier and it was believed the Duke would try to repeat that success. By mid July, it was common knowledge that the Duke had a sizable army and fleet of ships gathered at Le Tréport, poised to cross the Channel and land at Pevensey. But we were caught out. The fleet went further west and landed at Portsmouth, and the cry went up that we must move fast.

"Dear Lord," I prayed, "please keep Matilda safe."

I knew she was in Winchester, not far from the enemy force, and that she was expecting her first child.

The King led us north-west into Surrey and then south-west into Hampshire, thus ensuring the Duke could not reach London. We got as far as Alton, where we met the Duke's force. We were astonished that he had made so little progress. Why hadn't he taken Winchester? Could my prayers really have been that effective? I didn't know, but I gave the Almighty my praise and thanks anyway.

The two armies faced each other and ... there was no battle, but barons from both sides met to thrash out a settlement. I was amazed at the result. The Duke renounced all claim to the English crown! He did get something to justify the expense of the invasion; I believe he was promised a substantial pension and also most of King Henry's lands in western Normandy. Part of the agreement returned Ranulf to his bishopric in Durham. I don't know what kind of double game he had been playing.

Once the peace was negotiated, all the leaders went to Winchester and naturally I went too. We entered the city on the 31st day of July, where I was pleased to find Matilda undaunted.

"I would have done everything in my power to stop the Duke getting his filthy hands on the King's treasury," she said.

When I saw the steely look in her eyes, I knew she would have done it.

The treaty was formally ratified two days after our arrival, the first anniversary of the death of the previous king. So, King Henry had survived his first year and I hoped that now there truly could be peace and that the Queen would give him an heir.

Her baby arrived the following February – a girl, not a boy, but healthy.

"We are calling her Matilda," she told me when I visited, "but privately we call her Aethelic."

The child was a few weeks old by the time I saw her. I mentioned her name and she opened wide her blue eyes, gave me a hard look, frowned and bunched her fists as though she was going to punch me.

"My!" I laughed. "She's certainly got the spirit of Ironside!"

The Queen laughed too.

Against this happy background, a drama was being played out by the King. The Duke's invasion had revealed too many leading men whose loyalty was now suspect, some having openly sided with Curthose. One such man was Robert of Bellême, a rich but very unpopular landowner whose "sins" included building, without a licence, a castle at Bridgnorth in Shropshire. The King had a long list of his offences and when Earl Robert failed to answer these, not having appeared at the Easter court in 1102, he was declared an outlaw and the King set out to deal with him.

The Queen presided alone over the Whitsun court in Westminster, but she not only had her pedigree to help her, she had also been well-schooled in how to act like a queen. Still only 21, she was magnificent and I was proud of her.

By the autumn, the King had dealt with his errant baron and some others. I suspect that, unknown to most of us, he was quietly dealing with any barons he didn't trust.

A son and heir arrived in October the following year and was named William. He was given a second name, that of Aetheling or its Norman equivalent Adelin, a reflection that he had Anglo-Saxon ancestry and was the throne-worthy one. The King and Queen were delighted, as were we all.

We enjoyed a time of peace, but Archbishop Anselm was in exile again and underneath the surface the King must have been angling to increase his own support and reduce that of his brother. I did hear that the Duke had made an alliance with the disgraced Earl Robert and that made him an enemy of the King. Soon after this news broke, in the summer of 1104, King Henry took a large fleet across the Channel and made a state visit to his city of Domfront and others in the area. He and his entourage travelled unopposed through Normandy; indeed, I think the Duke was powerless to stop him, showing just how weak he was in comparison with King Henry. I did wonder if this indicated that there could soon be outright war between the brothers, the prize being total control of Normandy.

The imposition of heavy taxes on us in England that autumn and the following spring strengthened my suspicions. In March I visited the Queen and she made sure we had the opportunity of talking without others hearing our conversation.

"I think you may know what the King is planning," she began.

"An invasion of Normandy?" I suggested.

She nodded.

"He has been waiting for a good excuse and now has it," she explained. "Lord Robert Fitz Hamon has been captured by two of the Duke's commanders and is in prison in Bayeux. The invasion will be to release the King's good friend."

"And wrest the Duchy from his brother?"

"The people cry out under the Duke's unjust rule."

I raised my eyebrows. The Duke had never been known for his good government. I suspected him guilty of incompetence rather than cruelty, but the King of England could easily make a good case for his takeover of his father's lands.

"What worries me," she said, grasping my arm, "is what Edgar will do. He has kept himself out of the brothers' quarrels, but if the future of the whole Duchy is at stake, he may choose to fight for his friend Robert."

"Against his niece's husband. An invasion will put Edgar in a very difficult position," I agreed.

CHAPTER 43

Edgar had sent me the occasional letter, so I knew he was in good health. He was obviously very much in touch with the Duke and had told me of the birth of a son to Robert and Sybyl a year before King Henry's son William was born, but this news had been followed by that of Sybyl's death, when her son was about five months old. Each ruler now had an heir, so a provision to be each other's heir no longer applied. If King Henry wanted Normandy, he'd have to conquer it.

An invasion force left England in April of 1105 and was led by the King, his Queen being delegated to rule in his absence. She remained in Westminster and so it was easy for me to keep in touch with the King's progress. She received a letter soon after Easter and shared some of its contents with me.

"They landed at Barfleur and have met no opposition," she reported. "They were able to celebrate Easter at Carentan. The King says the church was full of chests and goods of all kinds, including farming tools, because the people in the area have been suffering much from robbers. Bishop Serlo of Sées took the service and preached. He begged the King to take control and restore law and order. The King tells me he responded by standing up and saying, 'I will rise up and work for peace in the name of the Lord and will devote my utmost endeavours to procure, with your help, the tranquillity of the Church of God'. But the Bishop hadn't finished his sermon and the next part is very amusing."

She grinned at me before proceeding.

"The Bishop then turned to the cutting of their hair and the trimming or shaving of their beards."

"What?!"

"It's true," she cried. "I've heard churchmen deplore long hair and beards which make them look like billy goats. It's too womanly, they say." She paused. "You'll never guess what happened."

"Go on," I urged.

"It so happened that the Bishop had a pair of shears in his baggage. He pulled these out and ... well, the King didn't have much option. He had to let the Bishop cut his hair! And then the Bishop cut off the long locks of most of Henry's leading men. They must look like a flock of freshly shorn sheep!"

We laughed together and I was pleased she was so relaxed about the campaign. There could be much more serious news later.

In fact, the campaign was aborted. It was quite hard for me and others to find out what had happened. All we knew for sure was that the King returned to England in August – without having conquered the Duchy. From rumours and snippets of information (the Queen would not talk of it), I learned King Henry had taken two cities after Easter and had been besieging a third, when he hesitated. He'd been threatened with excommunication! He held peace talks with his brother during the week of

Pentecost, which was at the end of May, but they couldn't reach agreement, and King Henry finally met the exiled Archbishop of Canterbury in late July, when they did some kind of deal, the outcome of which was that the King was *not* excommunicated and the Archbishop could return from his exile.

There were some further delays, but the King was able to renew his campaign in July 1106. We waited for news and it was a long time coming. Then I received a summons from the Queen.

"Andrew, at last we have a report of the campaign," she said.

I tried to read her face. She wasn't smiling and, for a moment, I wondered if the news was bad.

"The King engaged Duke Robert and his forces at a place called Tinchebray," she told me. "The date was the 28th day of September. Isn't that the date when King William's landing at Pevensey is remembered?"

"I think it is."

We never celebrated it, of course!

"There was a battle. The King offered the Duke a peace deal, of some sort, but Robert rejected it. So, they fought it out. The battle lasted about an hour and many died, but the King triumphed."

I looked hard at her.

"You're not rejoicing as I would expect," I commented.

"Among the men the King has taken prisoner is Edgar."

"Oh, so he did fight for the Duke."

"Yes, and now he is my husband's prisoner." She grasped my hand. "Pray he is merciful!"

There wasn't much else we could do. It was hardly a surprise that Edgar had chosen to fight alongside his sworn brother, but King Henry wouldn't have been pleased.

The Queen had no opportunity to plead face to face with the King for the release of her uncle, as the King remained in Normandy. There was much he had to do to restore law and order in what had been a troubled land.

So, Christmas was celebrated in the King's absence. I couldn't help thinking about the contrast between our King and the King of Kings. Jesus had been born into a very humble family, had grown up as a carpenter and then had exercised a preaching and healing ministry before being brutally executed. Yet he had conquered – conquered death and the devil – and given us hope. He had never lifted a sword or any other weapon. But we humans were forever fighting and breaking oaths of loyalty. I could understand why King Henry felt the necessity of campaigning in Normandy, for society there was anarchic and the ordinary people suffered much. However, I still felt some sadness that after eleven hundred years we still had not found a way of walking with Christ and being at peace with our fellow human beings.

About the middle of January, there was an unexpected arrival at the court in Westminster. I

312

happened to be there when a group arrived from Scotland headed by ... David!

"My dear brother, you are very welcome," the Queen greeted him, "but what brings you here and with no forewarning?"

"I have sad news," David responded.

The three of us sat slightly apart from everyone else.

"Our brother Edgar has died," he reported.

"No!" the Queen cried.

"He hadn't been well for a while," David continued. "He had been in the habit of fasting, as our mother had."

"I remember very little about our mother, as I was sent away at such a young age."

"She worked hard, ate sparingly and rested little. Edgar had become something of a monk in the last year. Maybe he knew his time was short, for he has now passed into the other world."

"Are you here simply to report this?" I asked. "I get the impression this isn't just a visit."

"You're right, Andrew. I am not welcome in my homeland."

"Who is King now?" the Queen enquired, anxiously.

"Our brother Alexander has taken the throne and been universally accepted. There will be no fighting."

"Praise God for that!"

"But he and I don't get on. Edgar has left me Cumbria in his will, but Alexander doesn't want me ruling any part of his kingdom, even as his vassal. I feared for my life, so have come to seek King Henry's help."

"He's still in Normandy," she explained, "but you're welcome here, dear brother, and we will do what we can to help you. First, I'll give orders for your accommodation and that of your retinue."

Lent began on the 27th day of February, and still the King was in Normandy. The Queen always took Lent very seriously and she was frequently seen in London walking barefoot to a church service (she visited many churches in this way) and ministering to those with leprosy. She would wash their feet (not just on Maundy Thursday) and was reported to have kissed their diseased hands as well. The people loved her.

At the end of March, the King returned to England. It was still Lent, so there could be no great feast, but it was clear the Queen was pleased to see him. I'm sure young David was able to put his case, but the King had other pressing matters to deal with, so there was no immediate resolution of the Scottish issue.

In the King's retinue was a familiar face – Edgar!

"We heard you were a prisoner," I told him.

"I was. King Henry captured several of us at the Battle of Tinchebray, but he has released some of us. So, Andrew, I am a free man!"

"What of the Duke? Is he still a prisoner?"

Edgar grimaced.

"He is, and likely to remain so. King Henry has brought him over to England. I fear he will be a prisoner for the rest of his life, unless his brother were to die soon."

"He has a son, doesn't he?"

"Yes, William Clito." He sighed. "Clito is Latin for aetheling, but he has a slim chance of getting a throne. The King has put him into the care of a Norman magnate. He's only four, so no threat, though I suppose he might be one day."

"So, what now for you?"

"Without Robert in Normandy, I feel I'd be better off here in England. I think the King will give me somewhere to live quietly. I'm getting a bit too old to fight any more wars."

"That's a shame. Young David might need an army to get his brother to implement King Edgar's will."

CHAPTER 44

King Henry's time was taken up with some problem to do with the church and he did not immediately consider David's situation. Then Edgar gave me some news.

"The King has invited the new King of Scotland to come to London to do homage to him," he explained. "King Edgar was a vassal of the English crown and Henry intends the same should apply to Alexander."

"No army going north for the moment then?"

"Probably no army at all. King Henry always prefers the diplomatic option. He likes to talk, not fight. He gets better results and it's cheaper."

"The burden of taxation has been very heavy for this last campaign in Normandy. We've all been complaining."

"But at least there is peace in England and now, for the time being, there is peace in Normandy. I reckon the King will find a way of helping David without waging war."

"What if Alexander doesn't come?"

"The invitation is really a command," Edgar snorted. "If Alexander has any sense, he'll make sure he comes. It'll be interesting to see what happens when he does appear."

It was a couple of months before the new Scottish King came to do homage. I wasn't privy to King Henry's conversations with Alexander, and when everyone was present the brothers stayed well apart, so there was no public wrangling, but many were aware of the tension between them.

Prior Turgot had also come south, having joined the Scottish party at Durham. He had come for a special reason.

"Andrew, come here," the Queen said. "I have something to show you."

I moved to her side and could see she was holding a beautiful manuscript.

"Prior Turgot brought this for me," she explained.

"What is it?" I was very curious.

"I remembered his visiting my mother just before she died and I knew she had used him as a confessor, so I commissioned him to do something for me."

I was intrigued.

"I don't remember much about my mother, but many have said how saintly she was. I asked the Prior to write an account of her life."

"He has written about Margaret? Oh, that's wonderful!"

"There are so few people left who really knew her. Mary and I came south when we were young. Our brothers were often away in other households. Edie was the one person who knew everything, for she was present when my mother was born, but she and your father are long since dead. I felt the Prior was my best option."

"It is very commendable of you," I replied. "There will be others who will want to read of her life, a life characterised by her faith and dedication to God's call on her."

"Sadly, my brothers have not so far followed in her footsteps. I am hoping the King can bring them to an agreement, one which lasts."

An agreement was reached and we all hoped it would last.

"There'll be no need to send an army," Edgar told me.

"Alexander has capitulated?"

"He's been forced to accept David can rule some of his kingdom. It should have been a sizable area – land south of the Forth including Teviotdale and stretching as far west as the Solway, but for the present, he's only getting Cumbria. I suspect he might get the rest later."

"So, Alexander has done homage and lost part of his kingdom. Didn't the King give him something to encourage him to agree to this?"

Edgar smiled.

"One of his bastard daughters," he chuckled. "Not the prettiest either. She's Sibylla. Her mother was a nobody, but the King acknowledges Sibylla as his, so she has status at court and the King will provide a substantial dowry." He paused. "He's been doing this on the Continent."

"Doing what?"

"Marrying off his illegitimate children, creating strategic alliances with the offspring of his fornication."

Alexander returned north and David took possession of his lands, though he was a frequent visitor to the English court.

King Henry had to return to Normandy the following year, as there was trouble there again, but by then he had given Edgar an estate in Huntingdonshire, where the erstwhile aetheling could live out his days in peace.

The King had yet to arrange marriages for his two legitimate children. At the age of only seven, Matilda was betrothed to Henry V of Germany and the following year went to live in Germany.

"She fancies herself married to the Holy Roman Emperor," Edgar commented to me one day. "She's been strutting around saying she's going to be an empress. She's got some spirit, that one."

The betrothal of William Adelin took place in 1113, when his father needed to make an ally of Anjou. The King also arranged another match that year – for Prince David.

"Who is she?" I asked Edgar.

"Matilda of Senlis, Countess of Huntingdon. She's a widow, a bit older than David, but she has extensive lands in Huntingdonshire and Northamptonshire." He smiled. "She's actually the daughter of Earl Waltheof. I fought with him against the Conqueror, so she has Anglo-Saxon blood in her veins."

"David's become a very devout Christian of late," I commented. "If he ever becomes King of Scotland, I could see him trying to pursue some of the reforms Margaret tried in vain to make."

There had been another marriage that I knew nothing about. I usually saw Edgar when he came to the court at Westminster, but my travels took me on one occasion close to his estate in Huntingdonshire, so I called on him. He was delighted to see me and showed me around. His hall was next to a farm which was well managed and brought him in a good income.

As we sat at table sharing a simple meal, a small child ran into the room.

"Dada!" she cried, throwing herself at Edgar.

He pulled her up onto his lap and kissed her cheek.

"Andrew, this is Margaret," he explained. "Isn't she lovely?"

She was a pretty girl with curly fair hair and bright blue eyes.

"She's my daughter," he added proudly, and then smiled broadly at my look of surprise.

"I am married," he said. "She is my legitimate issue. Her mother is Alfleda, a local woman of true Anglo-Saxon stock. Margaret has no Norman blood in her veins. Do you, my beauty?"

The child simply chuckled.

"I had no idea you had a wife," I said.

"No, I don't bring her to court. She would be ... a little overwhelmed, I think. We're happy enough here."

Before I left, I did meet the elusive Alfleda. She had a kind and gentle face and I guessed she was about thirty. She was clearly very shy of me, but I could see she was a good mother and she was obviously making Edgar happy in his old age, so I praised God for that.

Edgar had now passed 55 and I was nearing 50. We reckoned we had a few more years left in us. I was still acting as a merchant, but much of the hard work was done by my son Walter. My younger son Richard had taken up the travelling role which my brother Wulfgar had pursued, so we managed well enough as a family.

It was good that we had links in many parts of Europe, for Normandy was in turmoil again. King Henry had crossed over there in 1116 and had not returned to England. There was trouble with France – yet again!

Here in England, the Queen had proved to be a very capable regent and the King also had some wise and able men he could trust. One of these was the man I remembered from the fateful hunt in the New Forest (I had never been on a hunt since), the one who had clearly encouraged the King to seize the crown. He was a Beaumont, but we came to know him as Robert of Meulan. He was clever, but self-effacing, and totally loyal to King Henry. However, about this time, he retired to a family monastery, worn out by the strain of government.

In the year of Our Lord 1118, the King was still in Normandy. One of the problems he faced there was the support given to William Clito, the son of Duke Robert. He was still a youth, but he was a useful tool for those who wanted to oppose King Henry's rule. Sadly, the King had some implacable enemies, which even he, with his numerous illegitimate children offered in marriage, could not placate. Some enemies simply had to be conquered with an army – which was paid for by us, his English subjects! So, we hated wars in Normandy because our taxes rose.

The campaign was not going particularly well, but there was one great blow none of us had foreseen.

At the end of April, I had an urgent message to go to the palace at Westminster. I had not expected to be ushered into a private area, where the Queen was lying in a bed.

"Are you ill?" I cried.

Her bloodshot eyes looked in my direction, but I wasn't sure she could see me.

"Andrew," she whispered, "I don't think I have long."

"But you are young and strong. Whatever is the matter?"

"Some sickness has seized me."

"You've caught something from one of those sick people you visit."

"Maybe, but I can feel the tug of heaven. God is calling me home."

I was speechless, truly shocked. She wasn't yet 38. I stayed with her for a while; she was happy to let me talk of our family and all that had happened. She even smiled when I told her of Edgar's daughter.

"I pray my children will serve Our Lord well," were her final words as she drifted into sleep.

She went to be with Our Lord on the 1st day of May and all London wept, for she was truly loved. Whether the King wept I have no idea, for he was far away, fighting to keep his Duchy. The Queen was buried at Westminster, though I did hear another church wanted to have her tomb. Many churches and monasteries afterwards received lavish gifts in her memory.

The following month we heard Robert of Meulan had died and it felt like the passing of an era. The King had now been on the throne for eighteen years and there had been peace in England.

We had no idea that a truly tragic death would soon turn our world upside down.

CHAPTER 45

Peace finally came to Normandy in the late spring of 1120. The treaty was a great triumph for King Henry and we all rejoiced back in England. He did not immediately return, as there was still work to do to implement the terms of the peace deal, but, by the end of November, we heard rumours he would soon be back, though it was late in the year for crossing the dangerous English Channel.

King Henry left Barfleur in Normandy on the 25th day of November and arrived safely in Winchester. William Adelin and many of the younger members of the court travelled in a new ship, named The White Ship. This had been offered to the King for his journey, but he had declined it, and thus it was available for what was described as a rowdy mob of young people.

I had gone down to Winchester, as it was the first time I had seen the King since his Queen had died and I wanted to give him my condolences. He talked about what a good wife she had been and how he missed her. He added he had ordered a tomb-light to burn forever at the site of her burial. We then shared a few memories and it was good to see him smile.

I became aware though that there was something afoot in the court. Men whispered in groups and I saw some openly weeping. I was puzzled, yet no one explained to me what was the matter. The King had returned triumphant, so why the gloom?

Then I saw Count Theobald of Blois cajoling a young boy, pushing him roughly and speaking to him so urgently that I could see the boy was shaking. I was about to step in when the boy rushed across the hall to where the King was sitting and fell at his feet.

"Sire, there is dreadful news!" the boy cried.

The whole court froze.

"What's happened, boy?" the King asked.

"A ship has sunk and there is only one survivor."

"What ship?" cried the King, springing up. "Not The White Ship?"

"Yes, The White Ship."

"And who has survived?"

"Only a butcher. All others perished."

"My son?"

"Prince William has drowned."

The King slumped down onto the floor and began to weep uncontrollably. A cleric came to his side, but nothing could be done to comfort him.

I turned to a man standing near me.

"Do you know what happened?"

"Most of us have known for a day, but we were too afraid to tell the King. The crew and most of the passengers were drunk. In the dark, the ship hit a rock. It's a miracle even one man survived. He spent all night clinging to a piece of wood."

"Were there many on-board besides Prince William?"

"Very many young men and women, the flower of our noble youth. Hardly a family is unaffected."

Now I understood – the whisperings, the weeping. This was a tragedy of the greatest import. The King's heir was dead, and the peace deal he had so recently concluded was in tatters.

"God help us all," I quietly prayed and felt the tears run down my cheeks.

I stayed at court for a couple more days, but there was no way I could help. Indeed, there was no one who could console the King. He was distraught. So, I returned to London and, as soon as I could, I went to tell Edgar, who wept at the news. Later, when he was more reconciled to the dreadful event, we talked of the succession.

"The King has other sons, people like Robert of Gloucester, but none that are legitimate," Edgar commented, "and no bastard can be crowned."

We looked at each other.

"Well, one was," he conceded, "but he conquered us. King Henry's successor must be legitimate."

"Perhaps the King will marry again and have another son. But if he doesn't, who could take the crown?"

"Duke Robert has a son, William Clito, but I doubt the King would want him to succeed, as he's fought Robert most of his life and still has him in prison."

"At court, they mentioned the King's sister, Adela, has a son. He is Stephen of Blois. He should have been on The White Ship, but he had a sick stomach, so chose to stay on dry land."

"His sickness saved his life!"

"Indeed," I agreed. "His brother Henry is Bishop of Winchester and he could be a powerful ally. Count Theobald is another brother."

"We had better pray for another legitimate son," was Edgar's conclusion.

This prayer looked as though it could be answered when King Henry the following January married Adeliza of Louvain. We prayed and we waited, but there was no sign of a child being conceived.

Edgar was still in good health when I had more news to share in the late spring of 1124.

"Word has come from Scotland," I told him. "King Alexander died on the 23rd day of April. King Henry is in Normandy dealing with another rebellion and will have to wait for David to do homage, so David's already gone north to be installed as King at Scone."

"No fighting?"

"No fighting," I answered, shaking my head. "Alexander and Sibylla had no children and since her death two years ago, I think everyone has accepted David will be the new King, but they may not have expected that to happen just yet."

"So, Scotland has no succession crisis," Edgar mused, "but England ..."

We were all very concerned over what would happen when King Henry died. He was still only 56, but life could be fickle, and proved so the following year for Empress Matilda. Her husband, Henry V of Germany, died in May and her father recalled her to his side.

By September in the year of Our Lord 1126, the King had reached a peace agreement with the rebels in Normandy and he returned to England with Empress Matilda. King David travelled down from Scotland and it was announced there would be a great council to be held at Windsor at Christmas.

Edgar wrote to me to say he was now confined to his bed, but he urged me to bring him a full report. We were both sure the council had been called to discuss the succession.

It was early January before I was able to go out to Huntingdonshire. I was shocked at how frail Edgar was.

"I don't think I've got long," he croaked. "Do stay for a few days. Now tell me about the council."

"The King and all the leading men of his court met at Windsor, but the final conclusion of the proceedings was in Westminster on the 1st day of January."

Edgar had closed his eyes, so I touched his arm gently.

"I'm listening," he whispered. "Go on."

"I wasn't present at the discussions, but there was enough talk in the court for me to pick up what was going on. The King wanted his heir to be Empress Matilda and her male heirs, but there must have been some who favoured William Clito."

"He has a better claim," Edgar commented quietly.

"True, he is the grandson of the Conqueror, but if King Henry backed him, it could look as though Henry should never have been King, that he grabbed the crown Robert should have had."

The eyelids flickered open and a slight smile spread over his face.

"It's possible Bishop Roger of Salisbury put Clito's case, though I can't be sure," I added. "People close to the King, like his son Robert of Gloucester and like King David, would back the idea of Empress Matilda."

"England's never had a woman."

"I know, but at Westminster all the leading men and bishops and abbots, they all swore to support the Empress and her heirs, if Henry should die without a legitimate son."

"Astonishing," was Edgar's response. "What's she like?"

"The Empress? Bit imperious."

"Needs a new husband."

"She needs that to provide the heir," I responded. "I suspect King Henry will be working out now whom she should marry, and that person may well not be a Norman. I think there could be trouble."

I let Edgar rest and chatted to Alfleda. She told me a good marriage had been secured for their daughter and that she herself had family who would support her. She didn't seem to be afraid of a future without her husband.

"He won't last long," she told me. "He has been hanging on to life because he wanted your news."

The next day, I sat with Edgar again. His face was pale and he seemed hardly to be breathing. He must have heard me for he opened his eyes.

"I've been thinking." His voice was very faint. "I've had a long life."

"Yes, you have," I agreed.

He shook his head slightly.

"It's been a failure." He paused in his weakness. "I have nothing to show for it. The grandson of a king ..." He sighed. "But Margaret ... she did not fail." His tone was factual, not bitter. "Her son sits on the throne of Scotland and her daughter was Queen of England, the mother of an Empress."

"Will England accept the Empress as a ruler?"

"I think it will, but agree there could be trouble." He paused to get his breath. "I cannot say why, but I'm convinced that she will provide a son who will rule England and provide the royal line and ... and you know what that means?"

"The royal blood of Edmund Ironside lives on in the rulers of both England and Scotland. Is that what it means?" I asked.

"They did not win. Cnut the Dane. William the Norman. The House of Cerdic is not conquered."

His eyes were unusually bright. He thought of himself as a failure, but found comfort in the conviction that the line of Ironside would triumph.

"Fetch me a priest, Andrew."

His confession done, his sins forgiven, he slipped quietly out of this world, and I prayed he would rest in peace.

ENDS

If you have enjoyed this book, please email the author at fenflack@btinternet.com.

Historical note

There are several sources for events of this period. Besides the Anglo-Saxon Chronicle, there are the writings of people like William of Malmesbury, Orderic Vitalis and Symeon of Durham. These writers do not always agree, so I have sometimes had to choose the most plausible account. Queen Matilda commissioned Turgot to write about her mother, Margaret; the nature of the work is hagiography, but still useful. The names of Margaret's children are known and roughly their order of birth, but not the years of birth. Edith is said (by one chronicler) to have had Robert Curthose as a godfather, suggesting she was born when he was campaigning there in 1080; I have her born then, but have not made Robert her godfather. The chronicler also had present William the Conqueror's Queen, which is highly unlikely!

We know a great deal about the Norman Conquest, but the lives of Edgar and his sisters are usually overlooked or make only brief appearances, yet I hope I have shown that they did have an impact on history. Margaret's deathbed scene is one of the most famous such scenes. Edgar was reported by William of Malmesbury, who was writing in 1125, to be still alive and living in Huntingdonshire, but the date of his death is unknown.

When Henry I died, he named his daughter, the Empress Matilda (sometimes called Maud), as his successor, but, as Edgar had predicted, there was trouble. William Clito had died in 1128, but another grandson of William the Conqueror, namely Stephen of Blois, seized the throne and there was civil war for nearly eighteen years. Stephen was married to Mathilde, the daughter of Mary, Queen Matilda's sister, so the Empress and Mathilde were first cousins; Mathilde played a significant part in ensuring that the Empress was not crowned. Finally, it was agreed that the Empress's son would be King after Stephen. He was crowned Henry II on 19th December 1154, the first Plantagenet King and a direct descendant of Edmund Ironside. The Danes and the Normans did not win in the end.

Fen Flack